FIRE AND STONE

The Legend of Tena, Book 4

KARRI THOMPSON

Editing by Jennifer Murgia
Proofreading by Appalachian Proofing

ISBN (Paperback): 978-1-7323731-8-1
eISBN: 978-1-7323731-9-8

Library of Congress Control Number: 1-13607310631

For John and Kyle

CHAPTER 1

I stared at the Cup of Queens, rubbing my thumb along its embedded Landaffen words and symbols. The royal feast celebrating the joining of the cup with its stone and the defeat of the Hanllants left me joyful yet uneasy. I'd welcomed the filling of the cup with snow-berry wine, but as an attendant poured the honey-sweet, fermented juice into it, my hand shook. When it was one-fourth full, I stopped him. Soon it was my turn to speak.

Mom, Uncle Dean, Phyllis, Dad, Todd, Thriss, Brell, and I sat in the Aludene palace on the same side of a long, pine table on a raised platform facing the citizens of Aludene. Behind us, King Mutu, Queen Jussik, and their young son, Prince Pakak sat on their thrones.

Half-hidden in the folds of my thick gown, the walrus tusk lay in my lap. The tusk had been cleaned, polished, and its deadly point fitted with a golden cap, but nothing could erase the memory of where I'd seen it last...protruding from Daveen's chest when he'd held my family captive and tried to force me to take him to the aurora borealis.

I remembered it clearly: Daveen's eyebrows had come

together, cheeks ghost white, and mouth agape in a twisted cry of pain and anger. I'd driven the tusk into his body with my whole weight, and with a final push, knocked him to the cold floor. The ring of blood at the tusk's entry point had expanded and dripped, pooling onto the ice of the Aludene palace floor. His leg had jerked twice, his head had lolled to one side, and his eyes had fluttered closed.

My fingers cold and stiff, I'd immediately worked the wind, encasing my family and friends with quick magic. Through the swirl of cold air and splinters of ice, I'd kept my eyes on Daveen, watching for any signs of life. His blood-stained lips had parted, and his fingers had unfurled. Leaving Daveen and the other Hanllants behind, I had worked the wind, carrying us to safety before we'd known whether Daveen was alive or had died. Either way, the Aludene were safe.

The wind had stopped, and we had landed in the snowy meadow outside of Stan's cabin. The aroura borealis had danced as light exploded from my fingertips, and the stone joined its cup in a display of Landaffen magic and colored lights. Later that evening, we'd sat in Stan's living room, rejoicing in our escape and the restoration of the cup, but I'd still felt on edge.

Steam had risen from the piping hot bowl of soup, warming my hands and cheeks, but a deep chill had run down the length of my back, biting into the base of my skull. My stomach had turned, and I'd held my breath.

I'd thought I heard something outside the window behind the couch—the crunch of snow, the crack of a twig, a hand clumsily rested against the cabin's exterior—I couldn't tell. When I looked, I could have sworn I'd seen a quick flash, a smudge of a non-distinct dark color, but the glare of lamplight upon the glass had made it impossible for me to be sure.

I'd ignored it, blaming it on my nerves, but after I'd finished my soup and set my bowl on the table, Daveen's face had appeared in my mind. As his eyebrows rose into sharp points, his lips had curled above his teeth, and blood had dripped from the corners of his mouth. His eyes had narrowed into tight slits, and as his stormy eyes burned into mine, he'd pulled the tusk from his chest.

"Hosh de meechh," he'd sneered with a throaty growl, cursing me for stabbing him.

With each word, bloodied saliva had sprayed from between his teeth. I'd gasped, drawing in a quick breath and frantically wiping Daveen's imagined spit from my face, and the image had faded.

"Laura, are you okay?" Brell had asked.

The pit of my stomach had lurched, my throat spasmed, and I vomited, doubling over as I reached for my empty soup bowl. My attempt at containing my regurgitated meal had failed, and instead of spewing into the bowl, it splashed against the coffee table and dripped onto the rug.

Mom and Stan had come to the rescue with a wad of napkins and an old rag. Breaking into tears as Brell held me, I'd apologized again and again for throwing up on the rug. But something else still bothered me—when I saw Daveen's face, I hadn't been trying to see him with all of my senses. The vision had come abruptly and without any warning.

My upset stomach was blamed on what I'd been through that day, and it wasn't until the next morning that I told Brell what I'd envisioned and what Daveen had said when he'd jerked the tusk away.

"Are those real words, or was it just my imagination?" I'd asked Brell, choking as I held my tears.

He'd squeezed his lips together and spoke. "They are real. I know them."

"But I fully know Landaffen now. Why can't I translate them?" I asked.

Still looking at me, he'd tilted his head down and took both of my hands in his. "They are old words of a dead language, the first tongue of our kind. Words I only know because, as a prince, my studies included the antiquated language my royal ancestors once spoke."

"Then that can only mean one thing." I shuddered. "My vision was real! But what I saw took place yesterday!"

"You have seen the past, something Landaffen magic cannot do."

"Then how can I . . ." I sighed, shaking my head.

"You are The One, Laura. And you drank from the Cup of Queens. You have abilities of no other. Besides acquiring heat magic, there is no telling what else you might be able to do."

I squeezed his hands, and the muscles in my neck tightened. "What did Daveen say?"

Brell closed his eyes, sucking in a breath as he slowly opened his eyes to meet mine. "He said that 'the true will prevail.'"

"True as in truth?"

"No, 'true' as in fullbloods. You are of half race, which means your ancestry contains human blood."

"So what? I'd huffed, crossing my arms as Brell tried to console me.

"Do you think he's alive?"

"I do not know."

Later that day, an Aludene protector had found the bloodied tusk in the corner of the palace, and from my vision of the past, I knew what Daveen had said as he'd yanked it from his body and tossed it on the floor. And now here I was, the next day, in the Aludene palace with the tusk and cup as I waited to speak.

Resting my gloved hand upon the tusk's surface, I shivered as goose bumps formed on my arms. From under the table, I reached for Brell's hand. He gently held mine between his palms and smiled.

"I love you," he said softly.

His coat had been exchanged for a traditional Aludene parka, made from the sloughed wooly skin of a nausern, an animal similar to the gorthen in the Wventorin Grove. The parka's fur collar was lifted, meeting the points of Brell's ears, and creating deep shadows along his jawline. Sharply contrasting his pink lips and ocean-blue eyes, the fur gently cradled his handsome face, and his cheek bones appeared more prominent.

My chest warmed and the heat from Brell's hand extinguished the chill in my arms. "I love you, too," I whispered.

Blocks of ice that made up the front wall of the palace had been removed, exposing the throne room to a large courtyard encased with a three-sided circus-like tent made from sloughed off nausern pelts and held up by wooden beams.

The citizens of Aludene sat at tables decorated with pine branches and purple honeyberries. Fire flicked from small firepits placed at the ends of each row, their tendrils of smoke escaping through a multitude of holes in the tent's center. The smell of baked salmon and stewed shellfish permeated the crisp, evening air.

At one end of the courtyard lay the three large pouches containing the clothing Mom, Uncle Dean, and Phyllis had worn the day they were snatched from Berkshire County by Daveen. Next to those were the packed-up supplies and luggage that Thriss, Todd, and I had taken with us. Deciding he wanted to visit Wventorin, my dad had packed a suitcase and set it among our bags.

Flying or taking a train back to Berkshire County wasn't possible, since Mom, Phyllis, and Uncle Dean didn't have government-issued IDs with them. Driving from Juneau to Boston was an option. Dad could rent a mini-van, but the drive would take forever, so at the end of the feast, I planned to perform quick magic.

King Mutu rose from his throne to speak, and Brell leaned toward Mom, Dad, Phyllis, and Uncle Dean to translate the king's words.

King Mutu nodded at his wife and turned to the crowd. "It is time," he announced.

I slipped my hand from Brell's and stood. Carrying a wreath

of laurel, twigs, and pine needles, Queen Jussik came up behind me. As I lowered my chin, she set the delicate crown on my head. I held my breath as the soft sprigs sunk into my hair.

The king raised his goblet, and everyone followed, lifting their glasses. "To The One, heir to The Cup of Queens," he said. "Descendent of Queen Tena and her daughter, a half-race and grove born, The One will maintain the balance between the keepers of groves and humankind." His chest expanded with a big breath, and the fur on his tunic fluttered as he exhaled. "The Hanllants have been defeated." He nodded in my direction. I sat down and shifted uncomfortably in my seat. "When it is time," he continued, lifting his glass higher. "The One will lead all into a united front of harmony and peace."

There were cheers, loud human claps, and soft pats as the Landaffens tapped two fingers against their palms. Mom blinked her teary eyes, and Dad took her hand and held it on the table.

Uncle Dean beamed, his smile wide and cheeks shining. "My famous niece," he whispered to Phyllis as she dabbed the corners of her eyes with her fingertips.

"Thank you," I said in both languages and raised the sacred cup.

The smooth surface of the Cup of Queens flashed, reflecting the torchlight of the sconce closest to me. Closing my eyes and tilting back my head, I set the goblet's rim against my bottom lip and took a long sip. A second gulp emptied the cup, the nectar's acidic aftertaste making my nose crinkle.

A ray of white sunlight poked through the hole in the domed ceiling, igniting the empty gold-framed niche in the wall with bright light. Holding the cup by both handles, I walked to the back of the room and returned the goblet to its home.

The Cup of Queens sparkled, igniting in a flash of gold, silver, and bronze. The dull, oval stone at its center absorbed the light, radiating with its own humble beauty. Beside the cup, I set the tusk from Queen Tena's beloved walrus and turned to face the thrones.

Propped upon its front limbs, Queen Jussik's faithful flippered pet sat next to her on the icy floor. Lifting his bristled cheeks and chin, the walrus softly whistled and clicked, and I imagined it missing one of its gold-capped tusks like that of Queen Tena's Humshu.

"Shhhh, Nome," Queen Jussik whispered, and gave her walrus a pat on the head.

My face grew hot, and the tips of my fingers became too warm to bear. While pulling off my gloves, I stood and took a deep breath.

"Thank you," I continued in Landaffen and stuffed my gloves into my coat pocket. My pulse pounded in my neck. I glanced down at my shaking hands. "I, um, I want to start by saying how grateful I am. For all of you. For believing in me and giving me your support." I smiled, my lips trembling.

"We have the cup. We have the stone. The lights in the sky made it whole. And it has been returned to its rightful place in Aludene." I glanced over my shoulder.

"But none of this would have been possible without your support. Without your trust. And without your faith in who I am and what I've been fated to do." I licked my cold lips.

"Believing in myself, believing that I really am The One, is something I've been struggling with since I first discovered I was a half race." I swallowed hard.

"But with the encouragement, training, and hospitality I've received from the Wventorin, the Tulix..." I smiled at the king and queen. "And the Aludene, I have embraced who I am and, when the time comes, I promise you that I will do my best to lead us to peace." I lifted my chin and spoke a little louder. "I will be ready. We will be ready."

The group applauded. I heard a whistle, and knew it came from Uncle Dean.

"Until that time comes, I will continue to develop my skills as a Landaffen and as a leader while honoring my role and duties to both worlds."

Delicate clapping interspersed with Uncle Dean's hearty applause erupted for a third time. When I lowered my chin, the clapping thinned and stopped.

"But doing this has come at a great price. Sacrifices have been made and Landaffen lives lost, their bodies taken by the earth." I swallowed hard and took a quick breath. "The guilt I hold for those no longer with us is heavy on my heart and will remain there until it is my time to join the trees." I lifted my head. "Unfortunately, as we work toward unity, I cannot promise peace among ourselves." My heart beat hard in my throat, and I exhaled slowly. "To restore the cup, we did defeat the Hanllants." I glanced at the king, "but we do not know for sure if the Hanllants have disbanded or if they plan to regroup with a new leader if Daveen did, in fact, succumb to his injury.

My shoulders tensed. "We also don't know if there are others like the Hanllants who plan to rise against our efforts in the future. And when the time comes to enter the human world, we do not know if there will be resistance and war before there is harmony and peace."

I tightened my jaw and raised my voice. "But I do know this: I will not let you down. We will stay true to what's fated to come, and none of our hardships and losses will be in vain."

Queen Jussik ran the top of her index finger along the watery lash line of her right eye and rubbed away a tear with her thumb. My eyes watered, and I sniffled to suppress my own tears.

"Thank you." I held my hands at chest level and nodded.

The people stood up and clapped. Copying my family and clapping palm-to-palm, many of the Aludene applauded even louder than Uncle Dean. I sat down, and my chest warmed as Brell drew his arm around my waist and pulled me against his side.

"Those are the words of a true leader," Brell whispered.

Brell's soft breath against my ear sent chills up my arms, but my insides quivered and I knew if I held up my fingers, they would be shaking. I clasped my hands together and placed them in my lap.

"Thank you," I said and set my hand on his thigh. "But right now, I really don't feel like a leader," I whispered back. I wrung my hands into fists. "I wish I had the same confidence in myself that they seem to have in me."

"They have confidence in you because you have already proven yourself to be someone who is meant to lead, can lead, and will lead." He placed his hand on mine.

"Let the feast begin," the king said, opening his arms. "And this day shall forevermore be known as The Return of the Cup of Queens." He motioned to the Cup of Queens as it sat in the niche, winking in the sunlight.

Attendants delivered clay pitchers full of winter berry wine and plates of food to each table. Uncle Dean's nose wrinkled as steam rose from the cod fillet on his plate. His mouth turned down at the corners.

I laughed. "What's wrong, Uncle Dean?"

"I'm not much of a fish eater," he groaned.

"That's true," Mom joked. "He's never been one for seafood. Unless it's formed into a stick and breaded, he won't touch it."

Uncle Dean chuckled. "Now hold on, Marg, that's not completely true. If you want to see a man who loves his seafood, put a pound of Alaskan king crab legs and some clarified butter on my plate." He half rose from his seat and scanned the courtyard.

With my fork, I swirled a tender flake of cod in a creamy white sauce and ate it. "I'm afraid that's not on the menu."

"If it cannot be caught with a hook and string, then you will not see it here." Brell smiled and took a bite of boiled seaweed.

"Then they are sure missing out," Uncle Dean said. "I know what they oughta do." He pierced his fork with a piece of roasted turnip. "Make an agreement with those mermaids to have crab delivered weekly. Right up through there."

He pointed to the center of the courtyard where a child held a handful of raw fish over a large hole cut into the ice. Four dolphins poked their heads from the water, and as they bobbed with opened mouths, the child dropped fish into their throats. The child patted the dolphins' rubbery heads and returned to his table.

"How cute," Thriss gushed and leaned closer to Todd. "I would like to feed those beautiful creatures before we leave.

"You're out of luck, Dean," Dad said. "The first time I saw those women in the water, they were trying to free the crabs I'd caught."

"Landaffens eat seafood. Maybe those women wanted *your* crab for *their* dinner." Uncle Dean laughed.

Brell swallowed his forkful of cod. "Those beings were not Landaffen. Until Laura retrieved the stone, we did not know of their existence. How Queen Tena knew of these creatures and made them the keepers and guardians of the stone is still a mystery."

"Well then, I guess I'll just have to fill up on what I hope is spinach." With a twirl, he loaded up his fork with steamed seaweed. Leaning closer to his plate, he smelled the blob of mashed turnips, made a sour face, and chuckled. "You can't say much about their taste in food."

"You're being rude." Phyllis gave Uncle Dean a playful whack on the upper arm. "Look at these beautiful, handmade parkas and boots the Aludene have given us." She smoothed the fur of Uncle Dean's sleeve. "The least you can do is show some appreciation by eating everything on your plate."

"Oh, all right," he groaned.

A trio of musicians cut across the courtyard to a small stage, carrying stringed instruments and wooden flutes. A pair of percussionists joined them. Within minutes, an irregular tribal rhythm combined with the warm, mellow tones of a violin and the delicate wafting melody from the flute filled the grove.

Queen Jussik approached our table holding a wooden basket. "It is time for the Marezka," she said. "Our traditional dance."

She held up her arm. A thin strip of leather strung with clay beads and seashells hung from her wrist.

From the basket, she handed me several bracelets and set a pile of them in the center of our table. She moved to the next group, continuing to pass out the bracelets. Uncle Dean let out a deep groan as Phyllis tied the bands to his wrists. Dad turned to Mom and stuck out his wrists.

"I don't know, Clark," Mom said. "Unless something's changed in the last two years, you have two left feet." She lifted one eyebrow and crossed her legs at the knee.

"Come on, Marg," Dad said. "It'll be fun."

"Oh, all right," she grunted, and slipped the bracelets onto her wrists.

Uncle Dean stared at the ice, shaking his head. "If I slip and break my neck..."

Etched with a wave-like pattern and lightly sprinkled with snow, the slab of ice covering the ground was designed to be slip-proof, but when Uncle Dean stood, he lost his footing and had to grab the table to catch his balance.

"You can do it, Dean," Phyllis said.

Following the Aludene's lead, everyone at our table joined the Landaffens by forming parallel lines and facing our partners. When the music started, we copied their steps the best we could and joined the musicians by holding up our hands and flicking our wrists to the beat. As we danced, the soft clicking of shells intertwined with the music, creating a soft melody in rhythm with our steps.

Uncle Dean's awkward shuffle could hardly be called dancing, but Phyllis's graceful moves made up for her partner's lack of agility. My dad did have two left feet, but Mom wasn't much better at trying to follow along.

Thriss's moves were delicate, yet full of power, and Todd was in full half-race mode, his steps polished and coordinated. As always, Brell was the epitome of Landaffen poise and elegance, and I could only hope I looked smoother on my feet than I felt.

Where sewn sheets of nausern pelts draped over the tent's frame, light from the setting sun snuck through the cracks in the canopy, igniting the courtyard with a warm orange glow. As Brell bowed and I curtseyed, our bodies entered a thick band of bright light where it reflected against the ice and illuminated our faces.

Forming two lines, we separated from our partners, and my mom ended up next to me as we stood across from Brell and my dad.

"Mom," I whispered from the side of my mouth. "Dad told me he's going to be staying with you while he's visiting Wventorin. I'm surprised you said yes to that."

"I'm surprised, too, but he said he'd pay half the rent," she whispered back. "And I hate to admit it, but I'll feel a lot safer with him there."

"Yeah, I will, too. I don't want you to be alone right now."

"But I'll still never forgive him for what he did to us—that lying, two-timing, son of a—"

"Mom!"

"Okay, okay," she huffed under her breath.

Following the other dancers, we took two steps forward, two steps back, and twirled.

"But knowing he's a smildt, doesn't it all make more sense now?" I asked and shuffled my feet a beat behind everyone else. "You know, his need for adventure and taking off all the time."

"So what? That's not an excuse for cheating on me and spending money we didn't have," she said, gritting her teeth.

"Just try to be nice to him for my sake," I said. "Once I figure out what I need to do next, I'll be leaving again, and I'll feel better if he stays with you."

We smiled, curtsied, and did another twirl.

The Marezka ended, the music shifting into a slow, romantic melody with faint drum beats and a flute solo. Small children circulated the courtyard with baskets, collecting the musical bracelets, and those who remained on the dance floor moved closer to one another.

Mom sat down at the table. When Dad sat next to her, she folded her arms and turned away from him.

"Hold your hands up like this," Brell said softly in my ear.

With his elbows bent, he raised his hands. I set my palms against his, and he moved forward until his chest was inches from mine. My heart beat hard, and my chest warmed.

"Now what?" I whispered.

Brell smiled, his light-blue eyes dancing with the same magic they held the first time we danced together in Wventorin. A strand of his dark hair fell across his forehead, escaping the furry Peter-Pan-style cap that he'd been given to wear.

"We step forward and back as we move side to side."

I followed his lead, accidentally stepping on the toes of his boots and laughing as I did it. But within minutes, I'd memorized the simple repetition of steps and body twists as we repeatedly moved from facing each other to being side by side.

The dress I wore, a gift from the queen, was an inch or so too long, and with each twirl, the fur trim at the bottom brushed the ice like a broom, sending a dusting of soft snow against Brell's ankles.

It was the traditional outfit worn by Aludene's royals: an A-line skirt and matching long-sleeved tunic made from the buttery-soft skin of a young nausern, a rarity since only a couple calves per herd actually shed their hides before their skin thickened up at adulthood.

A crimson-dyed thread of seagrass wove an intricate pattern across the bodice. In the foreground, a whale lifted its head from the sea. Upon rolling waves, an iceberg poked from the water, and a pair of seagulls flew overhead. A fur-collared cape hung over my shoulders.

Brell's breath hit my cheek. "You are so beautiful," he said.

The king had given Brell a leather tunic with fur trim. Like my dress, it was embroidered with crimson seagrass. At the center of Brell's chest, a pair of dolphins poked from the water, and V-shaped objects in the sky represented non-descript birds.

A wool scarf poked up from the top of Brell's tunic as did wool socks from his low-cut boots.

The sun dropped below the tree line of the grove. Flames danced from a series of stone fire bowls, and as the fire flickered in the crisp evening air, it reflected like a summer sunset upon the ice floor.

"And you are so handsome," I said, dropping my chin but keeping my eyes on his.

"You are my only dance." He kissed my forehead. "And soon you will also be my wife."

His words sent a sweet chill up my back, bringing me to the first time we'd danced together. Thriss and Todd danced next to us, palm to palm like Brell and I, dancing a traditional Wventorin dance to the foreign Aludene tune. Todd dared to brush his lips against hers, and I heard her give a small laugh as light as butterfly wings and whisper to him, "Not here, silly."

Mom and Dad were back at our table talking between sips of wine. Mom's eyebrows crossed a few times, but she eventually smiled, lowering her head when Dad touched her arm.

Uncle Dean and Phyllis joined them at the table, Uncle Dean lifting his glass for a refill when an attendant passed carrying a jug of snow-berry wine. Phyllis snuggled against his side, and he wrapped his big bear of an arm around her waist.

He told Phyllis he loved her. The music was too loud, and they were too far away for me to hear, but the warm glow in his eyes gave away his words.

A gust of icy wind pushed through the tent flaps. Fire crackled in their pits, whipping with the breeze, and the trumpeting from a woolly mammoth resounded through the courtyard. I flinched as the music morphed into a deep melody with long flute notes and heavy drumbeats.

I stared at Phyllis and Uncle Dean. My heart jumped as I remembered them bound, gagged, and shivering uncontrollably as they sat on the floor of the throne room while Daveen toyed with my emotions, threatening to take their lives and the lives of others I loved.

They were all in danger because of my Landaffen fate. My family and friends' worlds of conventional worries and simple pleasures would never be the same again. And though I knew they'd be under the protection of the Wventorin when they returned home, their safety was no guarantee. To maintain the balance between humans and Landaffens, I was the missing piece of the puzzle, but my presence made the puzzle more complicated and dangerous than complete.

Daveen would never give up. I could feel it in every nerve of my body. My heart beat hard, and my palms burned against Bell's hands as heat radiated through my core. Daveen would never let me win. He wasn't dead. And his fight wasn't over.

"He's still alive," I whispered.

"Who?" Brell asked. "Daveen?"

Watching the smoke from the fire bowls rise to the top of the tent, I tilted back my head. The smoke gathered, stretching into thin wisps, and snaking through the hole in the center of the tent. The moon was full and bright. I closed my eyes, and Daveen's face creeped back into my thoughts, his eyes squeezing into slits as he snickered.

Brell gently curled his fingers around my hand. "Laura, are you okay?"

I let out my breath and snapped my head down. "Yeah, I'm fine. I..."

"There is nothing to fear. Protectors are stationed inside and outside the grove's perimeter. Even if Daveen is alive, there are not enough members of the Hanllants left to force their way inside Aludene without being caught."

"I know. I'm just feeling anxious."

He brought my right hand to his lips and kissed it. "You know you are my only dance," Brell said. "But I think Prince Pakak would like the pleasure of having this one." Brell smiled.

Pakak stood next to us with one hand raised in my direction. "The One Called Laura." He lifted his hand higher. "Will you—"

I glanced at the thrones. Queen Jussik saw me and smiled. "Yes, of course," I said and took his hand.

"Thank you, the One Called Laura."

"Please, just call me Laura," I said. "You don't need to be formal with me."

Like the music, the dance was raw and tribal, requiring the stamping of feet and clapping of hands in rhythm with the drums. Prince Pakak met every beat, his timing perfect as his little boots padded the ice and gloved hands came together over his head. When I missed a clap or stomped at the wrong time, I laughed and Pakak giggled, his shoulders jumping.

The instrumental song ended, shifting into a slow melody with the soft whistling of the flute.

"Thank you, Prince Pakak," I said, giving a curtsy as he bowed.

We walked to the edge of the dance floor and stood next to an ice sculpture of a killer whale and its calf.

Pakak brushed his red nose with his hand. "Thank you for saving me. Thank you for saving our grove."

"You're welcome, Pakak." He blinked at me with watery eyes.

I set my hand on his shoulder. "I'm so sorry about what happened to you. If only I could have restored the cup without anyone getting mistreated and hurt."

"Do you believe he has joined the earth?" Pakak asked. "The One Called Daveen?"

I stared at the snow at my feet. "I don't know for sure, but something inside me tells me he's still alive."

"But you want him dead." He took in a breath, opening and closing his eyes. "Though I have only seen the turn of ten seasons, my senses are strong, and your feelings concerning him are deep, making your emotions easy for me to read."

I smiled at Pakak and remembered the first time I saw him. I'd thought he was older than he is because of his height. It didn't take long to see his true age from his action, but even at ten, he could read me better than I'd like.

"I do, but if he *is* dead, that means I killed him." I stared at the ice sculpture. "By defending myself, I've hurt people, but I've never taken a life. Ending someone's hope for a future and taking someone away from their family and friends is something I hope I never have to do."

Pakak drew back his shoulders. "I would kill him. If he were here right now, I would cut his throat."

He pursed his plump lips and opened his parka. A dagger hung at his waist, sheathed in a leather holder. Its golden handle gleamed in the flickering firelight. Bending down, he patted the bulge of a dagger strapped to the outside of his left calf.

"I am ready," he said. "I am a warrior. I will fight at your side to protect Aludene."

"Thank you, Pakak." I lowered to one knee to meet him eye to eye. "And I will welcome your help as a warrior *when* you are grown. But I want you to promise me that if anything happens while you're still a very young prince, that you'll run from danger and hide until the fighting is over and you are found."

He stamped his foot. "I cannot make that promise. The one called Daveen made me cry, and that is something I will never let him do again. With my voice and my weapons, I will fight against my enemies."

"There is nothing wrong with crying, Pakak. He made me cry, too. Many people have cried because of what he's done."

Pakak's eyes shifted from mine. A hand touched my back.

"Laura," Brell said. "I believe they are ready."

I looked over my shoulder. Mom, Dad, Phyllis, Uncle Dean, Thriss, and Todd stood next to the pile of bags and supplies, a collection of hiking backpacks, long duffle bags containing our tents and extra weapons, and Dad's luggage.

"Before we go, I'm going to change out of this dress," I told Brell.

As I headed to the palace, Pakak grabbed my hand. "When will you return to Aludene?" he asked.

"I'm not sure. Right now, I need to focus on getting back home and deciding what I need to do next."

"Heat magic," he beamed. "You need to learn heat magic."

"Exactly. Whatever heat magic is, I need to figure it out." I gave his hand a squeeze and let go.

CHAPTER 2

om, Dad, Phyllis, Uncle Dean, Thriss, and Todd
waited for us next to the exposed square of frozen
soil. I forced a smile when they saw us coming
toward them.

"Why do I have to make a grand exit and do quick magic in
front of the entire colony?" I groaned.

"Your magic is more powerful than anything they have ever
seen," Brell said. "Your presence here will be added to their
histories and become legend."

"We're ready, Laura," Dad said.

I tucked my laurel crown into one of my bags and put on my
parka.

Uncle Dean rubbed his gloved hands together. "As ready as
ever," he added.

"We have a lot of explaining and apologizing to do," Mom
said.

When Mom, Uncle Dean, and Phyllis used Stan's phone to
call home, they'd found out that their friends and coworkers
were sick with worry, thinking the three of them had been the
victims of foul play.

"More like *lying* and apologizing. Now that we have our stories straight, it's time to convince our friends that we haven't been abducted by aliens." Uncle Dean chuckled.

"And I need to get Molly back to my barn," Phyllis said.

Thankfully, one of Phyllis's neighbors took in Molly so animal control wouldn't take her.

King Mutu signaled to the musicians. The music stopped and the Landaffens gathered, forming a large circle around us. I stepped onto the frozen dirt, knowing that the closer I was to the earth, the easier it would be for me to conjure quick magic, especially if I was barefooted.

"You can do this," Brell whispered and clasped my hand.

On the inside of the circle, the king, queen, and little prince took their places across from Brell and me.

Brell walked forward. "It has been an honor," he said in Landaffen and bowed.

"Thank you for your assistance, protection, and continued hospitality. As the rightful keepers of the Cup of Queens, you have fulfilled your role and duty to Queen Tena's legacy. Your loyalty and dedication to our people will not go unwritten or unsung. Restoring the cup has opened a new chapter in our pursuit for balance and peace, and this would not have been possible without the Aludene."

Brell smiled, nodding at the crowd, and the people cheered. As he blinked and inhaled deeply through his nose, his released breath took the form of a misty cloud. I exhaled slowly between tight lips and saw my own breath.

It was suddenly much colder in the courtyard. Prince Pakak hugged himself and shivered, but no one else seemed to be alarmed or bothered by the sudden change in temperature. I pulled my parka closed at my neck.

A muffled series of pops and claps followed like a flag flapping wildly in the wind. My pulse pounded and my hands shook. Instinctively, I shoved my hand under my coat and wrapped my fingers around the handle of my sword.

At the main opening into the tent, a protector was resecuring a tent flap that had come free. With the breeze, the leather fluttered between his fingers as he tied the strap to a stake in the ice floor. I let go of my sword and freed the air in my lungs.

"We leave here today, knowing that the Cup of Queens is safe," Brell continued. "And on behalf of my parents, King Vaylan and Queen Sennille, the Wventorin give you our gratitude and allegiance."

"Thank you," King Mutu said. He nodded, holding up one hand, and I nodded in return.

I took off my boots, resting one hand on Brell's shoulder to keep my balance. My feet burned and became numb as they pressed into the divot of frozen soil.

"Get closer," I said. "You all need to be touching me."

Brell scooted our belongings into a compact pile near my feet and put his arm around my waist. Mom and Dad stood behind me with their hands on my shoulder. Thriss and Todd stood at my left holding hands as Thriss kept her hand firmly pressed to the center of my back. Uncle Dean and Phyllis moved to my right and held my right upper arm.

Closing my eyes, I inhaled through my mouth, rocking backward as my lungs filled with air. I raised my hands, bringing them perpendicular to my body and exhaling through pursed lips. I opened my eyes. A small funnel of wind spun under my open palms. As I worked the wind, the funnel grew, engulfing our supplies and brushing against my knees.

"Get closer," I shouted above the whip of wind.

Our circle tightened, and Mom rested her chin above my shoulder as she and Dad inched forward. Plucking the air with my fingertips, I created a whirlwind that split and reformed when we were at its center.

As I raised my hands, the funnel's velocity increased, and the twist of wind thickened and blurred as small particles of ice, powdery snow, and pine needles joined its spin.

"Don't let go of me," I ordered as I remembered everything King Hurrlan had taught me.

My feet continued to burn against the frozen soil, taking me back to the patch of earth outside of the Boston airport. *No! Not there!* With the jerk of my head, I shook away my thoughts. The sweet pressure of Brell's hand filled mine, and he mouthed, "You can do this."

My palm warmed in his, and as the cold wind brushed my cheeks, I closed my eyes and remembered standing with Brell on a ridge just inside the grove's entrance at high moon. It was the first time I'd seen the Wventorin Grove.

A village set within acres of trees—ornate, wooden tree homes glistening with gold filigree and jewels, rope bridges with steps of wood and polished stones; windows dancing with candlelight and pathways aglow with torch light.

The smell of flowers filled my nose—soft, powdery, and sweet. Ivy stretched over rooftops and under doorways, hanging like damp, shaggy beards. An owl hooted, and a choir of frogs croaked above the ever-constant chirping of crickets.

See it with all of my senses. Feel it. Hear it. Smell it.

I took a sharp breath, my chest rattling as I exhaled against the whirl of air. My arms floated upward, bobbing like buoys in a restless sea. The tips of my fingers grew numb, stretching and thinning like a rubber band, and I knew I was slowly becoming one with the wind.

My shoulders expanded, the sensation of nothingness reaching my collarbones and trickling up my neck as if thousands of tiny needles were pricking my skin.

A field of night-blooming flowers, their tiny white buds opening as a beam of moonlight shot through the clouds. Moss covered stones. The fresh night air, cool and ripe with the fragrance of damp wood.

I heard a scream. The wave of nothingness dissipated, and the muscles in my throat tightened. I became aware of my body. A strange pushing and pulling sensation throbbed through my chest, and my stomach reeled as if I'd dropped from the sky.

Someone yanked my hand. A voice boomed and hollered. Another scream cut through the maelstrom of snow and forest debris. Cut short, pinched off, and snatched by the wind, the voice died.

Fingers pressed into my thigh. My feet burned. I opened my eyes. We were still in Aludene!

Beyond the band of wind, swords flashed, and arrows flew. The colonists darted left and right. Moonlight pierced through holes in the tent's canopy. Ropes dangled from the holes, some loose and others pulled tightly, as those I assumed were Hanllants slid down the ropes to the floor.

Mom and Phyllis sat at my feet holding my legs as Dad and Uncle Dean spread their bodies over them.

"Stay down. Get behind our belongings!" I ordered.

Thriss nocked an arrow. "I cannot see well enough! I do not know where to aim," she cried, dropping her bow and grabbing her sword.

Todd wielded a sword in one hand and held up the other, the side of his hand angled to give a blow. With a kick, I wrenched my leg free from the hand poking through the wind.

A voice I recognized cut into the funnel, its bitter evil hiss burning in my ears. "Get her now! Before it is too late!" Daveen screamed.

The funnel slowed. Pinecones and ice chips dropped to the ground, but weaving the air with my fingers, I maintained the whirlwind's spin. A pair of hands broke through the funnel, fingers stretching to grasp me, but I ripped my arm away, and with the other hand, continued to work the wind.

"Brell!" I screamed as a sword sliced through the cone of wind. Swinging his blade, Brell countered its blow.

"Go! Leave! Take them home! I will stay here and fight." Brell's sword dripped with blood, and his pant leg was torn.

"No!" I screamed. "I'm not leaving you!" An arrow flew past

my head. Gasping and grunting, I plucked the air, sustaining the wind's momentum.

"Go! Go!" he shouted.

Mom screamed. She let go of my legs, and I dropped to my knees next to her. She lay against the ice, her ribs victim to an arrow.

"Mom! Mom!" I shouted, lowering one hand to reach for her.

A spray of arrows followed, some joining the blur of ice and debris while others pierced through the funnel. I shielded my family, curling my body over them. As Brell, Thriss, and Todd used their swords to deflect the incoming arrows, the ting of metal echoed against the wind.

"Mom!" I cried.

Mom gasped, her lips trembling, and the arrow's staff jerked with her next breath. She reached for the arrow, and Phyllis stopped her.

"No, or you'll bleed to death," Phyllis explained.

With the shaft of the arrow between his fingers, Dad pressed his hand against Mom's wound. "She needs a doctor! We have to get her home!"

"Go! Now!" Brell shouted. "I will protect your wind."

"No! Come with us," I screamed.

He crouched to one knee, rolled from the funnel, and disappeared.

"Brell!" I cried.

Thriss grabbed my shoulder. "He is not coming back!" she shouted. "Let us leave! We must go now!"

Raising my trembling hands and strumming the air with my fingers, I closed my eyes and concentrated.

Fields of flowers. Tree homes with stained-glass windows. A bird's chirp. The moon, round and yellow.

An arrow buzzed past my ear, and I imagined a bumble bee with its fuzzy, alternating stripes and legs thick with pollen.

Mom groaned, but I kept my eyes closed and worked the wind.

Grass under my feet. The clap of owl's wings. The bubbling and burbling of a stream.

The funnel shook, and I parted my numb legs to keep my balance.

My serene vision shifted, and I remembered Brell on the forest floor and Gressim standing next to him. A white-tipped sprout poked through the damp soil, coiling at Brell's feet. A tangle of vines slithered and spiraled, curling around his ankles and calves, snaking between his thighs, and encompassing his waist.

"He is gone. Do you not see what has happened? The earth is going to take him," Gressim had said softly.

My thoughts muddied, and I forced them to change.

"Laura! You can do this," Thriss urged.

A field full of peaceful gorthen. The stone pathway leading to my tree home. Thriss's lontee.

A spray of snow hit my face. I smelled smoke. Something heavy and limp dropped against my tingling legs, and my vision shifted.

Snow entered my mind's eye, its hard, thick surface reflecting the sun. In fluffy lumps, the snow bubbled and brewed. The frozen floor parted. Gray, leathery vines pushed up from the crevice and twisted around Dassh's body.

His face was pale, nose red, lips purple, and blue eyes vacant. I reached for his hand.

"Laura!" Todd shouted. "You've got this! Don't give up!"

I shook my head.

Grazing horses. Doves perched in a tree. Shields and swords gleaming in the armory.

My body expanded, rejoining the wind. Light-headedness came to me in waves, splashing into my neck and shoulders. My fingers stretched, becoming one with the funnel. Mom sighed and her breathing relaxed, for when there is nothingness, there is no pain.

"You did it, Laura!" Todd shouted.

I fell to the ground, landing onto my side. In the moonlight, I saw a small tree.

"Brell," I whispered. "He needs my help." Digging my elbow and forearm into the snow, I tried to push myself up.

"Hesh de non lane vee vey!" someone screamed. A series of grunts and Landaffen swear words followed.

Snow crunched, shuffled, and flew.

"What's happening? Who's yelling?" I tried to push up from the snow.

"Hold him down! Do not let him get away!" Thriss shouted. "He is making himself unseen."

"I got'im," Uncle Dean said. "As long as I can still feel him, this rascal ain't going anywhere."

"Laura? Are you okay?" Dad put his hand on my shoulder.

A smaller hand pressed against my forehead. "She will be fine," Thriss said. "It took much energy to conjure this magic, and maintain it for so long, while taking six people with her. She will need time to recover."

Pushing the heel of my boot in the snow, I rolled onto my back. The sky was ink black. I took a deep breath, taking in the smell of an old campfire. As I stared at the stars, my head spun, and the twinkling pinpoints of starlight swirled until I closed my eyes and opened them again.

"Mom?" I turned my head, forcing the words from my tight throat. Tears pushed to the corners of my eyes. Mom's head was in Phyllis's lap, and Dad held Mom's hand.

"I'm okay, Laura. I'll be fine," Mom said between shallow breaths.

"What the hell? It didn't work! We're still in Alaska!" Todd whined.

I patted the snow with my hands, and the flakes gave easily, flattening against the ground. "This isn't Alaska."

"Laura's right. Look! There's your house, Marg. We're home," Phyllis said.

I rolled my head to the other side. Uncle Dean was on the

ground, straddling a flailing blurred figure. "Todd, run inside and call for an ambulance," Uncle Dean said.

"That is something we cannot do. The humans will want to find the owner of this arrow." Thriss grabbed the hand of Uncle Dean's captive and pinned it to the snow. "We will take her to Wventorin."

"She's right," Mom moaned. "I don't want to deal with the police. Take me to the grove."

"There's an old sled in the barn," I said. "You can pull her on that."

"I'll get it," Todd said and rushed toward the barn.

"She's having trouble breathing," Dad shouted, his forehead wrinkling with worry. "I'm pretty sure the arrow punctured her lung."

Thriss readjusted her hold on the captive's arm. "Our healers have experience with this type of injury. Using hollow thorns, they draw blood and fluid from the lungs." The captive stopped fighting, and Thriss let go of him. "It is also safer in the grove."

"Safer?" Dad threw his hands in the air. "It was supposed to be safe in Aludene," he added, emphasizing the word "safe" in an irritated tone.

"I have to go back," I cried. "Help me up." I rose to one elbow. The muscles in my arms trembled, and I dug my fingers into the snow to keep myself from collapsing.

"No! You are going to Wventorin with us," Thriss said as she helped me stay upright. "It is too soon. You cannot return until your strength comes back."

In a fast jog, boots clumped across the thin snow bed as Todd returned with the sled and two of Molly's blankets. Dad laid one blanket across the sled and rolled the other into a pillow.

I sat up a little higher. "But Brell—"

"You are in no condition to fight, and when you are ready to return, you will not be going alone," Thriss insisted.

Dad and Todd lifted Mom onto the sled. Phyllis put the

rolled blanket behind her head to keep her propped against the inside of the sled's handle.

"We do not know enough about our new enemy," Thriss said. "He is not from Laramiss."

Thriss shifted, so I could see past her.

The Landaffen had given up trying to be unseen and was no longer blurred. He lay on his stomach with his head turned in my direction. With one knee pressed against the center of the Landaffen's back, Uncle Dean knelt next to him. As the Landaffen struggled, sneering and cursing, Uncle Dean tightened his grip on the Landaffen's pinned wrists.

"Okay, on your feet, you son of a gun," Uncle Dean said.

Todd ran to the other side of the Landaffen, and as Uncle Dean slid his knee from the Landaffen's back, Uncle Dean and Todd jerked him to his feet. Two circles of bright red blood remained in the indent of snow where the Landaffen had laid.

With its mohawk of compacted, trimmed red feather, reminiscent of a centurion helmet from ancient Rome, his helmet lay in the snow like a dead cardinal with spread wings. The Landaffen's hair was black, thick, and cut straight across his forehead. Todd shouted for Thriss to retrieve the helmet saying it could give us a clue as to where the Landaffen came from.

The Landaffen's bow, quiver of arrows, and a type of sword I didn't recognize sat on the snow behind my uncle. With its white, triangular, teeth-like shapes embedded into its long blade, the sword was more like a club that could be swung or pounded onto its target.

Fighting with his elbows and feet, the Landaffen kicked and twisted. At one point, he threw back his head, giving Uncle Dean a bloody lip.

"Damn you," Uncle Dean shouted. He dabbed his lip with the back of his hand and, with the toe of his boot, stuck the Landaffen behind his knees, forcing the Landaffen to stagger forward.

Shifting my weight, I rolled to one knee. Thriss hooked her

arm with mine and pulled me up. When my feet were firmly planted, she let go of me.

"I have something to calm the Landaffen," Thriss said.

On her toes, she gracefully jogged through the crust of snow towards our pile of belongings.

As Dad and Todd loaded our supplies onto the sled, Thriss dug through one of the half-destroyed bags. I stumbled to the pile and yanked an arrow from my dad's suitcase. Another arrow protruded from one of our duffle bags. At both arrows' points of entry, the material was singed black and melted.

The arrow's head was black with soot, and at the base of its shaft, some kind of fibrous material had been wound, tied, and ignited. With my touch, the material turned to ash and stuck to my gloves.

I tossed the arrow in the pile, grabbed my backpack, and slung it over one shoulder.

"Okay, let's go," Dad said.

He threw the sled's rope handle over his head to his waist and headed toward the woods, pulling the sled behind him. Phyllis stayed at Mom's side, walking next to the sled.

Thriss approached the Landaffen.

"Neve des umh, lunkg, qualv," the Landaffen shouted, telling Thriss she was a dirty, misguided lover of Tena. Based on his accent, he wasn't from Laramis, Aludene, or Tulix.

His fur parka was unbuttoned, revealing a muscular chest and abdomen. A shallow cut ran diagonally from his collarbone to his sternum, and with each heavy breath, the run of broken flesh and blood glistened in the moonlight. Leather pants covered the Landaffen's legs. His feet were clad with the same type of boots the Aludene wore, but his socks didn't poke up from the top the way the Aludene wore theirs.

From under thick black brows, his dark eyes narrowed, dancing with hate and fury. A necklace of large, almond-shaped, green leaves hung about his neck. His ears were pointed, but they weren't as long as the other Landaffens I'd met.

In muscle mass and weight, he was bigger than Uncle Dean, but he was shorter and stockier than my uncle, and had unusually wide shoulders and a long torso. Like all Landaffens, his movements were graceful, but they were more sporadic and rigid than fluid and controlled.

Thriss grabbed the Landaffen's jaw, digging her fingers into his cheeks. Todd pulled a dagger from its sheath, and the Landaffen stiffened as Todd held the blade against the Landaffen's neck.

"This will keep him calm," Thriss announced. From a small paper envelope, she sprinkled white powder onto his tongue. When she was done, she clamped the Landaffen's mouth shut with her hand, glaring at him as he swallowed.

Within seconds, the Landaffen's eyes fluttered and closed, but his legs stayed firm to the ground, cranking in a slow, clumsy walk as Uncle Dean and Todd guided him. They joined the path Dad made with the sled, dragging the Landaffen's feet as the Landaffen tottered with them.

I held up a charred arrow. "Have you seen this before?" I asked Thriss. "Thank God one of these wasn't used to shoot my mom."

"No," she said. "That arrow had fire. I do not know of any colonies that use such weapons."

"Where do you think he's from?" I flexed my hands, feeling the blood rush into my extremities. Tensing my legs, I bent one knee at a time, lifting my feet from the snow and slowly lowering them.

"That, I do not know," she said, shaking her head.

"Laura!" Dad shouted.

They'd reached the tree line, and Dad stood waving his arm for us to catch up with them. Uncle Dean and Todd quickened their pace, the Landaffen's legs awkwardly shuffling.

"Go ahead and catch up with them, Thriss."

Rotating my shoulders, I took a deep breath and arched my back. My boots crunching through the snow, I walked to the small tree I'd seen earlier. At the sapling's base, the snow was melted, exposing a ring of earth. I dropped to my knees.

"Laura, are you okay? What are you doing?" Uncle Dean shouted from over his shoulder.

"A Landaffen died here," I said. "He gave his life for me. His name was Dassh."

CHAPTER 3

As the winter wind rose and died, the sapling swayed left and right. Thriss lowered next to me and delicately held the topmost leaf. With her index finger, she stroked its vein from tip to stem.

"Dassh was my friend," Thriss said. She looked up at the moon and clasped her hands. Her bottom lip trembled. "I feel I am to blame for his death." She gave a hard sigh, and the air exiting her lungs temporarily blurred my vision. "He was here, protecting you, because I had talked my father into approving his request to do so. Dassh believed in the legend of Tena, vowing to sacrifice his life for you if needed." She touched the tiny trunk. "But at the time, I was naive. I thought Daveen had been defeated, and now..." Thriss dropped her head.

"It's not your fault." I put my arm over her shoulder and drew her to my side. "There's no way any of us could have predicted I'd be attacked again. Please, don't blame yourself."

Pressure built behind my eyes. With my next breath, I straightened my back and stood, locking my knees. A warm tear rolled down my cheek. The muscles in my legs tensed. I flexed my fingers and closed my eyes. My pulse spiked, my heart jumped, and Brell entered my mind's eye. As my lungs expanded, I sensed he was weak and scared, but at least he was alive.

Bringing my palms together, I exhaled through tight lips. "I need a minute, Thriss. You don't have to wait for me. I'll be right behind you."

Breathing slowly with my eyes closed, I imagined the Aludene courtyard—rows of wooden tables bedecked with pinecones and branches of evergreen. The tent, billowing with a cold breeze. Fire bowls, their flames licking the wind.

"You misjudge my abilities to perceive, Laura," Thriss said. "I do not believe you will be right behind me. You plan to go to Aludene."

I opened my eyes. "I do, but can you blame me?"

"No." She stood and lightly brushed her hand across one of the sapling's tender limbs. "Are you able to feel Brell? Sense that he is alive?"

"Yeah, but that's it. My emotions are heightened, but I'm too weak to feel much more than that."

"I cannot blame you, but I believe it is a risk you should not take." She blinked her teary eyes. "You still need to recover from using quick magic."

"I've recovered enough. I have the strength needed to return alone."

"You should not go by yourself. Wait a little longer, and I will come with you."

"No, you can't." I set my hand on her arm. "I need to enter Aludene unseen by all. Keeping both of us unseen would be impossible after traveling again." I licked my wind-chapped lips. "Besides, they need *you* to get into the grove. I don't think Todd can do it."

"But you are also needed. You cannot be..." She lowered her head. "Killed," she said softly. "Or captured. You must be kept safe. You are The One."

"I know, but at the same time, because I *am* The One, I'm

the only person with the ability to help Brell and the Aludene colony right now."

"Do you have a plan?"

"No, but I have a strategy—the element of surprise."

As we stood facing one another, I clasped her shoulders with my hands. "Take care of Phyllis and my family," I said. "As soon as I find Brell, he and I will return, and we'll figure out what all of us need to do next."

"I will," she said.

I dropped my hands from her shoulders, and we hugged. "Please be careful," Thriss said. "Take this." She pulled her quiver and bow from her back and helped me slip them onto mine.

"I will," I said. "While I'm gone, find out as much as you can about that Landaffen. I'll text Todd as soon as I have cell service."

"Laura!" Uncle Dean shouted.

"Tell them goodbye for me." I walked from where Uncle Dean could see me.

"I will," Thriss said. "Find a new tree," she said in Landaffen, which was the Landaffen equivalent of "good luck" and "break a leg" combined.

I planted my boots in the snow, grinding them to the top layer of soil. Holding out my hands, I worked the wind, and the air at my feet swirled.

"Thriss! Laura!" Todd shouted.

Taking deep breaths, I continued, weaving the wind into a tight funnel around my body. My fingers trembled, and my teeth chattered from the cold.

"Where's Laura?" Uncle Dean shouted.

Sucking in a fresh breath of cool air, I closed my eyes and decided to go to a place where I knew there wouldn't be any Hallants, until I regained my strength from using so much magic. Envisioning our former camp site, I pictured the flat expanse of snow where we'd pitched our tents and the sharp slope of the snowbank behind it.

My skin stretched and pulled. I joined the wind, spinning into nothingness until my feet landed softly, sinking into a snow bed much thicker than the one I'd just left. It was colder here, too. Pulling my parka closed at my neck, I scanned my surroundings. When I saw two indentations in the snow where our tents had been, my heartbeat slowed, and my shoulders relaxed.

It was snowing. Flakes of ice caught the breeze and fell diagonally, glistening in the moonlight. A full moon hung in the cloudless sky, giving enough light for my sharp, half-race eyes to see without using a flashlight.

My arms and legs were weak, but I trudged through the snow toward the edge of the woods. The snow and wind increased, producing a slurry of erratic flakes, obstructing my vision. To my right, a large boulder protruded from the base of the mountain, marking the entrance to the Hanllant's cave, something I thought had been completely buried and made unusable by the avalanche. When I'd passed it on our way to Aludene earlier that day, the boulder hadn't been visible.

Halfway across the field, I saw another huge, box-shaped rock at the tree line that hadn't been there either. Shielding my eyes with my hand, I squinted to get a better look. The boulder moved, undulating forward. I unzipped the side pouch of my backpack, pulled out a pair of binoculars, and slung its strap over my head. The thing reared, but its girth told me that it wasn't horse. My hands shook and teeth clattered as I brought the lenses to my eyes.

I gasped and took a step backward. It was a woolly mammoth! On its back lay a saddle-like blanket and upon the blanket sat little Prince Pakak!

The mammoth crashed through the snow, bumbling into the clearing, and cutting to my left. With his arms around the creature's neck and his hands clasping fistfuls of raggedy fur, Pakak lay forward against the mammoth's back.

Every few steps, the mammoth shook his massive head. Pakak rocked with him, ducking as the shaft of an arrow piercing the beast's ear swung toward him. Staggering clumsily, the mammoth dragged his feet in a mad rush and pushed against the weather, his motion restricted by another arrow sticking from his hindquarters.

I moved forward, ploughing through the snow to intercept them. The wind's speed increased in intermittent gusts, sucking up the freshly fallen flakes and blowing them in a frenzied frozen dance as they joined the blasts of snow.

The mammoth continued its labored run, bobbing its great head as Pakak swayed atop its back. The muscles in my thighs burned, and I was out of breath, but I increased my speed, waving one arm over my head.

Pakak sat upright, pulling the tufts of fur in his hands. The mammoth stopped and raised its trunk.

"Prince Pakak!" I shouted, but the wind pulled my words in the opposite direction.

Pakak kicked his heels against the mammoth's back. The creature changed course and resumed its tortured run in my direction.

The prince lifted his spear. I raised my other arm and lifted onto my toes. "It is me, Laura!" I yelled as the wind continued to steal my voice.

Between the thick fall of snow and the dim light of the moon, I didn't see or hear Pakak's spear until its metal point caught the moonlight and the shaft whizzed through the wind. I dove left, summersaulting onto my back. Popping up onto one knee, I sunk a foot into the snow bed.

"Pakak!" I screamed. I drew my sword, angling the blade across my chest to shield my body.

The prince slipped from the mammoth's back, wielding his

own tiny sword, and came toward me, pumping his arms at his sides as his little legs gracefully skipped across the snow.

He sliced the air in front of me, and I leaned back, dodging his blow. He struck again, and I deflected his blade with mine. His arm flew behind his chest, but he maintained his grip and lunged, aiming for my throat.

I skirted right and spun to face him. He cut from below, bringing his blade within inches of my chest. I blocked his blade with the edge of my sword, and using my full weight, knocked his sword with such force, Pakak stumbled backward onto his rear.

Like a mad bull, the mammoth curled his trunk under his jaw, dropped his head, and rushed toward me. His shaggy fur, thick with ice crystals, sparkled, and powdery snow flew from the top of his head.

"Pakak! It's me, Laura!" I shouted again, pushing up from the snow. With my other hand, I yanked off my hood. The mammoth lumbered forward, ready to ram me with the flat part of its skull.

"Laura! Laura!" Pakak stepped into the mammoth's path, and the beast slowed to a stop.

Dropping his sword, the prince ran to me, kicking up snow. We hugged, Pakak wrapping his arms around my waist and pressing the side of his face against my side.

"I am sorry. I did not know it was you," he cried. "I did not know you were alive. Aludene was attacked."

"I know. That's why I came back. I wanted to stay, but I needed to get my family home, and we'd captured a Hanllant who tried to keep us from leaving." He released me, and I lowered to meet him eye to eye. "Have you seen Prince Brell? Do you know where he is? He stayed behind to help." I swallowed hard and took a deep breath.

"I do not know where he is now." The little prince wiped snow from his eyes. "But I saw him in the grove, fighting with bow and sword." He crossed his arms. "My mother would not let me fight. She put me on Tontan's back and told me to take Tontan from the grove."

"Your mother did the right thing." I set my hands on his shoulders. "How many attackers were there?"

"I am not sure. There were more than I could count." He whimpered. "Maybe thirty or thirty-five."

"Did you recognize any of them?"

"Yes, the one who held a knife to my throat in the palace." He sniffled and ran the sleeve of his parka under his nose.

"Noth," I sneered. "His name is Noth."

"And the one who told you to make the Cup of Queens whole. He was also there."

"That's Daveen. He's their leader."

"Daveen did not fight. He tried to stop me when I left the grove, but his body was wrapped in a bandage, and his horse was afraid of Tontan." Pakak bit his trembling bottom lip.

"Do you remember anyone else?"

"A girl. She was chained to his horse. It was the same girl he was with in the palace. She tried to pull me from Tontan's back."

"Nenmie," I lowered my head while remembering how she'd protected me from Daveen. "I can't believe she's still alive. I thought for sure Daveen would have killed her for helping me."

"Tontan knocked her away with his trunk. She fell and Daveen pulled her chain to make her get to her feet." Pakak demonstrated with a yank of his hand.

I sighed, shaking my head. "Tell me about the others."

"They had dark hair and dark skin like the Aludene, but they did not dress the same way we do. The Aludene do not wear red helmets and green leaves around their necks."

"The attacker we took home with us was wearing the same thing." I rubbed my chin. "What was happening when you left?"

"My father's hands were tied and Noth was taking him into the palace. The Hanllants made the Aludene stand in the courtyard. They formed a circle around my people and would not let them leave." With the back of his hand, he brushed away a frozen tear.

My pulse pounded in my neck. The urge to run to Aludene and hold Daveen still while I slid the blade of my dagger across his throat was almost too strong to control, but I lacked the mental and physical strength to make myself unseen by all. To enter now was suicide.

I exhaled slowly, stretching my fingers, and relaxing the muscles in my arms. "Did anyone follow you here?" I scanned the field, peering through the thick fall of snow.

"I do not think so. Tontan and I were attacked before we left the grove."

"Are you okay?" I looked him up and down for any signs of blood.

"I am fine." He stroked Tontan's shoulder. "Only Tontan was hurt. One arrow was on fire."

The fur at the arrow's point of entry was singed, exposing a circle of pink flesh. A trail of frozen blood ran from the wound to his knee, sticking to his straggly strands of fur in dark red clumps. He kept the leg below his injured rump bent and supported his weight with the other three. Tontan's injured ear was extended, the arrow dangling freely instead of rubbing against his face, but his other ear was clamped against his head.

Pakak sheathed his sword and pulled his spear from the snow. Dropping his spear into a loop on Tontan's blanket, he tightened the strap holding the blanket in place on Tontan's back. Attached to the blanket were several coils of rope and a small leather pouch.

Pakak jumped, grabbing a clump of Tontan's fur at his withers and climbing onto the animal's back. "Hold Tontan's head," the prince said as he rotated to the mammoth's hips.

The mammoth lowered his head, and I stood in front of him with a hand on each of his cheeks.

"It's okay, Tontan." Admiring the graceful curve and gleam of his tusks, I ran my hand from the base of one tusk to the ball of gold capping its tip.

Pakak grabbed the arrow's shaft, and in one motion, plucked it from Tontan's hip. Tontan jerked his head from my hands but kept the rest of his body still. The prince flung the arrow to the ground.

"I need snow," Pakak said.

I handed the prince a fluffy ball, and the prince packed it against Tontan's raw skin and puncture wound.

Pakak spun to Tontan's head and gave the top of the mammoth's head a pat. "Pulling the arrow through his ear will make the tear bigger." Tontan flapped his injured ear, and the prince caught it in his hand. "The arrow must be broken in two."

I held the mammoth's head, telling him he was a "good boy." With one hand on either side of the arrow, Pakak snapped its shaft in half. As the prince slid the arrow free, Tontan wrapped his trunk around my waist. Pakak tossed the arrow to the snow, and Tontan raised his trunk and trumpeted.

"Please save my people," the little prince said. "I will help you fight. Jump on Tontan's back. He is ready to take us to the grove." Pakak patted the blanket behind him.

I put my hand on Pakak's shoulder. "I need to make myself unseen by all when I'm in the grove. But my magic is still weak from traveling here. While I'm gone, I know a place where you and Tontan will be safe."

"No! I want to fight!" Pakak crossed his arms. "Take me with you."

"I know you do, but until the grove is secure—"

"But—"

"No, Pakak! You are the Prince of Aludene; it is your duty to stay alive, so one day you can lead your colony. Your mother sent you from the grove. She wants you here—not there—and we are going to obey her wishes. I'll come back for you as soon as I can."

I checked my phone. I'd lost three hours but gained them back when I left Massachusetts, so it was just after midnight.

"I am old enough to fight. I can take care of myself," the prince mumbled.

I took Tontan by his right tusk and led him toward my old campsite where the snowbank behind it would be just high enough to conceal him from the tree line and the field.

The mammoth's feet sunk hard into the snow, but the high wind and snowfall were enough to cover them.

"I want to come with you. I want to fight alongside my people," the young prince huffed, but I ignored him.

The wind slowly died. The snow fluttered in vertical paths, and by the time we reached my old campsite, it had stopped snowing. In the moonlight, Tontan's sunken footprints sharply contrasted with the bright snow. My prints were also visible, but I didn't dare use my energy to work the wind and blow them away.

"It is colder here than in the grove," Pakak huffed as he jumped from the mammoth's back. "Tontan's cold, too."

"Tontan's not cold." I knelt on one knee and buttoned up the topmost button of Pakak's parka. "His fur coat was made for weather much colder than this." I smiled. "In fact, if you snuggle up with him, I guarantee you will stay perfectly warm, too."

Pakak threw his arms around my neck, and we hugged long and hard while he sobbed on my shoulder. "Please, do not leave me here," Pakak cried. "The grove is the only place I know."

"Is this your first time outside the grove?"

He nodded yes against my shoulder.

"Do you know how to make yourself unseen?"

"Yes, but I have only seen the turn of ten seasons. I cannot maintain the mask for very long."

"What about Tontan? Can you make him unseen with you?"

"No, I am too young for that magic. I can barely work the wind." He lifted from my chest but kept his hands on my shoulders. "But I can speak the other language—the one you use with your family. The scouts taught it to me."

"That's great, Prince Pakak! Being able to speak more than one language is very useful."

He half smiled. "How long are you going to be gone?"

"Not long. I promise. I need to get you, and especially Tontan, back to the grove before the sun comes up. The last thing we need is for humans to see either one of you. It's bad enough that he's left his big footprints behind." I stamped the ground with my foot. "The snow is pretty packed. Even if I tried to get rid of them by working the wind, it would be tough."

"What if you..." His bottom lip protruded. "What if you are not able to return?"

"If I'm not back before the moon drops, ride Tontan into the woods as fast as you can. But don't enter the grove if you don't think it's safe. Instead, stay hidden in the trees, and do whatever you can to avoid being seen."

I unzipped my backpack, dug inside, and pulled out my camping shovel. "On my way there, I'll have to rub out Tontan's footprints and my footprints the old-fashioned way."

"I know how I can help." He smiled, and for the first time, I noticed he had dimples. "I will hide the footprints."

"I don't think that's a good idea." I unfolded the shovel and snapped the handle straight. "If a Hanllant enters the field, I'll have to make both of us unseen."

"But on snow, I am faster than you, and I leave no prints. Please. I want to help."

"Okay," I relented. "But you need to listen to me and do everything I say."

"I will."

"And promise to return here, stay with Tontan, and make sure he remains behind the snowbank." I sighed. "I don't even want to think about what will happen if he's seen by humans."

"I give you my oath that I will return here and stay with Tontan until you come for me," he said, holding out his hand for the shovel. "And if you are not here before the rise of the sun, I will ride Tontan into the woods and hide."

I handed Pakak the shovel, and Pakak gave Tontan a command, ordering him to stay. Leaving Tontan behind, the little prince and I retraced the path we'd taken. He walked behind me, shoveling snow into Tontan's footprints. Using the back of the blade, he repacked the snow and filled my tracks. Halfway down our path, we met the place where the brief snowstorm had done the job for us.

"Okay," I explained. "From this point on, you only need to worry about my tracks. As soon as we reach the tree line, run back, and hide."

The prince pulled off his hood. Cocking his head to one side, he lifted onto his toes. "Laura," he whispered.

"What?" I whispered back.

His eyes widened. "The trees. I hear them moving, but there is no wind."

I looked through my binoculars. The trees cast long shadows running north, but within those shadows, figures mingled.

"Run. Hurry. Back to Tontan," I ordered.

I grabbed Pakak's hand, and we darted toward the campsite. When we reached the snowbank above our camp, I slipped behind it, but Pakak came to a hard stop, jerking my arm and letting go of me.

"Pakak! What are you doing? Get down here right now!" I whispered.

He shook his head and disappeared.

Sinking my fingers into the snow, I climbed to the top of the snowbank and lifted my head over the edge. Pakak was in the field, skipping backward in a zig zag, smoothing out my footprints with the shovel.

"Pakak!" I whispered. "Get back here."

He glanced over his shoulder. I waved to him to return, but he ignored me. and stopped shoveling.

"Pakak, hurry! Before they spot you!"

A male voice shouted something in Landaffen. I peered through my binoculars and watched several figures emerge from the trees.

Pakak raised the shovel and waved it over his head. "It is my people looking for me."

Unease settled in my gut. Fear shot through my chest. "No! It's not them. It's the Landaffens who attacked us. Run."

"You are wrong."

"I'm not wrong. Please, trust me."

Pakak lowered his shovel, took a step backward, and turned to run. Dragging the head of the shovel behind him and dodging left and right, he smeared out most of the tracks I'd made when we ran to the campsite. At the top of the bank, he jumped, landing softly into the thick snow next to Tontan.

"Stay where you are. Don't move," I whispered.

He hugged Tontan's trunk and patted Tontan's shoulder.

Through the binoculars, I watched a figure on horseback appear through the trees. Many more followed on foot, wearing helmets with plumes of red feathers.

"What is happening?" Pakak whispered from below.

The winter air burned my lungs as I took heavy breaths to slow my heart rate. "I was right. It's the Landaffens who attacked Aludene."

In a single file, the group cut through the field toward the boulder concealing the cave.

"Laura—"

"Shhh. They're getting closer."

Desperately scanning the group, I searched for Brell. Daveen was in the lead on horseback, and Nenmie, chained at the neck, walked next to him. As she fell behind, Daveen jerked her chain, and she stumbled forward in a jog to keep up with him.

"I should kill you, traitor," Daveen snapped. "There is only one benefit to keeping you alive." He laughed. "As long as I cover that once-pretty, conspirator's face of yours before I have my fun."

"I have no will to live. Kill me!" Nenmie shouted. She straightened her back and lifted her head. "Kill me now, and let these beautiful pines make me one of them."

Nenmie's right cheek was puffy and bruised, and as she turned toward the moon, I saw that her chin, neck, and the fur on the collar of her parka were crusted with dried blood.

Daveen yanked the chain, hard. Nenmie tripped forward but didn't fall. "You will die at my hand. But it will not be today." He gave the chain another tug, and when its jingle reached Nenmie's neck, she lifted her head and cringed.

Noth rode behind them. He kept one arm tight against his chest, and I could only guess it was because of the shoulder wound Brell had given him. In a quick march, the others followed Noth. Similar in stature, they were wide shouldered with long waists and thick legs. Those injured came last, pressing blood-soaked pads of fabric against their wounds.

Releasing a pent-up breath, I lowered my binoculars and dropped my shoulders. The muscles in my back spasmed, and I drew my arms closer to my sides.

"I was wrong," Prince Pakak whispered as he crouched next to me. "Including the ones who are hurt, there are fifty-one."

"What are you doing up here? I told you to stay put," I whispered.

"I wanted to see what was happening."

He lost his footing and slipped several feet. Clogs of snow tore from the snowbank and tumbled to the base of the campsite. Tontan shook his head as one landed between his ears.

"Don't move," I warned. "Stay where you are. This ridge can't support both of us."

"What are they doing now?"

"There's a few more of them coming from the woods. One is on horseback and..."

My arms shook, and the snow under my elbow collapsed. Fumbling to regain my footing, I pushed up on one palm and planted the toes of my boots deep into the snowbank.

"What has happened? What do you see?"

"Caylent, Daveen's sister. I thought she'd been sent away. But obviously, she hadn't gone too far."

She held her head high, but the corners of her mouth drooped and the skin below her eyes was puffy as if she'd recently cried. Similar to the other helmets I'd seen, a hat with a mohawk of thick, red feathers sat upon her head. She wore a long fur coat, and as she rode, it draped over the back of her horse and swung.

"Who is with her? My mother and father? Do you see Prince Brell?"

"No. Except for Nenmie, it doesn't look like they've taken anyone else captive."

"Do you think...my mother and father are..." he sniffled and gulped.

"No, I don't. Your parents are more valuable alive. If he needs to, Daveen can use them to negotiate for something he wants."

"What do you think he wants? You restored the Cup of Queens. The cup has given you its magic. There is nothing to gain from owning it."

"For one, he wants me. It's no coincidence that we were attacked when I was working the wind, a time when I was most vulnerable. But I can't help but think there's another reason, too."

"Like what?"

"That, I don't know, but it's something I need to find out."

"Now what's happening?"

"They're getting ready to enter the cave."

Daveen pulled his horse to a stop, dismounted, and raised his hand. Caylent slipped from her horse and pulled her coat closed. A group of Landaffens broke from the line. With small shovels, they dug out the boulder and rolled it aside. Noth dismounted. Taking his horse and Daveen and Caylent's horses by the reins, Noth led the animals into a large cluster of pine trees. A few minutes later, he returned alone.

Holding his arm against his chest, Daveen limped to the mouth of the cave. With her arm around his waist, Caylent helped him to his knees, and with Noth at the rear, the three crawled inside.

The rest of the Hanllants followed, and when everyone was inside, Noth stuck his head from the cave. He gave a last look left and right, and from inside, the boulder was pushed back into place.

"What are they doing now?" Pakak asked.

"They're in the cave for the night."

"Now what?"

"We go to Aludene."

CHAPTER 4

"Nop tef, Tontan," I said, telling the mammoth he was a good boy.

I tightly gripped his saddle, bringing my hands around one of the horizontal cords on the blanket.

"This is how to make him go," Pakak said and demonstrated. He rode in front of me, using his feet to keep an even pressure against the sides of Tontan's body. "And this is how to make him go faster."

With a kick from Pakak, Tontan increased his speed, and when Pakak pulled the clump of fur in his hands to the right, the mammoth changed directions to cut diagonally to the tree line.

Though Tontan's strides were fluid, the side-to-side motions of his hips, the uneven snow, and the increase in speed made the ride bouncy.

"Now, it is your turn." Pakak slipped down Tontan's side to the ground, and I scooted closer to the back of Tontan's head, clamping my legs against his shoulder blades.

Pakak jogged to the start of our trail, and with the shovel, obliterated Tontan's footprints. By the time Tontan and I reached the trees, Pakak had caught up to us and was covering the mammoth's last set of tracks.

"That's good," I told Pakak. "I'm not worried about Tontan's footprints in the woods, just the ones in the open field. In the morning, his tracks will be the first thing they'll see when they leave the cave."

Grabbing a length of the mammoth's fur in his hands, Pakak jumped onto the gentle beast's back and resumed his position in front of me as I scooted backward.

"Ready your weapons just in case any of them stayed in the forest to patrol the entrance to the grove," I ordered as we passed into the first row of trees.

We unsheathed our swords, and Pakak did a Tarzan move, gripping Tontan's wooly coat with one hand and swinging onto Tontan's trunk. Curving his trunk into a hook, Tontan cradled Prince Pakak, as the prince unscrewed the gold balls from the tips of Tontan's tusks and removed them. Pakak tucked the golden caps into the pouch on Tontan's blanket. Tontan raised his trunk, and Pakak swung his leg over the animal's back to take a spot in front of me.

Packed with snow and ice, the pine trees' branches blocked the moon, making it difficult to see, but between trees where there was just enough space for the moonlight to sneak through, the snow bed glistened in shades of blue with black shadows.

With his trunk, Tontan knocked away the branches in our path, and Pakak and I flattened against the mammoth's back to dodge the low-hanging branches and icicles. We climbed the hillside, Pakak and I rocking with Tontan's undulating shoulders and uneven gate, while Pakak and I held our swords in front of us.

A thin fog encircled the trees, but as we gained altitude, the fog thickened, swirling in opaque clouds as Tontan's legs broke through them.

"Aludene is just ahead," I whispered. Reaching around Pakak, I grabbed a clump of Tontan's fur and pulled him to a stop. "Stay here with Tontan while I check to make sure it's safe for us to enter," I told the prince.

I slid from Tontan's back, and crept forward, weaving through the trees, and scanning the terrain in all directions. An owl flapped from a pine, taking flight, and I stopped and listened to the howl of a wolf.

Twigs snapped, snow chomped, and an Alaskan hare scampered into the brush ahead of me. I held my breath, and when the hare was gone, I continued forward, rolling my feet to make less noise. When the entrance to the grove was in my line of site, I stopped, hid behind a tree, and peeked around its thick trunk at the pair of pines marking the Aludene's entrance.

The pines' limbs were blanketed with snow, but with the grove's slightly higher temperature, the branches next to the disguised opening held only a slight dusting of ice. Next to the trees stood two Landaffens wearing red helmets, and though they were dressed in fur from neck to toe, the two shivered with their shoulders lifted, hugging themselves.

Broadswords were sheathed at their sides, and a bow and set of arrows hung over the back of the taller of the two. I concentrated, inflating my chest, and exhaling slowly until my body tingled, making myself unseen by all.

Taking long, controlled steps, I snuck to the illusive wall of evergreens protecting the grove. Keeping my back close to the trees, I side-stepped toward the entrance. One of the Landaffens yawned, and the other closed his eyes and dropped his head to his chest.

I took several steps in a row and stopped to watch them and listen. The taller one shuddered, mumbling that his toes and fingers were numb from the cold, and the other tucked his gloved hands in his armpits and nodded his lowered head in agreement.

The sound of a rustling tree branch broke through the woods. The Landaffens straightened their backs and placed their hands on the hilt of their swords.

"The One. She might have returned," the shorter one said.

"Or it could be Bando returning. He left to patrol the area

beyond the cave. But there are many creatures living in these woods so—"

A grunt cut through the night air, and Tontan trumpeted.

The skin on my spine prickled. I shifted my stance, concentrating on remaining unseen by all and wondering why Pakak and Tontan had left the snowbank.

"I do not know that sound," the taller one said.

Tontan burst through the pines toward the grove. I drew my sword, whispering to remind myself not to lose my concentration and become seen. Snow flew as the mammoth pushed between snow-covered tree limbs. Twigs snapped and branches bounced as he crushed low-bearing bushes.

Pakak screamed, a high-pitched throaty growl as he and Tontan entered the clearing in front of the Aludene's entrance. An arrow protruded from Tontan's right front shoulder and a spear from his rump, but the beautiful mammoth continued forward, limping, lowering his head, and using the flat plate of his forehead as a shield. As the shorter guard lunged toward Tontan, Tontan swung his head, puncturing the guard's abdomen with one of his tusks.

The guard teetered, fell to his knees, and sank into the snow. He choked and gasped, holding his hands over his belly wound as blood spilled from between his fingers. With the swing of his forehead, Tontan whacked the side of the guard's head. The guard's eyes closed, and he was still.

Remaining unseen by all, I lunged forward, taking the taller one down as he tried to avenge his partner by attacking Tontan with his spear. The Landaffen toppled face first to the ground, shrieking as I pinned his arms to the ice. He kicked and shot his fists behind him, aiming where he could feel my grip and weight pushing against him.

"Laura! Laura!" Pakak shouted.

"I'm here," I said and became seen as the Landaffen continued to struggle beneath me.

"We were attacked," Pakak shouted.

Holding Tontan's withers with one hand, the prince slipped down Tontan's side and unfastened the coils of rope from the mammoth's blanket. Pakak jumped to the ground and tied the unconscious guard's hands behind the guard's back.

"The Landaffen's wound is not deep. With help, he will live," Pakak said.

"How many attacked you?" I asked.

The Landaffen landed a hard smack against my ribs with his fist. Gritting my teeth, I hit his jaw with a back-handed elbow jab.

"I only saw one."

"Hurry, I need your help!" My knee slipped out from under me, and the Landaffen rolled onto his back.

Pakak ran to my aid with another length of rope. "Keep him still," Pakak said.

As the Landaffen lifted his back to fight, Pakak looped the rope over the Landaffen's shoulders and pulled the rope. It tightened around the Landaffen's body at his waist, sealing his arms at his sides. The Landaffen groaned as I pushed off his back and jumped to my feet. Pakak rolled onto his knees.

"I'm impressed, Pakak.," I said and made myself unseen by all again. "You are one smart and resourceful boy."

He smiled in the direction of my voice and put his hand on his hips. "As prince, from the turn of five seasons, I have been taught how to protect myself."

I kicked the Landaffen's hip. "Beside Bando, are there anymore of you in the woods?" I asked in Landaffen.

"I cannot see you. It is true. You are unseen by all." The Landaffen gasped.

"Are there any more of you in the woods!" I repeated.

He shook his head.

"What about in the grove?"

He shook his head again and licked a crumble of snow from his upper lip.

"He could be lying," Pakak said.

I took another coil of rope from Tontan's blanket, and as the Landaffen squirmed on his belly under my hold, I bound his ankles.

With his trunk, Tontan plucked the arrow from his shoulder, pinching the shaft between the nimble, two-finger-like tip. Shaking his head, he tossed it to the ground. Pakak removed the spear from Tontan's hip and packed Tontan's puncture wound with snow.

"He could, but—"

The tree limbs behind Pakak rustled, and I ducked, pulling Pakak flat to the ground. A hiss cut through the air, and an arrow shot over our heads.

The taller Landaffen squirmed in his restraints. "Bando!" he hollered. "Go to Mana Daveen! Tell him The One is here!"

"Oh, no you don't." I said through my teeth. "Pakak, stay here with these two. Wrap their ropes tighter if they try to get away." My arms and legs stopped tingling.

"Laura, I can see you," the prince said.

"I know, but I need to conserve my strength."

With my bow in hand, I rushed into the trees. Bando saw me and ran, knocking branches away with his forearms. I sprinted, cranking my arms hard, and with each step, lifting my knees as high as I could to pull my boots from the suction of thick snow.

Minus the helmet, from behind, Bando looked more human than Landaffen. Though he maintained a jog, his hips rocked unsteadily with each landed step, and his gait was clumsy and mechanical instead of graceful and smooth.

As the distance between us decreased, Bando peeked over his shoulder at me more frequently, and every time he did so, he'd either run into a branch or hit the brush of feathers on his helmet against a low-hanging limb.

He reached the edge of the forest. Just below the fringe of pines lay the open field of snow and the Hanllant's cave.

Nocking an arrow, I stopped and aimed for the center of the Hanllant's back. My blood pulsed hard in my neck, and I held my breath to keep my chest and arms steady. Bando slowed. His hands shaking, he reached into a cluster of bushes, battling the clumps of snow weighing down the shrubs.

The moon was lower in the sky, its light covering the landscape in a wash of icy blue. His lips trembling and eyes wide, Bando looked at me, breathing heavily, and I changed my target, lining up the trajectory of my arrow with the top of his right thigh instead of his heart.

He twisted, drawing something from the bushes, and I released the arrow, keeping my eyes focused on the patch of leather covering the top of his leg. In the moon's glow, a long, flat board with a point on one end and rounded corners on the other, flashed as it spun in front of him, shielding his leg. The whistling arrow pierced the object, and before I could draw and nock another arrow, he yanked the arrow from the board. Holding the board perpendicular to his body under his arm, he ran through the tree line.

I lowered my bow and rushed after him, stopping at the top of the ridge. Bando dropped the board lengthwise, placed his left foot toward the top of it, and kicked off with his other foot. Standing sideways with bent knees and arms slightly extended at his sides, Bando rode down the slope, weaving left and right with more poise than any snowboarder I'd ever seen.

"Dammit!" I screamed.

Lowering to one knee, I nocked another arrow and steadied my bow, aiming for Bando's butt. I released the string, and Bando fell forward into a somersault, his legs flipping into the air. He toppled onto his side, hitting a lone tree, and didn't move.

Behind me, the crunch of snow and creak of heavy limbs resounded through the woods. I turned, dropping my bow, and drawing my sword. I concentrated, trying to make myself unseen by all, but I was too exhausted, and my magic was spent.

"Laura, it is me."

Tontan broke through the trees. On the mammoth's back, Prince Pakak sat with his knees drawn behind Tontan's ears.

"What are you doing here? I told you to keep on an eye on—"

"I am," he said. He gave Tontan a kick and they moved closer to me.

Behind Pakak, the Landaffens lay, stomach-down across Tontan's back. Loops of rope attached them to Tontan's blanket, preventing them from jumping or sliding from the mammoth's sloped back. The shorter one was still unconscious, but the taller Landaffen snarled and shouted for us to set him free.

"There is room for one more," Pakak said as he motioned to the bottom of the ridge.

"How did you get the unconscious one up there?" I asked.

"Tontan helped, but I also had a little help from this." The little prince held up a dagger.

I took a closer look at the taller guard. A superficial cut ran across his throat and frozen blood stained his parka.

The cave was about a hundred yards from where Bando lay. As we made our way to the snowfield, I kept my eye on the rock concealing the cave's entrance and my hand on the hilt of my sword.

Bando lay in a fetal position with his head turned from us. His board and helmet lay several yards away, half hidden in the snow.

"Bando! Bando!" the taller Landaffen shouted, but Bando remained motionless.

"I will make him too numb to talk," Pakak said.

He packed a ball of snow in his hands, and as the Landaffen continued to squirm and yell for his comrade, Pakak stuffed snow into the Landaffen's mouth and throat. The Landaffen gagged and coughed, his saliva crystalizing at the corners of his lips and his cheeks turning blue.

"Okay, get ready," I said to Pakak.

I rolled Bando onto his back, and Pakak stood behind me

with his sword raised over his head. Bando moaned and his eyes fluttered open into slits and closed. As his head tilted back, I saw he wore a necklace made from flat, white beads. Each circular bead varied slightly in diameter and some of their edges were uneven. I'd seen a necklace like that before, but I couldn't remember where.

"He's out. Get more rope," I said and crossed the limp Landaffen's hands at his wrists.

Pakak held out the rope. "There is no blood. He did not meet your arrow."

"Nope. I missed. He fell riding that thing." I nodded in the direction of Bando's board. "And met a tree instead."

As I bound the Landaffen's hands and feet, Pakak retrieved the board and studied it. The board was taller than Pakak by at least a foot, forcing the prince to keep one end of the board in the snow as he held it.

"He rode it like a sled?" Pakak asked. "But there was no one to pull it."

"Yep, and he wasn't sitting. He stood on it. Used it like a snowboard," I said, combining the Landaffen words for snow and board.

Pakak tilted his head to the side and rubbed his chin with his gloved fingers.

"It's a form of recreation—a snowboard is a board people stand on and use to slide down snow-covered hills," I explained.

"Why?"

"Because it's fun. But in this case, he used it as a form of transportation. Snowboarding was the fastest way to get from the top of the ridge to the bottom. Good thing for us, he crashed."

"He does not understand snow." Pakak ran the toe of his boot along a deep skid in the snow. "He cannot read when it is hard or soft, wet or dry, compact or powdery. He did not avoid the crundt. That is why he failed."

"What is crundt?"

Pakak pointed. "It is when a flat crust of ice forms over softer snow. His board broke through the crust, dropped, and he lost control."

"Let me see that thing."

Pakak handed me the board, and I inspected it, flipping it over. It was way longer than a standard snowboard and made from wood instead of fiberglass. On its underside toward the rounded end, there was a centered, five-inch groove filled with splintered wood.

"He may not be able to read snow, but I bet he can read water." I ran my finger along the splintered remains of wood in the groove.

"How do you know?"

"It used to have a fin. This isn't a snowboard. It's a surfboard." I looked at the moon. "It'll be morning soon. We better get out of here." I tucked the board under my arm and swooped up Bando's helmet.

Tontan curled his trunk around Bando's waist and hoisted him onto his back. Pakak secured him to the blanket in front of the other two. I rode Tontan up the hill, and Pakak made our tracks disappear with the shovel.

As I rode, my posture stiffened, and my shoulders locked. Daveen's angry face materialized in my mind's eye, and I remembered a dream I'd had two nights before. In the dream, Daveen stared at the ground, his lips stretching over his teeth, and he shouted a word in Landaffen that I didn't recognize.

Waking up in a sweat, I had tried to remember the word, but as I replayed the dream in my head, the only sounds that came from Daveen's mouth was a mumbled word I didn't understand.

I'd told Brell about the dream, and he'd comforted me with a big hug and a reassurance that dreams weren't real, but it had still left me shaken for the rest of the day.

CHAPTER 5

When we reached the top of the ridge, Pakak popped onto Tontan's back with me. The unconscious Landaffens awoke from their stupor, and after several minutes of lethargy, the shorter one flailed with confusion, screaming to know where he was and why he'd been taken captive.

Bando and the taller one calmed him down, and the three wiggled closer to each other, bringing their heads together and whispering among themselves.

Whispering was unnecessary. Pakak and I could hear everything they said, and if their whispers were true and weren't part of a plan to fool Pakak and me, I could surmise that the only thing they felt they could do at this point was wait for the Hanllants to return and rescue them.

A spray of snow hit us as Tontan knocked a branch from our path. Pakak and I ducked as it snapped back into place.

"Have you seen a helmet like this before?" I asked Pakak. The helmet lay in my lap. I ran my fingers along the crest of dense, red feathers.

"I have not. It is not meant to keep a head warm."

"No, it's not. But it could keep a head cool." I thumbed the helmet's basket weave of some kind of dried grass. "It reminds me of something ancient humans—Romans—used to wear. I think they were called centurion helmets. They had this same plume or brush of feathers on them, but the Roman helmets were made from brass, and the plume was sometimes made from horsehair. They wore them to protect their heads during battle, but this helmet can't offer much protection."

"Then it is worn for decoration," Pakak said.

Bando jerked his body left and right, knocking me forward. I twisted toward him and clapped my hand in the middle of his back.

"Bando, what is the name of your grove?" I asked him. "And where is it?"

"We are Hanllants. We answer only to *Mana* Daveen."

I spun around and whispered in Pakak's ear. "What does *mana* mean?"

The prince shook his head. "That is a word I do not know."

I twisted at the waist and grabbed Bando by the shoulder. "Daveen is Laramis. What are you?"

"What are you?" Bando turned his head and sneered. Despite the cold, his face was red from the rush of blood as he lay perpendicular to the mammoth's back.

"I will tell you what you are not. You are not The One. You have stolen magic meant for Mana Daveen."

Holding a fistful of mammoth fur, Pakak swung his leg over Tontan's back and dropped onto Tontan's side. "She *is* The One!" Prince Pakak said sharply as he hung feet first above the ground. He squeezed his dark eyes into slits and pursed his lips until they turned white. "She is the descendent of Queen Tena. It is proven. It is law. Daveen will never hold her magic."

Bando licked his swollen lips. "Mana Daveen does not need the creed of a false legend for him to win power over humankind."

"The Legend of Tena is truth!" Pakak slipped his foot to the side of his other knee and smirked. "You are ruled by lies and loathing, a deception that can only be played upon by the weak. Daveen rules you with his hate for what is fact, and he has made *you* hate in return. Your loyalty is twisted."

Bando jerked his upper body toward Pakak, hitting my back in the process. The little prince drew his sword and pointed it at Bando's throat. "Do you want to be my first kill?"

"Pakak! No!" I said. "Right now, our priority is going to Aludene."

Pakak leaned forward, bringing his sword closer to Bando's throat. Bando lifted his chin and smiled. "I would be an easy kill, a coward's kill."

"Pakak! Put down your sword!" I ordered.

"I am no coward," Pakak said. "And you are not worth the spill of blood. At least not during this turn of my life." He slipped his sword into his sheath, and in one swift movement, jumped onto Tontan's back.

When we reached the grove's entrance, Pakak and I dismounted and drew our swords. Pakak took Tontan by the trunk.

"I'm going to go in first, unseen by all. Wait here for me. I'll come and get you when it's safe to enter."

Making myself unseen took every ounce of mental energy I had left. I stood between the two trees and gave Pakak a good-bye nod as my body tingled and faded. A small wind engulfed my body, sucking me inside the grove.

Six protectors guarded the entrance, four of them on mammoths. The mammoth's tusk guards had been removed, and coils of rope, spears, daggers, and quivers were attached to the mammoth's blankets.

Taking a deep breath, I scanned the grove. From a dozen homes and where a myriad of fire arrows had met their mark, whisps of white smoke twisted into the air. A circle of ash covered the courtyard where the tent once stood, and its icy floor was stained with soot.

The fire bowls that had provided warmth and light during

our celebration had been knocked onto their sides. Where the hot stones had fallen, holes burned into the snow and ice, leaving their edges blackened with soot. In several places, the ice floor was cracked, making deep crevices to expose the frozen ground.

Torches marking the grove's perimeter were lit, and in the firelight, I saw additional protectors guarding the grove's interior border. Fluffy, oblong mounds of slush dotted the ground throughout Aludene, and I lowered my head, knowing the marred snow marked where the earth had swallowed their dead.

As I left Aludene, tears burned my cheeks. I licked my cracked lips and tasted blood. When I was outside of the grove, I closed and opened my eyes, making myself seen.

"Laura, is it safe?" Pakak asked, running up to me.

"Yes," I said gently. "Take my hand."

With Pakak's hand in mine and Pakak's tiny fingers wrapped around Tontan's trunk, a gentle wind enveloped our bodies, and we entered the grove.

"Prince Pakak," one of the protectors said, rushing toward us. "It is Prince Pakak and The One," he announced, lifting his chin, and shouting into the night. "And they have three Mentsune with them."

"Autka, tell me," Pakak said to the other protector, "are my father and mother safe? Where are they?"

"They are safe. They are in the palace," Autka said.

"What about Prince Brell?" I asked. "Is he here? Have you seen him?"

"Prince Brell of Wventorin fought well," Atku said. "The Aludene are indebted to his skill and bravery. He was injured, but his wound appeared to be superficial and did not hinder his abilities."

"Is he in the palace?"

"No, when the Mentsune retreated, he followed them from the grove and has not yet returned."

"Mentsune?" I asked.

"Yes. I found a means to make one of them speak." Autka

shifted his eyes away from me. "They are Hanllants, having pledged their allegiance to Daveen, but they are from a colony called the Mentsune."

As captain, Autka wore a leather strap across his fur parka. Around his neck hung a pendant made from ivory. His hood was drawn tightly around his face, but like the other protectors, the hood's fur trim was pulled from one ear, keeping his hearing unobstructed and sharp. With wind-chapped and frostbitten ears, Aludene protectors were easily identified, and their permanently scarred and misshapen earlobes were considered a sign of bravery rather than a deformity.

Two days prior, I'd sat in the palace with King Mutu, Queen Jussik, Brell, Thriss, Todd, Captain Autka, and six additional protectors. On sheets of hand-made paper, I'd sketched out a crude map of the location of the cave the Hanllants had used, explaining how it was buried in the avalanche and no longer accessible to them. How wrong I'd been about that, though at the time, I had no idea the Hanllants numbers had increased, and they'd have enough hands to dig out the cave.

During that meeting, we'd come up with a plan—how I'd take my family and friends back to Wventorin, meet with the high council, and decide where to go from there when it came to the Hanllants. Unfortunately, our plans had to change.

Autka bowed. "The one called Laura," he said. "It is good to see you are safe and well."

"Thank you," I said. "I need to speak to the king and queen right away. The Hanllants have regained access to that cave I told you about. And there's a lot of them. Fifty-one. They went into the cave and left these three behind to guard the grove." I spoke so fast, I accidently broke into English. "Sorry." I took a breath, and in Landaffen, started to repeat what I'd just said.

Autka put up his hand. "You do not need to be sorry. I was a scout before I was a protector. I understood your words," he said though I slowed down and continued in Landaffen.

I nodded toward the Landaffens on Tontan's back. "Where is the Mentsune Grove?"

"We do not know. The name of his grove is the only information the captive would divulge when it came to its location." Autka's bushy eyebrows glistened with crystals of snow. He lifted one eyebrow and continued. "But we do know *why* we were attacked and *why* they chose to do so at that particular time."

"Why? To kill me and take the Cup of Queens?" I asked. A gust of wind snuck up my sleeves, and I shivered, realizing just how cold I'd been since leaving home.

"That should be discussed with the king and queen."

Autka ordered three protectors to leave their posts and apprehend our prisoners. Another protector kicked his heels, sending his mammoth in a cantor toward the palace.

"Tontan is injured," Pakak said as he patted the mammoth.

"Yes, Prince Pakak," said one of the protectors. "I will make sure he is attended to."

The protectors untied Bando and his comrades, and I pointed for them to take the helmet and board. Pakak and I followed in a heated walk as another protector holding a torch stayed at my side. When we reached the courtyard, Pakak let go of me, and Tontan, free from his Landaffen cargo, limped ahead of us to rejoin his herd.

"Tawshu!" Pakak screamed.

When he reached the hole in the ice, the prince dropped to his knees.

As I came closer, the glow of the protectors' torches revealed what Pakak had seen.

Tawshu bobbed in the water while a trio of dolphins used their noses and flippers to hold the dead member of their pod at the water's surface. Tawshu's jaw was unhinged, and his black eyes were dull and cloudy. The red-feather fletching of an arrow protruded at an angle from the dead dolphin's back, and when

Tawshu floated sideways, I could see the head of the arrow sticking from the mammal's side.

As Pakak reached out his hand, the dolphins nudged Tawshu to the edge of the ice. I knelt next to Pakak and put my arm over his shoulders.

"Tawshu," Pakak cried as he stroked the dead dolphin's rubber head. "This is Nantu. And Kash. And Lonta." Pakak patted the head of each dolphin as he said their names. "Tawshu was Nantu and Kash's son. Lonta is their daughter."

"Oh, I'm so sorry." I cupped my hand over my mouth.

One at a time, Nantu, Kash, and Lonta whistled, and Pakak whistled back.

"Do you know what they're saying?" I asked gently.

"I cannot understand it as words—only emotions. But I am sure you do not need me to tell you how they feel."

"No, I don't."

"It is time for them to let him go."

The remaining dolphin family lifted their heads. Tawshu rolled to one side, sinking into the sea. The three gave a final whistle, dropped into the water, and disappeared.

"Pakak!" Queen Jussik screamed as she and King Mutu burst from the palace.

The queen took her son into her arms and sobbed.

The king set his hand on his wife's shoulder and smiled. "Thank you, Laura," he said. "Thank you for bringing our son home." He offered me his hand. "Come. We have much to discuss."

I looked at the palace from over his shoulder. Where the palace door once stood, a collection of wet ash and scorched boards remained. The ice wall on the left side was partially melted, revealing the interior of the palace. On the left, a series of logs were being used to support and secure what was still frozen and solidly set into place.

"Prince Brell is not here," the king said. "And unfortunately, we do not know where he is."

"Yes, I know. Autka told me."

"Your prince did not flee a coward. He left after Aludene was secured."

"Do you think he was he trying to find Prince Pakak?"

"We do not believe so. In a state of panic and haste, the queen sent Pakak from the grove. Even I did not realize she had done so until the Hanllants had abandoned their fight."

"Autka told me these Hanllants were from a grove called Mentsune."

"Yes, that is the only information we have learned. Come," the king said and led me into the palace.

The king sat down at the table where we'd eaten dinner earlier that night. Autka entered the palace and joined us. Autka drew off his hood, set his hands in his lap, and told the king about the Landaffens that Pakak and I had brought with us and how the remaining Hanllants were in the cave.

In the niche, The Cup of Queens sat where'd I'd left it, but the cup was turned, making its stone hard to see from where I was at the table. A row of torches illuminated the royal hall. Pools of frozen blood stained the icy floor, and an attendant was on her knees, using a small torch to melt the blood and wipe it away with a cloth.

At the far end of the hall next to the queen's throne, a frozen pool of red was larger than the others. From the pool ran a wide streak of icy blood along with a series of smears on either side of it, one smear in front of the other.

Hand in hand with the queen, the prince pulled his mother to a stop when she tried to steer him away from the throne room.

"Where is Nome?" Pakak asked, his voice wavering.

The queen dropped her head. With the pat of his boots echoing upon the ice, Pakak ran to the large blotch of blood and followed the smears into another room. The queen went after him, and a moment later, the two emerged.

The prince walked up to me with his chin buried in the fur

collar of his parka and his little feet dragging. He raised his head, blinking away a series of tears.

"Nome, my mother's walrus, is dead," he cried.

"I'm so sorry, Pakak." I set my hand on his shoulder. My eyes were misty, and I looked up to hold my tears.

"How could they do such things? Do they not have a connection to all that lives in the natural world?"

"The Hanllants are bad Landaffens," I said. "It's obvious that they kill freely and kill without provocation or remorse. I think they killed your animals to send a message and a threat."

"A message that they are evil and like to kill?" His little voice cracked and with the back of his hand, he flicked a tear from his chin.

"Yes. And to let us know that if we ever get in their way again, they won't hesitate to kill those we love."

The prince sucked in his bottom lip and sniffled. "I said I would not cry again, and yet, I have cried."

"And I told you, there's nothing wrong with crying." I blinked, and instead of brushing my tears away, I let them roll down my cheeks and absorb into the trim of my parka.

"There will not be a reason for me to cry again," he said. He stood, stomped his foot, and rubbed his tears away.

Three protectors entered, using the points of their spears to push Bando and the other two Mentsune ahead of them. The Mentsunes' bindings had been resecured at their hands, and instead of being bound at the ankles, the three captives were tied together at their waists, forcing them to walk in a line next to each other.

"Put them in a cell away from the other one," Autka ordered.

"You should have let me kill them, Laura," Pakak snarled.

"Pakak, come with me," the queen said.

As the queen and Pakak left the room, the queen tried to take the little prince's hand, but he jerked it away. A few steps down the hall, he kicked the wall and ran ahead of his mother.

I joined King Mutu and Autka at the table. Several firepits

were lit, and as their warmth hit me in waves, I pulled off my hood and gloves.

Running his forearm across the tabletop, King Mutu pushed plates of half-eaten food, goblets, and dirty utensils away from his spot at the table. A goblet filled to the brim with winter-berry wine toppled against his arm. The wine splashed to the floor, but the king barely flinched. A plate broke, and he ignored it.

An attendant came to wipe up the spill, but with his hand, the king blocked her from reaching the table. "You have already done too much. Please get some rest," he told her.

She nodded, but quickly picked up the broken plate pieces.

The king pointed down a corridor on the left. "Those who are injured are being cared for and healed here." He motioned down a hall to his right. "And those without homes will reside here in the palace until their houses are rebuilt."

"And the earth took how many?" I closed my eyes to suppress my tears.

Autka exhaled through tight lips. "There were losses on both sides. Twenty-seven Aludene became one with the earth." He lowered his head. "Fighting until their last breaths."

I buried my head in my hands. A spell of nausea radiated from my gut to my throat. Looking at the burned-down wall to my right, I thought I was going to throw up. Taking several quick breaths, I ignored the charred palace frame and focused on the Cup of Queens. The cup glimmered and the melted ice at its base dripped to the floor.

"Twenty-two Mentsune did not survive the attack." Autka smiled, nodding his head. "This would not have been possible without your prince. Like I told you, Prince Brell fought hard and true. His fight put some of my protectors to shame."

"I wish I'd been here to help, but my mom was hit by an arrow, and it was too late to abandon the quick magic I'd created." I sighed. "I got back here as soon as I could."

"How is your mother?" The king swallowed and leaned closer to me.

"I think she'll be fine. She's being cared for in Wventorin. The others are there, too."

"Then your quick magic did not fail?"

"No, but I was only able to bring myself back here to help. I didn't have enough energy to bring more." I stared at the dripping candle at the center of the table, watching the flame flicker as the wind picked up, howling through the room. "I am so sorry all of this happened."

"It is no fault of yours. Please do not feel responsible for the action of others."

"It's hard not to." I folded my hands in my lap. "Autka said you were able to find out why the Hanllants attacked and why they attacked Aludene when they did." I flicked a glance at the goblet, admiring how the lithel glowed orange in the torchlight. "They obviously weren't here to steal the Cup of Queens."

"Yes." The king rapped his fingers on the table. "Autka was able to persuade one of them to speak. His name is Koaen. In case we need to question him again, we have kept him apart from the others, so he cannot be negatively influenced by them."

"What did he tell you?"

The queen returned, carrying a wooden tray containing three cups and a ceramic pitcher. Steam rose from the pitcher's spout, and when she placed the pitcher on the table, the smell of fruit and spice filled my nose and lungs.

"Lunkdol tea," the queen said. She set the cups on the table and filled them.

"Pakak?" the king asked.

"He is asleep," the queen said as she started back down the hall. "He will remain in our quarters for the night."

The king rested his hands on the table and interlocked his fingers. The skin under his eyes was dark and puffy. His eyelids drooped, and a cut on his forehead just below his hairline was crusted with blood. I was sure I didn't look any better.

I ran my fingers through my hair and brushed the stray strands from my face.

"Koaen said the Hanllants watched our feast from the trees, sitting on the limbs extending over our tent," King Mutu said. "Waiting for The One to work the wind and conjure quick magic. A time when the colony would be focused on you, Laura, and nothing or no one else. They attacked when we would be the most unexpecting and vulnerable."

"We were not prepared. This is my failure," Autka said. He locked eyes with the king, and one corner of his mouth twitched. "I am sorry. It will not happen again."

I picked up my cup of tea and used it to warm my hands. "It's not your fault, Autka," I said. "The Hanllants aren't capable of being unseen by all, but somehow, they were able to sneak into the grove. None of us thought they were capable of doing this, so there was no way we could have prepared for it."

"This is true," King Mutu said.

"We also didn't know if Daveen was dead or if he'd survived. On top of that, we'd also assumed the number of Hanllants was small enough for us to handle. There was no way we could have predicted that Daveen had additional recruitments."

"True again," the king said.

"But the question remains—how in the hell did they get into the grove?" I set down my tea and crossed my arms on the table.

The king looked down at his folded hands, lifting his fingers from the opposite knuckles and sighing. "We do not know." He glanced at Autka.

"We have asked Koaen many times, and that is a question he will not answer," Autka said.

Heat pulsed from my belly to my chest. I dug down the neck of my parka and clutched the pendent Brell had given me when I was a naïve, high-school student with a massive crush on the strange boy I'd met in the woods near my home.

I scooted from the table, and the legs of my chair raked the ice floor hard, scratching the ice. "Take me to Koaen," I seethed.

CHAPTER 6

"I doubt he will tell you more than he has already told us," the king said as I followed him down the hall to a door at the far end.

Autka raised his torch. The king unlocked the door and stood aside, so Autka and I could enter first.

The room was colder than the one we'd left, and I was tempted to put on my hood. The walls, constructed from wooden beams and blocks of ice, were solid except for a small hole in the room's corner where the ceiling had burned.

From where I stood, the moon was not visible, but its light sent a white beam across the floor. Koaen lay in the dark, inches from the wall with his legs stretched in front of him and one shoulder resting against a section of the room that was made from ice. A cuff of thick leather wrapped around one of his ankles, and from the cuff, a long chain tethered him to the wall. In the ray of moonlight sat a cup of water.

"I will say no more!" Koaen shouted. His voice was scratchy, and his pronunciations mumbled. When Autka held up his torch, I could see why.

Koaen's bottom lip was puffy, split, and bloody. The delicate skin above and below his right eye was purple and pulled tight from inflammation. At his cheekbones, his face bulged with bruises and cuts made from someone's fist. Red, finger-sized welts wrapped around his throat.

He'd taken off his parka, wadded it into a ball, and had tucked it under his elbow. His arm lay awkwardly upon the parka, and the bone at the top of his shoulder protruded in a lump without breaking the skin.

"Your handiwork?" I whispered to Autka and reached for the torch.

Autka handed me the torch, flicked his eyes away, and nodded.

I got down on one knee, keeping far enough away so Koaen couldn't kick me. His black hair was cut straight over his ears and across his forehead. He didn't wear a helmet, but his hair was flattened in a circular pattern, telling me he'd worn one, and it was either lost or had been taken away. He wore the same type of necklace as Bando, tiny round disks threaded tightly together. His body trembled, and he pulled his plump lips into his mouth to keep his teeth from chattering.

"I like your necklace," I said. "Tell me about it."

He tightened his eyes into slits.

I reached for the necklace. Koaen flinched and moaned when I lifted the necklace from his chest, and he moved his arm. The flat beads were not made from ceramic or clay as I'd suspected. The disks were smooth like a tooth and varied in shades from bright white to milky beige and pink, reminding me of the inside of a conch shell.

When I let go of the necklace, Koaen lifted his chin and flinched, raising one side of his mouth. His arm shook and his teeth continued to hit up against each other.

"That must hurt," I said, eyeing his shoulder.

"The ice has made it numb."

"I can help you. I'll pop your shoulder back into place."

"What for? In exchange for answering your questions?" He grimaced.

I nodded.

"I would rather suffer than turn my back on Mana Daveen."

"But you already have, haven't you?" I sat down and crossed my legs. "We know you are from a colony called the Mentsune, and your attack wasn't spontaneous—it was carefully planned."

He smiled but only one side of his puffy mouth rose.

"And somehow the Hanllants were able to enter Aludene without being noticed."

Koaen smiled wider and the split in his bottom lip filled with blood. "Maybe you are not the only Landaffen to possess quick magic. Maybe you are not the only one with the ability to become unseen by all." He turned his head and spit, the glob of blood and spittle freezing to the ice.

"No. Koaen. I am the only one." I leaned forward. "Who helped you get inside Aludene?"

He turned his head and spit again.

"Daveen's plan included capturing me, but as you can see, that part of your plan failed. And it will continue to fail and fall apart."

"Mana Daveen does not need you. He got what he wanted." He laughed, and it came out like a throaty cackle.

"What did he get?"

Koaen sighed and shook his head. "I will tell you no more."

"We know where the Hanllants are right now, Koaen. And we know how many of you there are. The Hanllants are outnumbered."

Koaen snarled. "That does not concern me. The Aludene king will not attack them. He lacks the fortitude and the nerve." Koaen glared at the king and spit again.

Coming up on one hand, I leaned closer to Koaen. With my other hand, I yanked the parka from under Koaen's arm.

As his head hit the floor, Koaen screamed, lifting his head to the moon, and giving a raspy howl. He hissed and kicked his heels against the floor.

"Tell me!" I shouted. "Who helped you get into Aludene?

What did Daveen want? He didn't take the Cup of Queens. Did he take something else from this grove?"

"Come, Laura," the king said. "Leave him in pain. He will tell us no more."

Autka helped me to my feet.

"Wait,' I said, and Autka let go of me.

Taking Koaen by the ankles, I dragged him from the wall, pulling him flat on his back. Koaen squirmed, gritting his teeth.

"Don't move," I told him.

Placing my foot against his ribs, I grabbed his right hand. Keeping his arm an inch from the ground and at a forty-five-degree angle, I pulled his arm toward me, using firm and steady pressure.

Closing his eyes, Koaen grunted but stayed still. When his arm muscles spasmed, I knew the ball of his joint had slipped under the lip of his shoulder cup. I let go, and Koaen released a big breath. With his feet, he pushed himself upright while holding his arm at the elbow.

"Here," I said and handed him the cup of water.

"You should have left him in pain," Autka said.

"There was no reason to make him suffer any longer than he already had."

Autka shook his head, and he and the king started toward the door.

"He did not need the cup." Koaen gasped.

"What?" I spun on my heels.

"Mana Daveen. It is not the *cup* that he needed. He still needs you, but that is something that can wait."

"Laura," King Mutu said. He stood in the doorway with the key ready.

We went back to the throne room. The king and Autka sat back down at the table, but I crossed the room to the Cup of Queens. "Did you hear what Koaen said when we were leaving? He said Daveen didn't need the cup."

"Yes, that was understood," King Mutu said. "The cup has not been moved."

I took the Cup of Queens from its niche and brought it back to the table with me. "Yeah, but there was something about how he said the word 'cup' like he was hinting at something." I set the goblet in front of me and took a sip of my tea. The tea was ice cold.

"If he did not need the cup, then he only needed the . . ." I turned the cup, so the torchlight reflected against the front of the cup and its stone.

"Then he only needed the . . ." I repeated and gasped. "The stone."

"Is that not the stone?" the king asked.

"Yes, it is, but . . ." I ran my finger along the stone's surface. "But it's chipped. There's a small piece missing that wasn't missing before. Look."

I handed the king the cup. He inspected it and handed it to Autka. "It does appear that a small fragment has been chipped away."

"It might have been dropped by one of the attendants while cleaning, or it could have fallen during the attack and someone replaced it without noticing it had been damaged," Autka said.

"I don't think so. If you check the floor, you won't find the broken piece. And if you ask if anyone found it knocked over and put it back, I'll bet no one did."

"Has the magic of the cup been compromised?" the king asked.

I took the cup from Autka and scraped the nail of my index finger against the place where it was chipped. "No, it's fine." I closed my eyes and ran the pads of my fingers across the stone and engraved lithel. "As if it has a soul of its own, I can sense its magic. Nothing has changed."

"The cup knows you," the king said. "And it knows you are its true possessor, and as so, you were the only one who could make the Cup of Queens whole."

I smiled as the heat of my palm warmed the cup. "I always wondered why Tena used this simple, black stone, and not some kind of sparkly jewel."

"Maybe Queen Tena was a humble Landaffen with modest taste," the king said. "And the type of stone bore no wealth or significance because only the magic in the stone mattered."

"I get that. Buy why *this* particular stone? There has to be more to this. And Daveen didn't take the whole thing, he only needed a sample of it, which means to find out what he's up to, I'm going to need a sample of it, too."

King Mutu nodded to Autka, and Autka left the table.

"We still need to figure out how the Hanllants got in here," I said. "They made their way into the grove and into the trees without anyone noticing. How was that possible?"

The king folded his hands. "We were distracted. There was music, drinking, dancing..."

"But still—"

"How do *you* think it was possible?" The king leaned back in his chair. "The questions you asked the Hanllant implied you believe there is a traitor among my people."

I exhaled slowly and shifted in my chair, bringing my elbows to the table.

"Isn't that the only explanation? I think—"

"Will this be sufficient?" Autka interrupted as he returned with a chisel and handed it to me.

I exhaled louder than I wanted to. "Yeah, this should work." I gently ran my fingertip across the blade. "Hold the cup for me."

Autka took the cup by its handles and held its base firmly against the table. Steadying the corner of the flat blade against the edge of the stone just above the spot where Daveen took his piece, I gouged the stone.

A chip the size of my pinky fingernail broke loose and bounced across the table like a rock skipping across water. Autka caught it and set it in the middle of the table. I picked it up and turned it in my fingers like a tiny coin.

The side of the chip that was part of the stone's outer surface was slightly darker than the other side. The outer surface was also smoother than the underside of it.

"The magic of the cup still hasn't changed, but I'd be afraid to take more from it."

"Laura," King Mutu said. "You haven't answered my question. Do you think there is someone, an Aludene, who has changed his or her allegiance?"

Autka straightened his posture. "I mean you no disrespect, but I do not believe you have the aptitude nor the title to question the integrity of the Aludene." His nostrils flared. "You are a half-race and still very new to our world."

The king gasped, and I rose from the table. Keeping one palm against the tabletop, and the other hand fisted, holding the stone, I leaned toward Autka and lowered my head to bring my eyes level with his.

"Maybe you are that traitor," I sneered. "There is no other way the Hanllants could have entered the grove. Someone had to let them in, and who better to do so than the captain."

Autka popped from his chair, pushing hard from the table. His chair fell backwards to the floor, but I didn't move. "I will not be accused of such things!" he shouted.

I straightened my back. "And I will not have my abilities and judgment questioned by you or anyone else." The muscles in my neck tightened, and I felt sweat pool at the top of my bra band between my breasts.

"Yes, I am new to your world, but I am not new to deceit, conspiracies, combat, and death—things you have never experienced until now."

His shoulders dropped, but his chest continued to heave. He was at least six or seven inches taller than me, but instead of lifting my head to lock eyes with him, I rolled my eyes upward, and stared at him, unblinking.

"Sit," the king ordered.

He tugged Autka's parka sleeve, and the captain lowered slowly without breaking eye contact with me. I sat down, leaned back in my chair, and crossed my legs. Autka and I didn't shift our eyes from each other until the king spoke again. I unbuttoned my parka at the neck.

"Autka, you will not question the authority or he actions of The One again. Do you understand?"

"Yes, King Mutu." Autka's voice was flat, lacking inflection.

"And Laura, I wish for you to trust Captain Autka as you trust me. He is not a traitor." He rested his fingers atop my closed hand. The wrinkles at the outer corners of his eyes softened and tears pushed to his lower lashes.

I uncrossed my legs and stared at his hands.

"If an Aludene compromised the safety of our grove, that person will be found," the king continued. Through the hole in the ceiling, he looked at the graying sky. "I speculate there are three to four human hours left before the sun trades places with the moon. We should sleep until then. I believe your quarters are still available."

"We can't rest before coming up with a plan," I said. "Brell is missing. Your son has been through more than any child should have endured, and Aludene is not secure. We need to find out who betrayed us, so we can stop them from doing it again."

"Yes, I understand. That is our current situation, but rest is needed."

"We can't wait until morning. I say we pull together all of your protectors and those willing to fight, and wait for the Hanllants outside the cave." I spoke fast, my eyes darting from King Mutu to Autka. "When they leave the cave, we'll surprise them like they surprised us, and attack, taking as many of them as prisoners as we can, including Daveen. With their numbers depleted and their leader captured, they'll have no option other than to abandon their plans."

The king's face hardened, one eyebrow rising and freezing in place, and when he spoke, his lips barely moved. "This is a small grove. We have had no threats until now." He shifted his arm, knocking over his cup of tea. The liquid puddled at his sleeve, but he ignored it. "We have..." The king dropped his head. "We *had* twenty protectors... Only thirteen remain, and I will not ask them or any other members of this colony to risk their lives."

My throat tightened, tears threatened, and I wanted to shout that Koaen had been right, and the king didn't have the fortitude or the nerve.

"Yes, you are The One," the king said. "The Aludene are the keepers of the cup. We have a duty to Queen Tena and the Cup of the Queens. But when you restored and returned the cup, we filled our obligation." He removed his hand from mine, letting his fingers trickle from my hand to the table. "I cannot sacrifice the lives of my people for anything more than that. We have done our part."

Autka turned to me. "The Hanllants came," he said. "They took what they wanted. If they return, it would only be for you, and the grove would be, once again, at risk."

"Don't you get it," I said, raising my voice. "This stone is only one piece to solving this puzzle." I opened my hand. The chip's sharp edge had made a pink line in my skin. "The Hanllants have plans much bigger than the one they used to bust in here, and we need to stop them before they get what they want—power over every living creature on this planet."

I glanced from King Mutu to Autka, but they kept their eyes from me. "I don't know their next move, but with your help, we can stop them."

"Their next move does not involve the Aludene," the king said. "What happens when you leave here cannot and will not involve this grove. I am sorry, but we cannot give you more than what we already have."

"Yes, you can. Aren't your protectors up to the fight? Don't they want to see the threat of Daveen and the Hanllants eliminated?"

"Of course, they are, and, of course, they do," Autka grunted. "They proved that today, many of them with their lives." A vein pulsed in his forehead. He hit the table with his fist, and the pitcher and cups rattled against the table. "But we will not fight against what is no longer a threat to Aludene."

"But they are a threat. They're a threat to every grove. You need to understand that!"

Autka stood, his shadow covering the table, and his wide, muscular torso blocking the torchlight. He grabbed my parka tightly at my throat, making it hard for me to swallow. His eyes, fevered and intense, seared into mine.

I closed my eyes into tight slits and took a deep breath. My heart beat hard in my throat, and the muscles in my arms and legs throbbed.

"I'm not afraid of you," I seethed. "Let go of me before you regret it."

"Autka!" King Mutu said and smacked the table.

Autka didn't move.

The pulse in my neck pounded. Bracing my left foot against the rung of my chair, I pushed off while swinging my forearm at Autka's chin. My elbow struck his left cheek, and he let go of me. Reaching behind me, I yanked my dagger from the sheath on my calve and scrambled over the table. Autka's chair teetered on two legs and fell to the floor as he leaned away from me.

"Don't you dare try to intimidate me ever again. Do you understand?" I said as I positioned my knife against his jugular.

"Laura, please," the king said. "Both of you stop this. We are on the same side. We need to work together."

"Not following my plan is not working together," I sneered, keeping my eyes locked on Autka's.

Autka lifted his chin. I lowered my knife and moved back into my chair without shifting my gaze.

"Do you understand?" I repeated.

King Mutu nudged Autka with his elbow.

"Yes," Autka said. His jaw was tight, and his black eyes lacked emotion.

"You can stay here tonight, Laura," the kind said. "But I ask that you leave at first sunglow."

"What about the traitor?" I huffed, shifting my eyes back to Autka.

"I will conduct an investigation myself. If there is a traitor among the Aludene," Autka said, "the traitor will be found and disciplined." A bead of sweat rolled from his brow.

"And interrogated," I added. "The traitor might have information that could help me. He could also be playing a role in another one of the Hanllants' plots."

The king pressed his palms against the table. "As I have already stated, the Hanllants have no more need for Aludene." He turned to Autka.

"If there is a conspirator," Autka said, "he has already done his part. The threat of another conspiracy is low."

"I disagree. Aludene was attacked because we underestimated what the Hanllants were capable of doing. We can't make that mistake again." I pushed up the table. "But I'll give you this: the threat of another attack will also be low," I snipped. "Because I am leaving tonight."

"You have had no sleep," the king said as I turned toward the door.

"And Prince Brell has not been found," I said over my shoulder.

"Please do not let Autka's earlier actions influence your decision to leave."

"I would never allow someone's ill-mannered behavior to bully me into doing something I don't want to do." I pulled on my hood.

"Mutu!" the queen cried as she dashed into the room. She stood in her socked feet while clutching the flounce of her leather sleeping gown to keep its hem from the ice. "Pakak is gone!"

"What do you mean gone?" King Mutu asked. He and Autka rose from the table.

"He snuck away while I was asleep." The queen wrung her hands. "I checked his room. His bow and sword are missing. I fear he has left the grove."

"Captain Autka, is this possible?" The king's eyebrows drew together, and the gray circles under his eyes became more pronounced.

"As always, there are protectors stationed along the grove's inner perimeter, but with our numbers compromised..." The chief looked to the side. "Prince Pakak *is* small, and he *can* move without sound."

"He's also resourceful and clever," I added.

"Put together a team and find him," he shouted to Autka.

The queen dropped at my feet and grabbed my coat. "Please go with them," she begged, clasping her hands in front of her. "Before we went to bed, Pakak told me how you saved him and how you fought to bring him home. He trusts you. He will do as you say."

With the flutter of her thick lashes, tears spilled to her cheeks. She strengthened her grip on my parka, pulling me toward her. "And you are the only one who can make yourself unseen by all."

"I think I know where he went. I'll go if Autka will do as I say, and if not, I'll go alone."

The queen let go of me. "Thank you. Thank you," she said. I offered my hand and pulled her to her feet.

"Autka will do as you say," King Mutu said. He shifted his eyes to the captain. "And so will I."

"Come with me," Autka said to me. "I will take you to our armory."

The queen sobbed in her hands. "Where did my son go? What do you think he wants?"

"Revenge," I said.

CHAPTER 7

"You carry the Sword of Tena," Autka said as he caught up to me.

Our team included King Mutu, Autka, me, and five protectors. I led the group, but as we neared the edge of the woods, the king jogged ahead of me. Tena's sword was larger than the one I carried before taking this one from Daveen, but I'd gotten used to its weight and balance.

"Yeah, I do. Do you have a problem with that?" I snapped. "Who do you think should carry it, if not me, a direct descendent of Tena?"

"No one. Queen Tena's sword should belong to you." He lowered his head.

"Then why did you mention it in the first place?"

"I used it as a talking approach?"

"A talking approach?" I'd been speaking solely in Landaffen since I'd returned. I was as fluent as ever, but I still had trouble understanding some of their expressions.

"Yes. It is a starting point to fracture the tension between us," Autka said.

"Breaking the ice—that's what humans call it. You should use that expression instead, considering where you live," I joked sarcastically.

"I am sorry for what I did." Autka said, his words rolling gently from his tongue as he hung his head. "I should not have put my hands on you. I should not have questioned your abilities." He sighed. "It is not your abilities that I doubted. It was my own." He exhaled, and his released breath formed a cloud in the air. "As chief protector, it is my job to keep the grove safe, and I failed to do so. I took the anger I had for myself, and I applied it to you instead."

"In the human world of psychology, that's called projection." My tone was sharp and cynical. I was too worried, tired, and annoyed to mask my emotions.

"It was wrong for me to do so. Again, I am sorry. It will not happen again."

When I didn't respond, he stopped walking.

I turned to face him. "Fine, I appreciate the apology and explanation. But I'm not sorry for suggesting you are a traitor."

"Do you think I am the traitor?" His chest puffed with a big breath.

I put my hands on my hips. "No, I don't sense deception." I looked him up and down. "I sense someone who is insecure and compensates for it by being a brute."

"Laura," King Mutu shouted.

I rushed to the edge of the ridge. Pakak had done a great job eliminating our tracks. The path Tontan, Pakak, and I had taken was rough in a few places where the snow was mostly large ice crystals and didn't smooth out all the way, but those spots were sporadic and didn't let on that they were once mammoth footprints.

Without any snowfall, the Hanllants' tracks were still visible. A trampled path of disturbed snow and boot prints ran diagonally from the tree line to the cave. I pulled out my binoculars and scanned the field. The gray sky made the moon less visible, but its light illuminated the landscape in a ghostly glow.

"Do you think my son is here?" the king asked me. His eyebrows buckled. "I do not see him."

On Autka's orders, the protectors lined the ridge on either side of us. Autka stood behind the king.

"Do you see that boulder?" The king nodded. "It's concealing the entrance to the cave I told you about. The Hanllants are in there right now."

"And my son?"

"I think Prince Pakak is hiding either there..." I pointed to the far end of the field where it dropped into my former campsite. "Or behind one of those snowbanks near the cave. From either location, he can watch and wait for the Hanllants to leave, and the minute he sees Daveen, I think Pakak will try to kill him."

"He is only a boy," King Mutu huffed. "A boy with a boy's judgement and skills. I do not understand what made him believe that he alone could assassinate their leader."

"He is also a boy who's witnessed the death and destruction Daveen leaves in his wake. Anger and hate clouds common sense and makes it difficult to see the consequences of one's actions. In his mind, he is doing what he thinks a prince should do—avenge the destruction to his colony."

"You are very wise for your age, Laura," King Mutu said.

"I learned a lot from King Hurrlan in the Tulix Grove. When he taught me how to use quick magic, he also taught me that being a good leader meant being able to not only sense emotions but understand what causes them as well."

"I would like to meet this king."

"Someday when all of this is over, I'm sure you will."

"What do you suggest we do, Laura?" Autka asked.

"I'll go to those two places and search for Pakak. I'll go alone. If the Hanllants are early risers, I can make myself unseen by all and retreat if I need to."

"I would like to come with you," Autka said. "You have had no rest. No time to renew your magic. If you are unable to remain unseen, I will be there to fight at your side."

"I agree you should not go alone," the king said. He set his hand on my shoulder. "Autka will not disappoint you."

"Okay," I sighed. "Let's go."

Considering his large size and weight, Autka was more agile in the deep snow than I thought he'd be. We followed the path the Hanllants had taken, but I could still see that his footprints weren't as deep as mine. He'd taken additional weapons with him, including a spear with three prongs and a backward-facing barb. A large sea-turtle shell with a leather strap screwed into the concave side of the shell served as a shield.

"These turtles did not give their lives for our use," Autka had explained when he'd pulled it from their armory. "These shells were collected from those already dead."

He'd offered me a shield and additional weapons, but Tena's sword, a dagger strapped to my calve, and my bow and arrows were the only weapons I felt confident using.

The cold air bit my cheeks and nose. I held my cupped hand over my face and exhaled, giving my skin a shot of needed warmth. "Let's check those snowbanks near the cave, and if he's not hiding there, we'll go to my old campsite."

"There is also a chance he will see us, and call us to him," Autka said.

"Or he'll run and continue hiding from us. He doesn't want to be found. He wants to kill Daveen."

At the bottom of the ridge, we quickened our pace, Autka insisting I stay behind him. He held the shell high and positioned it to shield both of us.

"It is low moon," Autka said, looking at the sky and shaking his head. "The night cannot hide us."

"All of them went into the cave," I said. "I'm guessing they'll be in there for a few more hours. The only Hanllants they left on watch were the three Pakak and I caught outside the grove."

"Then the Hanllants are either foolish or over-confident," Autka said. "A proper leader would have stationed protectors outside the cave."

We changed directions and moved toward the snowbanks. Autka did what he could to hide our footprints by working the wind. With one hand, he wove the wind into a small spiral that dug its vortex into the snow and sprayed the flakes in a circular pattern. With his other hand, he smoothed out any remaining lumps.

"I haven't seen that technique," I said. "I've never wound the wind so tightly before."

"It is used to free fishhooks that have been caught in seaweed."

"So, you can stir the water below the water's surface?"

"Yes, the rotating water pulls the hook free."

"That's cool. I want to learn how to do that."

"Laura, look!" Autka pointed. "There are tracks from the cave to the field." He traced the dull outline of one of them with his finger. "With the snowfall and wind, I cannot tell how fresh they are, but there are at least two sets of prints."

At this point, unless they came from a mammoth or horse, every set of tracks pretty much looked the same to me. The prints were deeper at the heal. Due to the thickness of the snow, there'd been a lot of toe-dragging, but the prints overlapped and there was a fresh film of snow covering them, so I couldn't tell how many Landaffens had walked there or when.

"Did you see these when you and Pakak went to the grove?" Autka continued.

"No, but we hadn't come this close to the cave."

A snort and high-pitched whinny sounded from beyond the bluff. "I have heard that sound before, but I cannot remember which animal creates it," Autka said. "We do not have them in our grove."

"It's a horse. The Hanllants have three with them. They're

too big to pass through the cave's entrance, so they keep them in those woods." I pointed to a cluster of pine trees.

"We are too far from the snowbank to take cover," Autka said.

"Take my hand. I'll make us unseen by all."

Autka took my hand, and though we both wore gloves, I could feel the strength in his fingers and the heat of his palm against mine.

"Don't let go," I said and concentrated, diverting my energy into making every atom of my body and anything touching me invisible.

From the top of my head to my nose, my body tingled like the prick of a thousand pins. The bristling continued, settling into my neck and shoulders, but when it reached my chest, it disappeared.

"Are we unseen?" Autka said.

"No," I sighed. "I guess I'm too tired." I rotated my shoulders one at a time. "But I think I can still do it. I just need to—"

A pair of pine trees shook, and clumps of snow dropped from their branches. There was another whinny and the chomp of crusty snow.

"Get down," Autka said and pulled me to the ground with him.

He dug the bottom edge of his shield into the snow and guided me to duck behind it. He rose to one knee, and in one smooth motion and using only one hand, positioned his bow in a notch at the top of his shield. He set an arrow against the bowstring and aimed for the trees.

Regaining my strength, I closed my eyes, tightening every muscle in my body. The tingling returned, stronger this time. I curled my free hand into a fist and inhaled through my nose. My skin prickled and grew numb, the sensation flowing down my arm and to Autka's hand.

He gasped, and I heard the clack of his bow against the shell as it slipped from his shield. I opened my eyes. Autka was on both knees.

"Are we unseen?" he asked as he resumed his stance on one knee and reset his bow.

"Yeah, I did it," I said. "Just don't let go of me."

I peeked over the top of the shield and looked through my binoculars.

Within the cluster of trees, a dark mass reared and bucked, its shadow dancing wildly. Pine branches rustled, twigs snapped, and a horse burst from between two pines. The black stallion, thickly furred and with four white socks, skirted left and right, dropped its head, and kicked his back legs.

"It's Ontah," I said. "Daveen's horse."

From where we were and through my binoculars, the horse was only the size of my hand, but with the stallion's grace, strength, and beauty, there was no doubt it was Daveen's.

"And Daveen is the rider?" Autka asked.

There was a figure on Ontah's back, but it seemed small compared to that of an adult rider. As the figure held onto the saddle horn with both hands, the figure's body flopped like it had no bones. Ontah reared, dropped, and spun, and the figure flattened against the horse's back.

Blood rushed into my cheeks. "Oh, no! It's not Daveen! It's Prince Pakak! We've got to help him."

We became seen as I let go of Autka's hand and ran, focusing all my efforts on the prince. With each stride, I threw my weight forward, and with high steps, wrenched my boots through the thick snow.

Autka passed me, holding his shield with one hand, and cranking his other arm, and I increased my speed by stepping into the prints he made. Daveen's horse bucked, and the prince slammed forward onto the horse's neck, his little body teetering against Ontah's backbone.

"Hold on, Pakak!" I shouted as I ran. The cold air froze my throat and I coughed, struggling to say more.

Side-stepping, Ontah threw back his head, lifted his front feet from the ground, and turned toward Autka. Ontah snorted and dug his hoof into the snow, pawing the hard-packed ice like a mad bull.

"Laura, help me!" Pakak screamed.

"Autka! Stop! And don't move!"

Autka slowed down and became still. I did the same, but when Ontah stopped moving, I crept forward, keeping my arms low and hands open.

"Laura, what are you doing?" Autka whispered. "The animal has lost all sense. He is dangerous."

"I know this horse," I said. "And he knows me."

Clouds of condensed mist shot from Ontah's nostrils, and his head bobbed in time with his heaving chest. A film of powdery snow covered his muzzle and chin.

"It's okay, Ontah," I said softly. "Remember me? Good Ontah. Good boy."

When I was six feet away, I stopped walking. Ontah's breathing slowed, but his ears remained pinned to his head.

"Pakak, listen to me, and do exactly as I say."

Pakak nodded.

"Carefully swing one leg around to meet the other, slip from his back, and then slowly move away from him."

"I, I can't." Pakak sniffled. His cheeks were chapped pink and trailed with tears. "My hand is caught." He tugged his arm to show me.

Pakak's hand had been small enough to slip through a loop of rope meant only for fingers. It twisted about his wrist, pinching the leather of his gloves where two sections of the rope met and wound.

"Can you try slipping your hand from the glove?" I asked him.

"I already tried. I cannot do it." His thin, plum-colored lips quivered. "My wrist hurts, and I cannot feel my fingers."

"It's okay. I'll get it loose."

The prince cried, his shoulders bouncing. Ontah curled his neck, lifted a hoof, and scraped the ground. Pakak screamed as the stallion's back moved under him. Ontah scooted sideways, kicking up snow.

"Ontah," I said gently. "Good boy. Good Ontah." I slowly lifted my hand and took a step forward. Ontah took a step backward.

"He will not let you near him, Laura," Pakak whimpered. His hood had fallen from his head, and when Ontah skirted forward or backward, the hood flapped against Pakak's back.

"Yes, he will. Ontah is an angry horse, but he is a good horse. His owner is the one who is bad. Ontah has been whipped, beaten, and scolded into submission, but his heart has not hardened. I can sense his gentle nature."

With his free hand, Pakak smoothed the side of Ontah's neck. Ontah jerked his head, and as Pakak squeezed his legs and drew away his hand, the stallion reared. Pakak flew forward and dropped back into the saddle when Ontah's front hooves met the snow.

Pakak's eyes grew wide. His jaw dropped and eyebrows lifted. "No! Do not hurt him!" the prince screamed.

"Don't worry. I'm not going to hurt him. Ontah is as scared as you are. I'm going to help both of you."

"No! Laura! Make Autka stop."

I turned to look behind me. Autka stood with his bow raised and arrow nocked.

"Autka, wait! Don't do it," I shouted.

Ontah neighed and snorted.

"There is not time to wait. Prince Pakak is in danger. The moon has dropped, and the Hanllants will awake."

"Just give me a few more minutes," I said. My heart beat hard in my throat, and the muscles across my back tightened and ached.

Autka spoke without moving, as the arrow remained pointed at Ontah's chest. "The animal cannot be soothed," he said.

"As Prince of Aludene." Pakak's voice trembled. "I order you to—"

The release of the bowstring sounded like the buzz of a bee. The arrow's shaft stung the crisp air with its whistle, but just in time, Pakak kicked Ontah hard in the ribs.

Daveen's mighty steed lunged forward, breaking into a run. The arrow whizzed past Ontah's shoulder, and the arrow's point sunk into the trunk of a tree.

In a frenzied gallop, Ontah burst toward Autka. The protector dove left, rolled to his feet, pulled an arrow from his quiver, and aimed.

"No," I screamed, pulling his arm. "You could hit Pakak."

He yanked his arm from my hands and raised his bow. I grabbed him again, and he shook himself free from my hold. I dropped onto my butt.

"Don't!" I warned. "It's not worth the risk. You agreed to listen to me!"

Autka sighed and lowered his bow. I stood and wiped the snow from my pants. Ontah's hooves flew, snow flung, and Pakak bounced awkwardly as the stallion tore through the field toward my old camp site. Beyond that, acres and acres of a great snow bed stretched away from the cave, and at the far end, sat Stan's cabin.

I cupped my hands around my mouth and shouted. "Hold on, Pakak! We're coming!" Even with his sharp Landaffen hearing, with the crush of snow and Pakak's screams, I doubted he heard me.

Pakak slipped from Ontah's back. Hanging by his wrist, the little prince's body twisted and spun as he kicked his dangling legs. I sucked in a sharp breath and held my hand against my chest.

"His arm will break," Autka said. "Or it may already be broken."

I held my breath as Pakak pushed off from the snow with one foot and leaped back into the saddle.

"Thank God!" I sighed.

"We will not be able to catch up to them," Autka said. "But I imagine the horse will eventually tire."

"Yeah, Ontah will, and when he does, we'll be there." I looked east. The horizon burned orange behind a distant mountain range, and the moon was the same color as the sky. "There is nothing more the king and your protectors can do. Tell the king what happened and take your team back to the grove."

"Laura," Autka said from over his shoulder as he turned to leave. "Don't forget about those footprints we saw."

"I won't. I'll be careful. Don't worry."

CHAPTER 8

At a jog, I followed Ontah's hoofprints. The set of unknown footprints became less visible the farther I went. Finally, they disappeared, leading me to believe they were made long before Ontah took off with Pakak.

Stan's house was no longer a dot, but Ontah and Pakak were. The sharp angles of the cabin's roof and its smokestack were easy to see against the rolling snow and gray sky. From the chimney, smoke curled and thinned as a strong wind pulled it south.

Ontah, a bouncing dot with another dot on his back, grew smaller and smaller no matter how fast I ran. At times the dot on his back moved to one side, and my heart would jump as I watched, hoping Pakak wouldn't fall off and dangle to break a bone. But the small dot stayed atop the larger one until they passed the cabin and disappeared.

When they were close to the cabin, I'd hoped Stan would go out on the porch with his morning cup of coffee to say to hello to the day, but it didn't happen. If he had, Ontah might have been startled and turned to run toward me, but unfortunately, it was still too early for the mountain man to be out of bed.

The farther I ran, the more my legs felt like they were

weighted at my ankles. My boots dragged, catching on the coarse snow, slowing me down with each step, and it was hard to keep my eyes open.

When Stan's cabin was only a few yards away, I contemplated knocking on his door and asking for his help, but I trudged along, deciding not to add any additional stress to his life when it wasn't one-hundred percent necessary.

The snow bed thinned, thanks to Stan's grooming of his acreage, and I was able to quicken my pace. But with the lack of snow, hoofprints were less visible, and I had to slow down to figure out which way Ontah had run.

As I continued following Ontah's hoofprints, the wind changed directions, and the sky turned white as it began to snow. Thick flakes fell diagonally, blurring my sight, and my heart dropped as I turned and watched Ontah's tracks and mine start to disappear with the falling snow.

Following what was left of Ontah's hoofprints, I broke into a run, sprinting passed Stan's cabin to a spot behind his barn where Ontah's tracks ran in a tight circle before straightening out again. I stopped and looked through my binoculars and didn't see anything other than endless snow and a set of trees at the base of a distant hill. My throat hurt, and one of the cracks in my bottom lip had reopened.

Behind me, snow crunched in the rhythm of quick, determined footsteps. I drew my weapon and turned, digging the toes of my boots into the thin snow and raising my sword. It could be Stan, though through his cabin windows, I could see that the inside of his house was still dark. Or it could also be a Hanllant, having awoken to find Ontah missing and deciding to follow the horse's hoofprints.

Sucking in a quick breath, I changed my stance, shifting my weight to my left foot, ready to make myself unseen by all if it was Daveen or one of his Landaffens. A blurry figure in a smear of color matching the sky and snow crept around the backside of the house, his head half-hidden by a sea turtle shell shield. I lowered my sword and dropped my shoulders.

"Autka, what in the heck are you doing here?"

His boots slouched to the middle of his calf. His eyelids fluttered from his lack of sleep. With each heavy breath, his crude Aludene armor, a thick, double-folded leather tunic, and the strap he wore as captain, ballooned and fell.

"It is upon King Mutu orders. I am to help you find the prince and be your protector inside and outside the grove." Slightly bent at the elbows, he held his arms out to his sides. His eyes darted left and right, and he took his next step toward me like he was walking on a tight rope.

"Autka, are you okay?" I asked.

"I have never been this far from the grove," he said without making eye contact with me.

"Don't worry. You'll be fine. I know this world better than yours." He straightened his back. "You can make yourself seen," I said. "I know the human who lives here. His name is Stan. He's the human who was here when I restored the Cup of Queens." I nodded toward the cabin. "So, if he sees us, it won't be an issue."

He drew back his shoulders, and his body solidified.

"Besides, just like me, you need to save your magic. The farther we go south, the more likely we are to run into humans. With our weapons and the way we're dressed, we'll need to be unseen."

Autka got down on one knee and studied the messy ring of indents that had once been distinct hoofprints.

"I'm guessing that Ontah was either startled, or maybe the prince did something to spook him." I shook my head. "Either way, Pakak is still on his back, and from what's left of these prints, it looks like they are headed toward town."

Autka stood. "Prince Pakak will be able to make himself, and maybe Ontah, unseen, but he will not be able to keep the mask for very long. If Ontah does not slow from exhaustion, we will not be able to catch up to them."

"Then somehow we need to move faster." I put my hands on my hips and sighed. The sun broke from the horizon. The falling snow glistened, and a band of sunlight illuminated the barn door. "And I know exactly how we can do that," I said, jogging to the barn door and lifting the latch. "I just need to get the key from —" I threw the door open. Sunshine bounced from the hood of Stan's truck. "Damn it! It's not here!"

"What are you searching for, Laura?" Autka asked, looking into the barn from over my shoulder.

At my feet were the faint tracks of a snowmobile, caterpillar tread between the smooth, ski-like trail made from a pair of front runners. "The snowmobile. It's—"

Autka spun, reaching one arm behind his back, and clasping his hand on my shoulder to pull me down. "Pretense," he said, ordering me to make myself unseen.

He ducked behind his shield, turning into a blur the same color as the barn. To conserve my magic, I wrapped my arm around his waist and ducked behind him.

Stan's dog, a black and gray husky named Bucky, ran to the front of the barn. Bucky stopped and growled, his lips peeling back to display sharp teeth. He couldn't see us, but he obviously smelled that we were there.

Snow chomped hard, the ice crystals crunching like thick-soled boots were sinking heavily and clumsily into the snow. A gust of wind spread a sheet of snow in our direction, and the wind whistled.

A human taking long, slow steps, appeared from behind the cabin. He wore an army-green coat and black snow boots. A folded dog leash stuck from his pocket. The coat was unzipped, and in the wind, a long, plaid robe in blue and green billowed from underneath it. Red, flannel pajama bottoms bulged from the top of his boots, and a black knit cap covered his head. He held a double-barreled shotgun and pointed it at the barn.

Bucky continued to snarl, lowering his head and straightening his curved tail.

"There's nothing in there of any value." Stan said. "So come on out of my barn and get off my property, or I'll sic my dog on you!"

Autka reached for his bow, and I pressed my chest against his back to stop him.

"Stan! It's me, Laura!" I said, switching from Landaffen to English and making myself seen. I pushed off Autka's back, letting go of his waist, and rose while raising my hands.

With his tail wagging, Bucky ran to my side and encouraged me to pet him by putting the top of his head under my palm. I scratched him behind the ears, and he licked my wrist.

Stan lowered his shotgun. "Laura!" He jogged to me, clomping through the snow and slipping twice. He gave me a hug.

"So, what's happening with those Landaffers?"

"It's Landaffens," I said and laughed.

"Yeah, Brell wouldn't tell me what was going on."

"What do you mean? When did you see Brell?" My breathing intensified, and my wind-blown, watery eyes filled with fresh tears.

"About one thirty this morning. I remember because the show I was watching had just ended. I was about to force myself to go to sleep." He sighed and dropped his chin. "Because I, um, haven't really had a good night's sleep, since um...anyway. But it's all over now...right?" Stan said slowly with one eyebrow raised.

"Not quite." I lowered my chin. "The Hanllants returned last night and attacked Aludene."

"On, no!" Stan huffed. He put his hands on his hips and shifted his eyes to the sky. "Do you think that's why Brell needed my snowmobile? So, he could get away?"

When Stan said the word snowmobile, Autka's eyebrows came together. He looked at me for an explanation, and I motioned for him to come out as I explained that it was a motorized sled.

Autka became seen and came forward. "I am Autka," he said

in English. "Captain of the protectors of Aludene." Autka bowed.

"This is Stan. He's a friend of my dad's, and like I told you, he knows about the grove and the cup." Stan held out his hand, and Autka shook it. Bucky lifted his nose, and Autka gave him a pet.

"He took your snowmobile?" I asked Stan.

"Yep."

With his nose, Bucky knocked the underside of my hand with his nose, so I'd give him a pet on the head. "I'm sorry, Stan. I never meant to involve you in any of this. It just happened. If I could take all of it back, you know, I totally would."

"I know you would." He took both of my hands in his, and I wrapped my gloved fingers around his gloveless hands. "But *I* wouldn't take any of it back," he said. "I was thankfully there when all of you needed my help, and I'll continue to be there, just like I was for Brell today."

"Tell me more about Brell. What exactly did he say and do?" I asked.

The snowfall lessened and the wind died into a chilly breeze.

"Like I said, he came to my door at about one-thirty this morning and asked to use the snowmobile." He glanced at the barn. "His eyes were so desperate, and his hands were shaking so badly. I knew it wasn't from the cold. Of course, I said 'yes' and gave him the key."

"Brell didn't say why?" I asked.

"Nope, he just kept thanking me and then took off on the snowmobile." He pulled the leash from his pocket and clipped it to Bucky's collar.

"Which way did he go?"

"Toward town, but who knows if that's actually where he went. He rode off in that direction though, and that's the last I've seen of him." Stan pointed to the south.

"And he didn't say when he'd be back?"

"Nope, I've told you all that I know. What kind of trouble is he in? Are the Hanllants still a threat?"

"Yeah, unfortunately they are, but we have other things to worry about right now." Autka and I exchanged glances. "Did you see a horse run by here, or hear anything unusual? It would have been about an hour or so ago."

"Nope, I'm sorry, Laura. I finally fell asleep and woke up just now with the sunrise."

"The prince of Aludene is on a runaway horse, and we think they're also headed toward town."

"Oh, no!" He shook his head. "Damn! I wish you could take the truck through this snow, but you know that's not possible until April."

"Yeah, I know. The only thing we can do is keep following what's left of the horse's hoofprints and find them before Pakak gets hurt or they're found by humans. We don't want to get the local police involved. The sheriff's a nice guy and everything, but with Pakak's ears and Pakak not being able to give the sheriff his address or his parents' phone numbers, it would create a situation I don't even want to think about."

"I wish there was something I could do," Stan said while rubbing his chin. "I know, I'll call Edna at the hotel and ask her to be on the lookout for a horse and rider, and if she finds them, to try to keep them with her until you arrive."

"Thanks, Stan," I said.

Autka tilted his head. "I hear a strange sound. A hum or a buzz."

"I don't hear anything," Stan said.

I held my breath and listened. A motor droned, its pitch changing as if it kept speeding up and then slowing down.

"I know that sound. It's a snowmobile! It has to be Brell!" My pulse jumped as I inspected the faint snowmobile tracks leading from the barn.

Even with the earlier fall of snow, some of the tracks were visible. I jogged from the barn and cut left on Stan's property where the ground sloped upward, dropped two feet, and flattened out again. At the bottom of the slope, a deep gouge in the snow bed indicated where the snowmobile had flown from the knoll and landed. Beyond the knoll, the tracks became less visible and disappeared.

Autka stood on the knoll, shading his eyes from the sun. "Something is there." He pointed straight ahead of us. "I cannot tell what it is, but it is too big to be Brell on a motor sled."

Bucky ran to the top of the knoll and barked.

"I don't see anything," Stan said, lifting upon his toes. "Those Landaffer senses of yours sure are amazing."

I laughed again. "Landaffen," I said, and looked through my binoculars.

When the set of dots in the distance came into focus, I sighed, dropped my shoulders, and smiled. "You're right. It is too big to be Brell on a snowmobile."

CHAPTER 9

"It's too big to be Brell on a snowmobile because it's Brell, Pakak, and the horse, Ontah." My chapped cheeks hurt from smiling. I sighed, lowering my binoculars, and watching Brell through clouds of my breath.

With one hand, Brell worked the throttle. With the other, he held Pakak on his lap. Ontah's reins were tied to the snowmobile's frame, and Ontah walked next to the snowmobile with his head down.

"Are they okay?" Stan asked.

"Yeah, I think so," I said as I adjusted the focus of my binoculars. "Pakak is conscious, but he's holding his left arm across his chest. His wrist might be broken. When Ontah took off, Pakak's hand was caught in a rope on the saddle horn."

"Broken wrist and maybe a broken hand, too," Stan said.

"Brell seems fine. And so does Ontah. The snowmobile isn't scaring him."

"Yeah, that horse has got to be dead tired," Stan said.

I dropped my binoculars and waved both arms in the air. Brell perked up and let go of the throttle to wave back. He said something to Pakak. The little prince looked in our direction but didn't move his arms.

"Oh, I think I see them." Stan took a few steps forward. "Those little black things moving out there."

"Yep, that's them."

When the snowmobile reached the bottom of the knoll, Autka and I ran down the bank to meet it, and Brell came to a stop. Ontah hung his head and nipped at the snow.

"No, Bucky," Stan said. "You're staying right here with me."

"Laura," Pakak said. His voice broke, and his bottom lip trembled. His eyes were red and puffy, and dried tears trailed from his cheeks to his chin in powdery white frozen trails of salt water. "I am sorry," he sobbed, his bottom lip protruding and shoulders jumping.

"I know you are," I said gently.

Pakak's hand was wrapped in Brell's wool scarf. Pakak cradled it against the forearm of his other arm and winced when he readjusted it.

"Bring the boy inside," Stan said once we reached him. "And I'll take a look at his wrist. I was a corpsman in the marines. I've treated plenty of broken bones." He tucked the butt of his shotgun under his arm and headed toward the cabin. Bucky walked at Stan's side.

"This man's name is Stan," I told Prince Pakak. "He is our friend."

Pakak nodded and Autka scooped up the little prince. When his lap was free, Brell got off the snowmobile, took my hand, and drew me into his arms.

"I did not know you were here," he said. "You should be in Wventorin where it is safe." He held my face in his hands, and we kissed. "I love you."

"I love you, too." His kisses came harder, and my feet practically slipped out from under me as he took me by the waist. "I had to come back," I said. "There's no way I could have left you here, especially while Aludene was under attack. I had to help them. And I had to find you."

He kissed me again and sunk his head against my shoulder as his hands pressed against my back. "And the others?"

"They're safe. They're in Wventorin." Chills ran up my arms as Brell's warm breath hit my neck.

"How is your mother?"

"She'll be okay."

Brell pulled away from me and held me by the upper arms. His eyebrows drew together, and he parted his lips. "I am sorry about your mother. She will receive the proper care and treatment in the grove."

"I know." With my next breath, I felt a bit lightheaded and steadied myself by dividing my weight between my feet.

"My sweet Laura. You have had no sleep or food." Brell cupped my chin in his palm.

I laughed. "I look that bad, huh?"

He kissed my nose. "No, you do not. You look beautiful. You are the most beautiful being, Landaffen or human, that I have ever seen."

"Yeah, right," I wanted to say, but I understood. Even though Brell lacked sleep, I felt the same way about him.

The skin below Brell's eyes was sunken and darker than usual. His full lips were chapped and peeling, making them look less full. The hair at the top of his head was flat and longer strands twisted awkwardly above his eyes. But he was gorgeous.

I brushed his hair from his forehead. The hair at his ears parted, revealing his ear's delicate curve and point. His eyes, bright and mysterious, sparkled with a longing to kiss and hold me and never stop.

My cheeks filled with heat. "And you are the most handsome being, Landaffen or human, that I have ever seen." I dropped against his chest in a hug. "So much has happened. There is so much I need to tell you."

He wrapped his arms around me and kissed my forehead. "And I have much to tell you. Come, we will take the snowmobile and Ontah into the barn."

Ontah munched at the snow. His thick fur was matted where sweat had accumulated and froze. His chin and the rims of his nostrils were crusted with ice. "He needs water," Brell said. "He will get 'cold sickness' from eating snow."

Ontah's legs shook as I took him by the reins and led him into the barn.

When Ontah and I were inside, Brell drove the snowmobile up the knoll, turned off the engine, and pushed it into the barn. As he took off Ontah's saddle and covered the stallion's back with the blanket Stan used for the snowmobile, he explained how he'd seen Ontah running with Pakak. He instantly knew something was wrong, and went after them on Stan's snowmobile.

He'd caught up with them just before they reached the town. At that point, Ontah had slowed to a trot and hadn't had the energy to do anything other than sidestep away when Brell parked the snowmobile and crept up to him.

I ran my hand down Ontah's neck.

Brell picked up an empty bucket. "I will bring him water."

Brell and I found Prince Pakak sitting at the kitchen table. Stan hovered over Pakak, attending to his wrist and hand. A tin first-aid kit with its lid open was at the center of the table. Across from Pakak, Autka sat drinking water from a mug and eating a toaster pastry. Autka and Prince Pakak spoke in English, so Stan could understand them.

I ran to Stan's hard-wired phone and called Todd. My call went straight to voice mail, probably because Todd was in the grove, but I left a quick, semi-detailed message, explaining what had happened to Aludene, and that Brell and I were at Stan's cabin. I told him to text me updates on my mom, and I'd try calling again when I had cell service.

"I made a pot of coffee, and you can pop some frozen waffles in the toaster or help yourselves to those," Stan said, nodding in the direction of the opened box of toaster pastries on the counter.

I poured Brell and myself a cup of coffee. Autka chose water, explaining that he'd heard of coffee and how bitter it was from the scouts in his colony and had no desire to try it.

Pakak's fingers and wrist were swollen and bruised. His index and middle finger were puffier than the others and the joints were discolored. I sat down at the table next to Pakak. While Brell filled the bucket with water and took it to the barn, I briefly told Stan about the attack on Aludene.

"They were in the trees above the tent and no one heard them or saw them?" Stan asked when I'd finished.

"Nope, not with their Landaffen grace and agility. That's how they've been able to escape *human* eyes—that, coupled with the grove's magic of deception and the Landaffen's ability to be unseen," I said and remembered Daveen as the grocery-store boy.

He'd jumped from the asphalt, catching the street-light cable in his hands and pulled himself up to stand atop it like a trapeze artist. As the cable gently bobbed and became still, he'd folded his arms against his chest, bowed his head, and leered at me with one side of his mouth lifted.

My emotions began to match what they were that day, and I shuddered, feeling faint as my pulse pounded in my neck.

As the memory continued, it changed, and Daveen's baseball cap morphed into a hood with fur trim, but his eyes remained dark and menacing and his half-grin maintained its bestial evil. A pungent, salty odor entered my nose. The rumbling of water filled my ears. A gust of wind blew Daveen's hood from his head, and his hair in sticky, blonde strands, flapped against the sides of his face and ears.

His eyebrows drew together, and his thick lips pursed. I'd never seen his face so tanned or the skin on his cheeks appear so thick and weather beaten.

"Bearing away," he shouted in Landaffen.

"Laura?" Stan said.

I blinked and Daveen's stern face faded from my thoughts. "I'm sorry." I gasped. "What were you saying?"

"I said his wrist isn't broken." Stan dug into his first-aid kit. "Just a couple of fingers. But from what I can tell, they're clean breaks. Taping them together should do the trick. And then when he's home, the Landaffers can fix 'em up the way they like to do it."

I took a deep breath to recompose myself, and Pakak nodded and whimpered while looking at his purple fingers. Bucky stood next to Pakak, wagging his tail, and when he tried to lick Pakak's face, it was one of the few times the little prince smiled while being tended to. Brell returned from the barn and sat with us at the table.

"I do not understand why the horse named Ontah did not listen to my commands. I do not understand why he did not bond with me." Pakak's eyes welled with more tears.

"Since he's been mistreated, Ontah is not like other horses. He's been bullied and beaten into obedience even when it wasn't necessary. He's used to Daveen, someone who is rough and cruel to him," I explained to the young prince. "With someone as light as you on his back, someone who is kind and gentle, he didn't know how to respond."

"I am sorry, Laura. I should have listened to you." Pakak sniffled and, with the back of his good hand, buffed away the tears on his cheeks.

"It's not your fault that Ontah behaved the way he did, but you're unfamiliar with horses and shouldn't have attempted riding one in the first place. On the other hand, it is your fault that your parents are worried about you and a lot of people put their lives in danger while trying to find you."

Pakak hung his head, and Bucky made a second attempt to give the prince a lick.

"You never should have left Aludene," I continued. "And from now on, you need to do as you're told." I took a long sip of coffee.

"But I want to help. I want to see the Hanllants suffer and do so at my hand. I want to watch the roots of the great pines pull Daveen into the earth." He lifted his head. The fine arches of his eyebrows flattened, and his cheeks, fresh with tears, shined white under the warm glow of the outdated pendent light hanging above the kitchen table.

"You want revenge."

"Yes." He sucked in his bottom lip.

Brell reached across the table and set his hand on top of Pakak's uninjured one. "Punishment given in return for one received. A repayment of evil for evil," Brell said. "Revenge is the product of hate and a haunting desire for vengeance. A secret reward for killing Daveen will not await you if Daveen is swallowed by the earth. Your sorrows will remain, and if you do not quell your craving to kill, your longing for retribution will consume your soul."

"But the earth has taken many of my people because of him. The Hanllants killed Tawshu." He made a fist with his uninjured hand. "They killed Nome. The Hanllants do not deserve life."

"We seek the Hanllants because they want to alter that which is fated to be. Our goal is not to destroy them. Our goal is to stop them from interfering with The One's destiny," Brell explained in a soft voice so Pakak would understand. "In doing so, lives may be lost, but only because we have defended ourselves."

Pakak yanked his hand away. "If they are all dead, they can no longer interfere."

"If they are all dead simply for vengeance, then we are barbarians and not the keepers of peace."

"Maybe I want to be a barbarian," the little prince snickered.

"You are no barbarian. You are the prince of Aludene," Brell reassured. "Someday you will be king, a king who understands balance and harmony, and you will be there to support The One when she fulfills her destiny." Brell leaned across the table and stared into Pakak's eyes. "You have much to learn, and in time, you will. But until then, you must listen to Laura and those who have already learned these lessons, and do as you are told."

"Prince Brell is right," Autka said. "You must do as you are told."

Pakak sat back in his chair.

"Prince Pakak, do you understand?" Brell asked.

"Yes," the little prince said as he stared at the table.

While Stan wrapped Pakak's hand and wrist with gauze and medical tape, I told Brell everything that had happened after using quick magic to return to Alaska. He kept his hands folded on the table while periodically shaking his head and asking questions.

When I got to the part about the little prince helping me capture three Hanllants, I made sure to highlight Prince Pakak's resourcefulness, heroism, and bravery, and Pakak's stiff demeanor changed. It started with a half-smile, and when Brell commented that no other child of ten seasons could have accomplished such a feat, Pakak straightened his back and scooted closer to the table. Pakak filled in my tale with additional details, beaming but grunting in pain when he used his bad hand to gesture and accidentally moved his injured fingers.

"Then we just missed each other," Brell said when Pakak and I finished our story. "When we were ambushed, I fought alongside the Aludene. We outnumbered the Hanllants, but unfortunately, we were also unprepared. Now it is clear that the Hanllant's mission was also one of distraction, so they could acquire a piece of the stone."

I pulled the chip of stone from my pocket and showed it to him.

"When the Hanllants retreated, and I knew there was no more I could do to help the Aludene, I followed the Hanllants from the grove and hid and watched. Daveen left two Hanllants to guard the grove's entrance and another to search the woods in case you had returned."

"Those were the three Pakak and I captured." I gave Pakak a wink, and he gave me a thumbs up, something Todd had shown him earlier that week. "Daveen wants me dead," I said, "He won't stop until I'm one with the trees and the Legend of Tena dies with me."

Brell shook his head, saying, "I do not believe that is so. He wants you alive. He told them you must remain earthside."

"Maybe he plans to force me to perform another task that would give him power."

"Maybe. I do not know," Brell said. He squeezed his lips together and shook his head. "The reason why was not discussed among them."

"And that is when you left?" Autka asked.

"Yes, on Daveen's orders, two of them broke from the group to 'prepare for their departure', and I followed them. I did not know Prince Pakak had been sent from the grove, or that you were here and had gone to look for him. You must have been at our old campsite and did not see me when I crossed the field."

"We saw Daveen, Noth, Caylent, and Nenmie go into the cave with the group, so the two Hanllants you followed must have been from Mentsune," I said.

"Yes, they wore helmets with red crests. They were called Nalaan and Lanie," Brell nodded as he recalled. "The one called Lanie wore a necklace made from large, green leaves, leaves I did not recognize. The one called Nalaan wore a necklace of thin white disks like the one you described seeing, but a pendant of lithel also hung at its center. I was too far to see its design, but when it caught the moonlight, it shone in gold, silver, and bronze."

"Do you think he holds some kind of rank among his colony?" I asked.

"I do. Before Nalaan and Lanie left the group, Nalaan and Daveen engaged in what appeared to be an exchange of harsh words. I could not hear what was said, but when Daveen approached Nalaan and shouted, rather than backing away, Nalaan lifted his chin and placed his hand upon his sheath."

"Then what happened?"

"I believe a comprise was made. They exchanged nods, and Nalaan left with Lanie."

"Where did they go?" Autka asked.

"They went to a small body of water, an arm of the sea, and now I understand how the Hanllants were able to travel after Daveen was deposed from his use of quick magic," Brell explained.

Autka tucked his hair behind his ear and slowly rose from his chair. Brell's eyes shifted right as he turned his head toward the front door.

"Footsteps," Autka whispered in Landaffen. "Of many."

"I hear them, too," Pakak said.

"As do I," Brell added.

I held my breath and listened. Snow crunched again and again, the crisp piercing of an icy crust and the grating compaction of ice crystals. Bucky barked twice, a deep *woof, woof*.

"Quiet, Bucky," Stan said. "Laura, what's going on?"

"We hear footsteps, a lot of them."

Brell got up and slowly walked to the window. He lowered to his knees and peered through the small gap where the curtain panels met. "It is the Hanllants," Brell said.

Pakak scurried into the living room wearing the homemade sling Stan had made him. "They are looking for Ontah. Please, do not let him be found. Daveen will beat Ontah for running away."

"I do not believe they are looking for Ontah," Brell said. "They are not headed toward the cabin. They are taking the same route the others took when they left to prepare for the Hanllant's departure."

Autka and I crept to the window and knelt on either side of Brell. The sun was low in the sky, creating long shadows against the snow as the Hanllants marched across the field. Riding Noth's horse, Daveen was in the lead. Behind him was Caylent on her horse. On her head sat the red-crested cap she'd donned the day before.

Still chained, Nenmie walked behind Daveen, her head down and bound hands stretched in front of her. As the horse sped up and lurched forward, Nenmie tripped and broke into a jog, lacking the usual Landaffen grace and composure.

I used my binoculars. As Nenmie turned her head to look behind her, I saw a bruise above her right eye that hadn't been there the night before. The bruise was thick and blue, forcing her eyelid to droop.

"There should be fifty-one of them," I said, "including the ones who are injured."

"Can I take a look?" Stan asked.

I pulled the binocular strap over my head and handed them to Stan. Making room, I scooted to the right, and held up the hem of the curtain to give Stan a better look. Bucky squeezed his head between us and licked my neck.

"Son of a bitch," Stan said as he looked through the binoculars. "That woman needs to be rescued."

"I know," I said. "But it can't happen now."

"When we are able to do so, we will do everything we can to free her from the Hanllants and Daveen," Brell said. "Her loyalty to him is weak, and though I am sure she fears Daveen's brutality if she betrays him again, I believe she will accept our help."

Noth walked next to Daveen and his horse. The Mentsune came next, trudging through the snow, paired up and in a row like a small army. A sled pulled by two Mentsune brought up the rear. Upon it sat a Mentsune with his leg wrapped, and behind the sled, another Mentsune limped along, dragging one foot across the snow.

"I have counted fifty-one," Brell said.

"Then that's all of them. They didn't leave anyone behind. Where do you think they're going?" I asked Brell.

"To the same place where I followed the others. They are leaving this land and going to another," Brell said. "Where that other place is, I do not know."

"How do you know they're leaving Alaska?"

"Well, look at that," Stan said. He lowered the binoculars and scratched his head. "They just disappeared. I can't see them anymore."

"As they've come closer to your cabin and the town, they have made themselves unseen," Brell said. "And they will maintain the mask until they reach their destination."

"But *you* can still see them? You Landaffers can see each other."

"Yes, to the Landaffen the unseen appears cloudy and less distinct, but they are still visible. Laura is the only one who can make herself unseen by all." Brell stood and pulled me up with him. "I know you are tired, Laura, and you have spent much energy using quick magic, but I believe we must go now and follow them before they set to the sea."

"Set to sea? How are they going to do that?"

"The Hanllants I followed went to the edge of the sea, and at that edge, there was a boat; a large boat with three sails."

I gasped, remembering my vision of Daveen saying, "Bearing away."

CHAPTER 10

"Sea travel is not a part of our histories or legends," Brell said. "It is something I would not have believed if I had not seen it for myself. Traveling distances upon the water is a skill we have not chosen to learn and master."

"I did not think so either," Autka added. He stood in front of Stan's fireplace, rubbing his hands together.

Pakak had fallen asleep at the kitchen table. His injured hand sat in his lap, while his other hand lay on the table, cushioning his head.

"A grove must be surrounded by vast quantities of land," Brell explained. "That is the only way we can use our magic to remain hidden and protected against humans. Because of this, water routes are far from any grove. There has also never been a need to use waterways."

Autka crossed his arms "To travel above water on a vessel that floats, sharing the sea with humans, is dangerous and unwise, but it is not impossible."

"A crew of fifty-one could work together to make the boat and themselves unseen." Brell took another look out the window. "And sails could be powered by strategically working the wind."

Stan returned from the kitchen. "Here, take this." He handed me a plastic grocery bag he'd filled with granola bars, bottled water, and toaster pastries he'd warmed and wrapped in aluminum foil. "You two need to eat something. You can eat on the way."

"Thank you," I said and tucked it into my backpack.

"And now let's get you two looking like humans." He ran down the hall and returned with a myriad of winter clothes, and a double ski bag Brell and I could use to carry our weapons. Brell and I sorted through the clothes and found everything we needed.

"This will really help, Stan," I said when I returned from his bedroom wearing a sweatshirt and ski jacket instead of my Aludene tunic and parka. I'd carefully transferred the chip of stone from my parka pocket to one on the ski jacket that closed with a zipper. "If I have trouble keeping Brell and me unseen by all the Hanllants, they'll just think we're humans—at least from a distance."

Already dressed in the sweatshirt, ski jacket, and snow pants Stan had loaned him, Brell stood next to Stan and Autka, holding the ski bag filled with our weapons.

"It is time for us to go," Brell said. "The Hanllants have moved beyond the field." He turned to Autka. "It is now safe for you and Prince Pakak to return to the grove."

I went to the kitchen and gently gave the little prince's shoulder a shake. "Prince Pakak," I said softly.

"I...where am I?" he mumbled without opening his eyes.

"We're still at Mr. Stan's cabin. The Hanllants are gone. It's time for you and Autka to go back to Aludene."

"You are not coming with us?" His eyes fluttered open, and he lifted his head.

"No, Prince Brell and I have somewhere else we need to go." I patted his shoulder. "How's your hand?"

"It does not hurt much. It is numb and tingles," he said, although he grimaced while lifting it to the tabletop.

Autka helped the prince get to his feet, and Pakak yawned and stretched, bringing his arms high above his head.

Stan, Brell, Autka, Pakak, and I exchanged hugs and handshakes, and following an Aludene custom among those who have fought alongside one another, Brell and Autka clasped hands in a position that looked like they were getting ready to arm wrestle while using the other hand to pat each other's backs.

Autka took my hand and held it between his. "You have restored the cup. You have defended Aludene against our new enemy. You brought Prince Pakak home and have continued to protect him." He smiled while slightly lowering his head. "The Aludene cannot thank you enough for all you have done." He tightened his grip on my hand. "And I cannot thank you enough for what you have done for my people. The Aludene will continue to help you fulfill the destiny that is yours."

"Thank you, Autka," I said. "I thank the Aludene people. And I especially thank you for helping me search for Prince Pakak and being ready to fight if necessary."

Pakak ran to me and gave me a one-armed hug. "Do you think the Hanllants will ever come back?" he asked.

Like mine, the rims of his eyes were red, and the skin on his cheeks dry and bright pink. I lifted his hood onto his head, pulled the strings under his chin tight, and tied them.

"No, they have everything they wanted from Aludene. There is no reason for them to ever return."

"What about you? When are you coming back?"

"I don't know, but I will come back. I promise." We hugged again. "Thank you, Prince Pakak. You are a very brave prince. I could not have captured those Hanllants without your help."

He sniffled against my shoulder.

The town, Gold Creek Valley, lay in the distance, dotted with black and brown structures—the biggest one being the motel belonging to Edna where Todd, Thriss, Brell, and I had stayed. Since Brell had already been to the place where we assumed the Hanllants were heading, we chose to remain seen and just keep our distance.

Finally having cell service, I checked my phone and read a lengthy text from Todd. They'd made it safely to Wventorin. Mom was stable and expected to heal without any complications, and King Vaylan and Gressim were busy questioning the Hanllant we'd taken back to Berkshire County with us.

I texted Todd back, telling him Brell and I'd found out that the Landaffen we'd captured, and the Hanllants' new recruits, were from a grove called Mentsune, and we'd be in touch again soon.

To give his aching hands a break, every half mile or so, Brell switched carrying the ski bag from one hand to the other. Stretching the fingers of his newly freed hand, he'd rapidly blink, wrinkle his nose, and groan. When Stan lent his ski bag to us, he couldn't find the ski bag's accompanying shoulder strap, so it had to be carried by a pair of handles at the bag's center. Brell tried pulling the handle up one shoulder, but it was too small to go farther than the center of his bicep, especially with the thick coat he wore.

The backpack I wore made my shoulders ache. My calf muscles burned, and my feet were numb, but like Brell, I pushed forward without complaining.

We dropped into a small valley and stopped to eat a granola bar and drink lukewarm coffee from a thermos. A snowbank lay ahead of us, making it impossible to see into the distance, but the trail of Landaffen snow prints continued, cutting a wide groove into the snowy mound. I eyed the semi-steep hike we'd have to make and groaned.

"I will take your backpack," Brell said. It was at least the twentieth time since we'd left Stan's that he'd offered to carry it for me.

"No, you've already got the ski bag, and it's way heavier than the backpack." I hooked my finger under one strap and pulled the pack higher onto my shoulder.

"I will carry both." He held out his hand, and I slipped the backpack from my shoulder and held it out to him.

"Only if we trade," I teased and jerked it away when his fingertips hit the strap.

Brell smiled and he lifted an eyebrow. "I will not trade. I wish to take both." Stepping forward, he snatched the backpack from my hands before I could pull it away.

"You brat," I joked, and scrambled to take it back as it slipped to the crook of his arm.

Losing my balance, I teetered on one leg, grabbed his arm to steady myself, and tumbled, landing butt-first. Brell fell on top of me face-first with his elbows locked and palms on either side of me.

Brell shifted, firmly planting his hands. "I will carry both." He gave my forehead a quick kiss.

"Nope." I said and laughed as I wiggled my arms up my sides and past his wrists.

"Then I will make a contract with you. I am going to say a word in Landaffen," Brell said and flashed me a mischievous grin. "If you cannot tell me what it means, then I get to carry our weapons *and* our supplies."

"You really think there's a Landaffen word I don't know?"

My smile slipped from my face, and I froze in place. Daveen entered my mind's eye— his heated face. Sweat dripping to a pair of black eyes. Red lips. Blinding-white teeth. "Hapeye," he'd shouted.

That was the word he'd said in my dream—the word I couldn't remember until now!

I closed my eyes, using all my senses to translate and understand the word. Nothing came to me, and I opened my eyes.

"Are you okay?" Brell asked.

"Yeah, I'm fine." I pressed my lips together and nodded. "I

will definitely take that deal! But then I get to tell *you* a word, and if you don't know what it is, I get to carry the backpack."

"I will take that contract," Brell said. "My word is *velletsemn*." He smiled, one corner of his mouth lifting.

It sounded familiar to me, but I had no idea what it meant. I closed my eyes and turned my head toward the sun, hoping I wasn't too mentally exhausted for the meaning of the word to come naturally to me.

I repeated *velletsemn* in my head and told myself to think like an Landaffen, but the only thing that surfaced was that it might have something to do with breaking or undoing.

"To undo?"

"That is not correct."

"Then I have no idea." I sighed. My shoulders and back were getting cold. "You win. What does it mean?"

"It is a very old word. When the Landaffens first came to be and the colonies were very few, agreements between groves were bound through marriage, the marriage between a prince from one grove and the princess of another."

"At one time, humans did the same thing."

"This practice continued until over the turn of five-hundred seasons, a prince in a grove called Vellet, a grove very far from Wventorin," his eyes widened, "fell in love with a member of his colony." A strand of hair slipped from his hood.

"Sounds scandalous." I pushed his hair from his eyes and let the tip of my finger run down the side of his face. "Especially because she wasn't a princess."

He smiled. "Very scandalous."

"Was the marriage allowed?"

"It was, but at the displeasure of many since it required the breaking of a long tradition. This breaking became known as the Velletsemn as the couple named their wedding night the Velletsemn. The word is rare and has all but been forgotten because the first ending of a tradition only happens once."

A snowflake dropped from his hood and landed on my nose.

He brushed it away. "When word of this unorthodox marriage spread to other groves and the children of royals expressed that they, too, should have the right to marry for love rather than to bind contracts, a council was formed so agreements could be ratified by representatives from each grove. *Shemn* means to diverge from something."

"Oh, I get it—diverging from a tradition. And Vellet is the name of a grove, something I wouldn't know instinctively because it's not a common noun."

"Exactly. That is why I chose this particular word."

"Hey, I was kinda close with 'undoing.' You think you're pretty clever, don't you?" I teased.

"Yes, I do." He parted his lips and smiled, and his eyes shone as blue as the icy shadows that surrounded us. "There is another reason why I chose that word. If it were not for the *velletsemn,* we could not marry."

The sun was low in the sky, spreading its golden beams across the vast expanse of snow, igniting the sparse blades of dead weeds and tall grass in a fiery shade of bright yellow. Gray shadows appeared ocean blue, and the dusting of snow on tree trunks sparkled like tiny, white crystals.

Shaded by the fur trim of his hood, the sharp curve of Brell's jawline and the delicate sculpt of his face were more distinct. His plump lips parted, and he bent his elbows, lowering his body to kiss me.

Wrapping my arms around his neck, I drew him against my chest, and his elbows gave, bringing the points of his elbows to the snow. Our kissing increased, and as the pressure of his mouth built against my lips, the snow's chilly bite dissipated, and the icy wind against my skin was no more.

I bent my legs, and his lower body dropped between my knees. His mouth moved to my neck and throat, and I tilted back my head as he kissed me. Shifting his weight to one elbow, he worked his other hand up the bottom hem of my jacket where his hand glided between the down-filled nylon fabric and my sweatshirt.

When his fingers touched my breasts, he stopped moving, inhaled deeply, and dropped his hand to my ribcage where he wedged his fingers under my side. He exhaled, his hot breath exploding against my neck, and I dug the heel of my boots into the snow and inched lower to bring his lips back to mine.

With my hands behind him, I ripped the glove from my right hand. He readjusted his stance, and I arched my back to make room for his arm to cradle me. Grabbing the zipper of his coat with my barehand, I gave it a yank, bring it mid-chest, and jammed my stretched fingers inside and under his sweatshirt.

Our kisses increased, our mouths open and tongues meeting. Skin against skin, my palm pressed his chest as Brell's pushed his lower body against the insides of my thighs. Twisting my wrist, I changed directions, blinding fumbling for the waist of his snowpants. My hand slipped, and my palm ran down the length of his upper thigh.

Rising onto one hand, Brell rose from my body and buried his head under my chin while breathing heavily. I brought my exposed hand to my chest, and while balancing on his palm, he lifted his head, took my hand, and kissed it.

"We must stop," Brell said. "The day will come when we are joined, and at that time, we will share a bedchamber, loving each other and enjoying one another's bodies." His breathing slowed. "Waiting until that time is becoming more difficult." His chapped lips were blood red, and the apples of his cheeks ruddy, contrasting sharply with his fair skin.

"I know," I said softly. I closed my eyes, and he kissed my hand again. "You and I are also breaking a tradition. You will be marrying one of half-race."

Taking both of my hands, Brell gave a gentle pull, rocking us upright to sit across from one another. "And I will be marrying The One," he said as he cupped my hands in his.

"A marriage that can only happen once." I squeezed his

hands. "Just like the Velletsemn."

We leaned towards one another for a quick kiss and got to our feet. Brell picked up the ski bag and reached for my backpack. I set my foot on top of it.

"Wait. What about my turn," I said as I pulled my glove onto my numb hand.

Brell lowered his shoulders and half-batted his eyes, which was the Landaffen equivalent to rolling them. "I had hoped your turn had been forgotten."

"Nope. Not a chance. You take my breath away but not my memory or my want to win." I laughed, and Brell smiled while shaking his head. "Ready?" He nodded. "*My* word is hapeye?"

Brell tapped his finger against his chin, and one corner of his mouth drew upward in a smile. "Are you sure this is a Landaffen word?"

"Yeah, it is. I mean, I think it is. Daveen said it in that dream I told you about. I didn't remember the word he'd said until now."

"Dreams are not real, so the word he spoke could have been a product of your imagination." He kissed my nose and snatched the backpack from my foot, throwing me off balance.

"Hey." I gave him a playful slap on the shoulder as he pulled it across his back. "Okay, you win...but..."

"But what?" he asked.

"I keep having visions." I dusted snow from my pants.

"When this happens, are you seeing with all of your senses?"

"No. They just come...unexpectedly."

"And you do not believe it is your imagination?"

"No, I don't. It's not like I'm thinking back to something from the past or thinking about the future. I mean, sometimes I do that. It's hard to think about what I've been through." I sighed. "But these visions are different. They come unexpectedly, and I don't know if they're real or if I'm remembering part of a dream."

"Tell me about these visions." Brell held my hand.

"They're of Daveen—always Daveen. I see his face, and he's mad and yelling."

"Yelling a word like he did in your dream?"

"Yeah, but honestly, Brell, the more that I think about it, the more that dream wasn't like a regular dream. Something about it was different. It was like I was having a vision of something real while I was asleep."

"I have not heard of that being possible." He squeezed my hand. "But then again, you are The One. I believe anything is possible when it comes to you."

I dropped against him in a hug and laid my cheek on his shoulder. "I don't know what to think."

"You are also lacking sleep and have not eaten a full meal. Your mind could be playing tricks on you. But in the future, when you have one of these visions or dreams, please tell me right away."

"I will. Thank you, Brell."

He kissed my forehead.

Trudging up the snowbank, we stood at its peak and surveyed the landscape. The town was two or so miles away. The marching row of Hanllants, a dark, blurry chain at the far edge of village, chose to walk around the perimeter of the town, while Brell and I decided to cut through it. Saving our energy and remaining seen, we wouldn't freak out any humans by leaving what would appear to be disembodied footprints.

"Hold on. Your ear," I said as we cut to the road leading into town. The knit cap Brell wore under his hood was lifted on one side, exposing the point of his ear. I pulled it down and gave him a kiss.

"By taking this route, we will reach the bay before they do. It is there that we will hide and watch and listen as they prepare to leave," Brell said.

The village lay at the base of a small mountain range, sparkling like a geode as the windows of its buildings and small shops reflected the rising sun.

"It's pretty, isn't it," I said.

"Yes, it is." Brell lifted his face to the sky, put his hands on his hips, and inhaled while closing his eyes.

A pair of rabbits cut across our path, scurrying to take shelter in a cluster of dead brush, and when we reached the town, an elk broke into a cantor and headed to the nearest row of trees.

We cut to the sidewalk on the main road. "Closed" signs hung in the windows of businesses, and all was quiet until a truck started up down the road. Its engine struggled, and its tail pipe spit out billowing clouds of white exhaust that smelled like burning motor oil.

I wrinkled my nose and fanned the air in front of me. "If I'm remembering correctly, the marina is just ahead."

"It is," Brell said. "And it is there we will follow the sea to the place where it narrows and flows between mountains of ice."

Like the town, the marina was quiet, its crabbing and fishing boats having cast off long before sunrise. Dad's boat was at the end of the last ramp. While Dad was gone, he'd let one of his friends move it here and use it in exchange for the boat's care and quarterly barnacle scraping.

"This is the first time I have seen your father's boat," Brell said. "It is a fine vessel, solid and strong like the real 'Laura' but not as beautiful." He winked.

I jogged down the ramp.

The boat's name, *Laura*, was no longer dulled by saltwater corrosion. It was freshly repainted dark green, and above the "L" a laurel branch had been added, circling the top of the letter like a halo.

"Ah, I had no idea my dad this," I said. "He must have hired one of the marina's deckhands to do it."

"This also looks newly painted," Brell said as he stood on the other side of the ramp.

I ran to join him. On the haul was the hand-painted image of a mermaid—Dad's once-imagined woman in the water that had given him the nickname "Crazy Clark" among his friends.

"I wonder if I will ever see a mermaid again," I said.

"It is doubtful considering that their role in the retrieval of the stone is complete. It also appears that you, your father, and Queen Tena are the only ones who have ever seen them."

"How do you think they knew to help me? The merpeople Queen Tena knew would have died long ago."

"When the agreement was made between Queen Tena and the sea people, it likely became legend, passed down from one generation to the next. Or it could be instinctual for them to help you, just like knowing the Landaffen language is more instinctual than learned."

"I'd love for you to see them." I got to my knees, dipped my fingertips in the water, and swirled them in a zig-zag pattern. "They are so beautiful."

"Landaffens of the water," Brell said. "Yes, I would like to see them."

We left the ramp and followed the shoreline to an inlet, leaving the village and marina behind us. As Brell had described, the inlet narrowed, and soon we were flanked by massive icebergs, pristine mountains of ice, appearing blue at their bases and bright white where the sunlight flashed against them.

The snowbed thickened, our boots sinking to mid-calf, and rolling banks of snow made it easy to hide if needed. I ducked behind a snowy hill while Brell set down our supplies and scaled a glacier to look for the Hanllants. I picked up the backpack and slung it over one shoulder.

"I see them." He whispered down to me. He slipped down the glacier, keeping his fingers and toes against the ice in a controlled fall. "We are close. This trail of ocean curves, opening into a small bay. There we will find the Hanllants' boat." He grabbed the ski bag and looked up at me.

"Don't even think about arguing over the backpack. There's no time for that. It's my turn," I said and gave him a kiss.

We picked up our speed, racing to increase our distance from the Hanllants, so we could find a spot to take cover and watch.

As we moved south, the ground flattened, and the inlet opened into a small bay flanked by another set of glaciers. In the bay sat a boat tied to a wooden pole.

"Come," Brell said, motioning for me to follow him.

Sidestepping, we squeezed between a tall row of ragged ice mounds and found rocks that were tall enough to sit on while peeking over the crags. From where we were, the boat was the size of my thumb.

"This bay must lead back to open water." I peered through my binoculars, scanned the deck, and found a pair of Hanllants. "I think I see the two that came to get things ready," I reported.

One Hanllant was at the railing, strapping back some rope, as the other on the deck mopped the floor of a small, wooden corral and stable with a half roof. A small, double-hauled boat sat on a rack behind the stable.

"Yes, I see them now," Brell said. "The one at the side of the seacraft is Nalaan, the one in which Daveen appeared to argue with before Nalaan and Lanie left."

"I bet Nalaan's the captain," I said. "That's probably why his helmet is more elaborate than the others."

On Nalaan's helmet, the mohawk of feathers squeezed into its raised pedestal were longer and fuller, and the helmet was made from metal instead of woven reeds. When he tilted his head, the helmet caught the sun, bouncing the sun's rays in all directions.

"Their boat has got to be at least one-hundred feet long, and it's completely made from wood. At that length, it's not a boat. It's a ship." I refocused my binoculars. "And it has two hauls, so it's actually more like what humans call a catamaran."

"Hauls?" Brell asked.

"Yeah, a typical boat, like my dad's, has one haul. But look at what this vessel's floating on—two parallel hauls spaced about thirty feet apart."

The deck was a long, flat platform made from wooden planks. A large cabin with glassless windows was centered on the deck. Behind it sat the corral and stable that one of the Hanllants was cleaning, and at the stern sat a grouping of large wood boxes.

A low railing wrapped the deck, its handrail overhanging the deck by a foot, and beneath the railing, port, and starboard were long benches. Under each bench lay long-handled paddles.

Three masts, their sails wrapped and tied, rose into the sky, and at the top of the second mast hung a white flag. As the wind picked up, the flapping flag momentarily straightened, and I was able to make out a symbol on the flag's center.

"There's a triangle on the flag," I said. "The top third of it is red, the second third is brown, and the bottom third is green." I lowered my binoculars. "Does that mean anything to you?"

"No, it does not," Brell said as he squinted into the distance.

"Maybe it's a symbol representing their grove."

"It could be, but that would be unusual. Groves identify by name and not by an emblem. And using flags to display designs of meaning and significance is also a human practice—not Landaffen."

I shook my head. "I have no idea where they're sailing, but I'd be afraid to travel on any type of watercraft that didn't have GPS and a motor."

Brell shot a glance at the sky. "On land, navigation by the stars is a Landaffen practice that could easily be adapted for use on the sea. And with a crew of fifty-one, the Hanllants can fuel their sails by working the wind as well as using the wind to smooth waves and defy the sea's squalls and waves.

"There they are," I said, ducking below the crag's peak and shifting left to sneak one eye between two crags while concealing the rest of my face.

Following my lead, Brell lowered to sit on the rock behind us and shifted, so he could see the catamaran without being seen from below. I raised my binoculars and looked through them.

Mounted on Noth's horse, Daveen was in the lead, followed by Caylent on her horse. Noth's horse walked stiffly, one knee buckling when they hit a patch of thick snow. With the end of his reins, Daveen whipped the horse's neck, and the poor creature jerked its head. Daveen pulled the reins hard with both of his hands, and the horse curled its neck downward and clomped forward, lifting each hoof with more caution.

I clenched my jaw as my heart sank, but at the same time, I was eased knowing that at least one of the Hanllants' horses, Ontah, was in Stan's barn, free from Daveen's abuse and torment.

As Caylent rode, she kept her chin to her chest. Her face was shadowed, and when Nalaan jumped from the bow of the ship to the shore to meet her, she did not raise her head.

He offered his hand, but she dismounted without his aid. A Hanllant left the arriving group, took her horse's reins, and led it to the bow of the ship where a team of Hanllants had laid a makeshift wooden ramp leading from the shore to the ship's deck.

Nalaan grabbed Caylent's face, sinking his fingers into the hollows of her cheeks and forcing her head upward. Her plump lips puckered with the pinching of her cheeks, and when Nalaan shouted at her, a vein in his temple pulsed.

Caylent responded with something Nalaan obviously did not want to hear. He raised his hand, his lips and eyebrows twisting with anger, but before he could slap Caylent's cheek, Daveen jumped from Noth's horse and caught Nalaan's hand in his.

Nalaan ripped his hand from Daveen and the two exchanged words, both Landaffens shouting with crossed brows and hand's wildly gesticulating. Caylent wiped her eyes and rushed up the ramp and into the cabin. Daveen followed her and Nalaan to the top of the ramp where he addressed the Mentsune and pointed like he was giving orders.

Noth led Daveen's horse up the ramp, onto the deck, and into the stable. Caylent's horse had already been corralled. Its bridle and saddle were removed, and a Mentsune was strapping a blanket to its back. Noth patted his horse's neck, nodded to the

Hanllant attending to Caylent's horse, and joined the others as they loaded onto the ship.

As the ship rhythmically rocked, Noth kept his balance by holding out his arms. When the catamaran bobbed, rising higher on one side, he fell against one of the masts and wrapped his arm around it.

Nalaan walked bow to stern with his hands clasped behind his back, nodding at his shipmates as they prepared to launch. Working without a bobble or disruption in their timing, the Mentsune were as agile as they were on solid ground, moving crates and rearranging their supplies.

Caylent burst from the cabin, ran to the railing, and folded at the waist over the water. Daveen came to her aid, patting her back as he turned his head from the ocean.

"Wow" I said. "I'd think with your amazing grace and balance, seasickness wouldn't be an issue for Landaffens," I said.

"What is seasickness?" Brell asked.

"It's when you're standing on a surface, like a boat, that keeps moving under your feet. It messes with your senses and the fluid in your inner ears. A lot of people get nauseous and dizzy because of this. The Mentsune have probably learned to move with the boat and don't get seasick. Obviously Caylent doesn't know how to do that," I laughed, "because she's throwing up right now."

Caylent rose and wiped her mouth with the back of her hand. Nalaan approached her, and Daveen moved aside while she and Nalaan spoke. I put down my binoculars.

"If they don't have a remedy for motion sickness, Caylent, and maybe even Daveen and Noth, are going to be in for a long, miserable ride. I'm not sure how the horses will handle it either."

"There is a powder we use for churning stomachs, but I am not sure if it will aid in this type of sickness," Brell said.

A sharp thumping sound came from the boat; a rapid succession of three thumps in a row.

"They have moved a drum to the back of the ship," Brell

said.

"Yeah, I see it." I rose a little higher. "They're getting ready to leave. I'm going to make myself unseen by all and go down there. Maybe I can find out where they're going."

"I will come with you," Brell said.

"No." I set my hand on his forearm. "It will be easier for me to stay unseen by all if I'm alone."

"Okay, but do not go on the ship. There are many Hanllants in a small space. They will be difficult for you to avoid," Brell warned.

"I won't. I'm just going to get close enough to hear them." I took off the binoculars and handed them to Brell.

"If you are discovered, my bow will be ready."

While I closed my eyes and concentrated, Brell strung his bow and readied an arrow. When I was unseen by all, I touched his shoulder. "I won't be gone very long," I said.

Climbing from our hiding place, I slipped between the rocky ice and made my way to the rock-covered beach. A flock of puffins waded at the shore, dipping their thick orange beaks into the water while others floated or swam at the bay's edge. As I neared the ship, the birds sensed my presence and took flight.

With their swords drawn, two Mentsune rushed to the railing above where I stood and scanned the beach. I held my breath, the pulse in my neck throbbing, and watched and waited, hoping I hadn't left any noticeable footprints. The Mentsunes nodded at one another, lowered their swords, and returned to their duties.

Caylent and Daveen stood side-by-side with their backs against the handrail. The sea lapped against the shore, and with each surge, the catamaran rocked. Its hulls scraped the sand making it difficult to hear what they were saying to one another.

As I crept closer, walking on the rockiest sand to avoid leaving boot prints, Caylent spun, hung her head over the railing, and puked. I turned my head and waited for the splashing to stop before I looked again.

Caylent coughed into a handkerchief and dabbed it against her lips. "I cannot do this, Daveen," Caylent said. "I cannot feel ill for the rise and fall of seven suns."

"You will not be ill for seven suns," Daveen said. "I also suffer from the moving water, but Nalaan has assured me that in two turns, we will learn the rhythm of the sea, and our bodies will no longer fight its dance."

Caylent placed her hand against her stomach. "Nalaan has assured us of many things that have not come to be."

"Shhh," Daveen said.

In return, Caylent said something, but she'd lowered her voice, making it impossible for me to hear her.

I looked toward the shore at the spot where I knew Brell was hiding and found his hooded head, a speck of black within the grey crags of rock. I took a deep breath and swallowed.

Tiptoeing up the ramp to the deck, I dodged the Hanllants as they worked to untie ropes and unpack supplies. Light on my feet, I wove between them and ducked when they handed items off to one another.

I passed the tiny corral and stable. The horses stood next to one another, and Lennch was with them outside the corral. While holding the reins of their halter together in one hand, to calm them, he ran his hand down their necks.

Caylent and Daveen were still toward the back of the ship. A swell rocked the ship, and Caylent grabbed the handrail with one hand and Daveen's shoulder with another. I stretched out my arms to steady myself, took hold of the railing, and walked three slow steps to get closer to them.

"Please," Caylent cried at a whisper. "I do not love him, and he does not love me. He is cruel and hateful and eager to inflict pain." She sobbed in her handkerchief. "You stopped him today, but you will not always be there to keep him tame."

"Nenmie would say the same about me." Daveen let go of the railing and sighed. "But you are blood, and his brutal treatment of you will not be tolerated in my presence."

"This marriage is wrong. It goes against our beliefs." She pressed her gloved fingers against her lips and turned her head away from her brother.

"But it does not go against the beliefs of the Mentsune." Daveen grabbed the handrail.

"But the Velletsemn?" Caylent leaned back over the railing and dry heaved.

"They know nothing of the Velletsemn. We follow their traditions. The pact has been made, and we will not break it," he whispered through tight teeth. "You will marry Nalaan."

"Please, Daveen." Caylent whimpered, her voice cracking.

"In time, love will come if you let it."

"No, I will never love him." She wiped her wet cheeks. "Let us find another way," she begged.

He grabbed his sister's arm, jerking her from the railing. "There is no other way. We need them. You know that. It cannot happen without the Mentsune."

A drum beat boomed across the deck. A horse whinnied, and Caylent hugged herself and shivered.

At the drum stood a Mentsune holding a stick, consisting of a long, wooden rod with a piece of stuffed leather tied to one end. The drum was wooden with a leather skin tied to its drumhead by a series of vertical ropes running the length of the drum's body. Standing waist high, the shell of the drum narrowed to a round pedestal, giving it the shape of a wineglass with a thick stem.

"We leave soon," Daveen said. "And this miserable land of ice will finally be behind us for good."

"And a girdled land of wet heat and rain will be better?" She crossed her arms. "I will feel like an animal in a cage."

"Nalaan said it is a land of sweet fruit and clear waters," He faced the channel, lifted his chin to the sea, and took a deep breath. "And bright flowers so fragrant, their sweet scent fills the air even when they are too far to be seen."

"Sweet fruit and fragrant flowers?" Caylent scoffed. "Have

you forgotten who I am, brother, or do you believe I have gone soft like Father?" She looked at him up and down. "Or maybe my brother, too, has gone soft?" she said in a teasing tone and smiled.

"Not soft," Daveen said. "Eager." One side of his mouth rose. "Heat magic will be mine soon."

The drummer hit his instrument again, and as the drum's thunder echoed against the glaciers, the crew rushed to the benches to retrieve their paddles. Both horses whinnied.

Pulling Caylent with him, Daveen moved from the railing. Skirting left, I avoided a blow from his shoulder, but the ship bobbed before I'd planted my feet, and I lost my balance. I fell forward toward the mast and broke my fall by catching a fluttering piece of the sail that had escaped its binding.

In a coordinated scramble, most of the crew reported to the benches and sat facing opposite the shore with their paddles poised across their laps. Four Mentsunes carrying long poles walked to the front of the ship. A team positioned themselves at the masts and started to untie the sails. I dropped and rolled away just as a Mentsune reached for the mast I was holding.

With my palms ready to push up from the deck, I squatted on one knee, waiting for a Mentsune pushing a wooden crate to get out of my way. When there was enough room for me to wedge between him and another Mentsune coiling a rope, I popped from the deck and turned to my side to squeeze through them. Accidentally bumping against the Mentsune with the crate, I stopped to see his reaction.

The sailor stared at the spot on his pants where I'd touched him. The drum sounded again. The sailor glanced at the crate, brushed off his pants with his hand, and continued winding the rope.

Wood scraped and rumbled, and a deep vibration penetrated the soles of my boots. I rushed to the front of the ship, cutting left and right to avoid hitting someone else. A group of sailors were at the bow, pulling the ramp from the shore where the ramp's underside scraped the edge of the deck before leveling out.

"Damn it," I mumbled to myself as I looked over the railing at the freezing sea below.

My only choice was to jump, and since the ship was moored in waist-deep water, there was no way I could jump without getting completely soaked and causing a huge splash.

Dripping with sea water and sand, the end of the ramp swung onto the deck. I gripped the handrail, flung my leg over the other side of the railing, and dropped against the side of the ship just as the ramp swiped the air where I'd been standing.

As my body hit the haul, air shot from my lungs, and I gasped, sucking in the cold air to catch my breath. Pressing my toes into the wood, I was able to take some weight off my hands and readjust my grip.

My heart beating in my ears, I held on while eyeing the sea below. Clasping the railing as hard as I could, I pressed my fingers into the rail, but they slipped within my gloves, making my hold weaken.

The drummer gave his drum another thump, and the Mentsunes at the bow sunk their poles into the water. I hung, my body swinging, as the sailors dug the tips of their poles in the sand and pushed off from the shore.

Swells crashed against the haul, and water surged back into the sea as the sand under the ship gave, and the ship rocked and bucked in the surf. Foam crested the waves and rumbled, spraying water on my pants. Tightening the muscles in my legs and keeping the soles of my boots on the haul, I stopped my body from banging against the ship.

Another drum beat. *Thump! Thump!* Another repositioning and push of the poles, and the ship bobbed from the shore. My teeth clattered and my hands and wrists tingled. I exhaled through pursed lips as I watched the water rise.

Timing my entrance with the ship's next pitch and break of waves against the haul, I held my breath and let go. Pointing my toes, I brought my hands together above my head and closed my eyes.

As I hit the water, my legs collapsed beneath me. I found the sand with one foot and sprung upward, opening my eyes and spitting when my face hit the cold air. I shook uncontrollably, my arms and legs convulsing.

If I stood on my toes, the water came to my chin. I couldn't feel my hands or my face. My breathing was short and frantic as if my lungs were stuffed with ice. The water rolled, and as my body lifted, I couldn't touch the bottom until I was between waves.

Thump! Thump! The drums boomed; their beat barely audible over the sound of water lapping against my ears. I rotated to see the shore.

Something struck my head hard, knocking me off my feet. A dull thud rang in my ears, and I fell sideways, rolling onto my back. A row of paddles came toward me, and I kicked and flapped my hands to get away from them.

A paddle hit my knee. Another jabbed my hip, pushing me underwater. Keeping my eyes open, I watched the series of paddles rise, scrape the surface, and dip back into the sea.

I kicked harder, cupping my hands and pushing the water at my sides, trying to steer from the boat and toward the beach, but my heavy boots kept me from making any real distance. The blade of a paddle cut the water above me. I released the air in my lungs, watching the paddle beat the bubbles as they rose toward the sunlight, and I sunk.

The heels of my boots hit the sand, and I twisted, losing my sense of direction and not knowing which way was up or down. Were my eyes opened or closed? My eyes stung, my head pounded, and everything was dark.

My chest hurt, my lungs aching for air. I flailed my arms, and my hand hit sand. In one motion, I straightened my arms and pushed my palms and toes against the sand. With a kick, my head popped to the surface.

I gasped, inhaling deeply, and balancing on the tip of my boot as I pressed my toe into the seabed. A wave slapped my face. Water entered my nose and made me gag. Between swells, I saw the beach and bounced on my toe and scooped the water with my hands to get closer.

When the soles of my boots were flat on the sand, I walked forward, dragging my stiff legs. Too numb to move, my arms hung at my sides. The tips of my fingers throbbed. When my chest was above water, I continued forward in a staggered march while looking over my shoulder. A jerk of my head shook some of the water from my ears.

The drumbeats continued, and the Mentsune paddled in time with each echoing thud.

Nalaan was at the tiller with Caylent, and Daveen and Noth stood behind them. At the center of the bay, the ship turned, and the paddlers rotated on their benches to face their new course.

Like the wings of a giant white bird, the sails peeled from their masts and billowed simultaneously, bulging outward in the direction the ship was heading. With their arms raised, wrists turning and fingers strumming the air, groups of Hanllants who worked the wind stood at the base of each mast. Unlike sails I'd seen before, these sails were upside-down with the triangle's point at the bottom.

"Brell," I tried to say when the water level dropped to my waist, but my lips wouldn't move, and the pathetic sound I'd produced was a mumble of gibberish.

I staggered to the edge of the beach, the weight of my clothes forcing my knees to buckle. The wind whipped, lashing my face, freezing my wet clothes, and I was too numb to tell if I was still unseen by all.

I looked over my shoulder. The ship had left the bay and was making its way down the channel that led to the sea. The Hanllants faced opposite of the beach, and the paddlers struck the sea with their paddles in a coordinated waltz of wood sticks and water to a drum beat I could no longer hear.

I licked my lips. "Brell! Help me!" My words, weak and broken, rode the wind.

"Laura! Where are you?"

"Brell!" I coughed, my body jerking.

The sticky sand sucked the soles of my boots like a leech. I couldn't lift my legs, and as I tried to crank my arms and use my momentum to push forward, my arms continued to dangle and wouldn't move.

The beach. The rocks. The glacier. They were a blur, a smear of white and gray. Something tall and black walked along the beach. It cupped its hands around its mouth and shouted.

"Laura! Laura!"

My head hurt. The landscape spun. I couldn't feel my body. I flopped forward to the ground. Planting my heels, I rolled onto my back.

"Brell! Brell!" I slurred and closed my eyes against the midday sun.

"Laura!"

"Brell! I am here." I tried to raise my hand and opened my eyes.

On his knees, Brell hovered over me, his eyes flicking back and forth, and brow wrinkling with worry.

I parted my numb lips. "Brell!" I gasped.

"You are still unseen by all," he said. He patted my body, found my hand, and held it between his. "You are wet. I must get you warm and dry."

"I can't feel you touching me." I exhaled, my body shuddering.

My chest tingled, a sharp, painful prickle, radiating into my hands and feet. I cringed, but my cheeks and lips barely moved.

"I can see you! You are seen by all!" Brell said. "You are injured. Your head. The skin is torn."

I shivered, my body spasming as my limbs shook and teeth

clattered. Brell lifted my back and slipped his hands under me. My body lolled to one side, and my eyelids trembled and closed.

⚜

"Where am I?" My lips felt like sausage links. The ground beneath me was hard and hurt my skin.

"We are in a shallow cave below the glacier. The wind will not touch you here. I need to get you in dry clothes."

He pulled down my hood and unzipped my ski jacket.

I blinked my stinging eyes and saw a helmet with a red crest. Small, dark eyes peered down at me. Lips curled, exposing teeth. "No! No!" I screamed, thrashing my head, and rolling from side to side. "Don't touch me." I slowly curled my fingers, trying to make a fist. My hands were cold, but the gloves I wore were soft and dry.

"Laura! It is me, Brell."

Hands held me down by my shoulders, pressing my back into the ground. I lifted my foot, drew my chin to my chest, and saw dry socks on my feet. My icy boots, frozen socks, and wet gloves lay next to me.

"Laura. Please do not fight me."

I blinked again. The helmet morphed into a knit cap. Brell's face hovered above mine. He parted his lips and smiled.

"Brell. Brell."

"Your head is bleeding. How did this happen?" He pushed strands of my wet hair from my face.

"I...I think something hit me...I can't remember."

I sighed, closing my eyes and concentrating. The memory surfaced. Water in my mouth and up my nose. My vision blurred and my eyes burned. Being so cold, I could hardly breathe. Then the blade of a paddle struck my head.

"A Mentsune," I gasped. "With a paddle. His paddle hit me."

"Did you become seen? Did they know you were there?" Brell

took off my jacket, my arms limp as he maneuvered them. He hesitated when it was time to take off my sweatshirt.

"No, they were...paddling the ship from the bay. I was...in the water...still unseen by all when I was hit."

"How long were you in the water?"

"I don't know. Seemed like...forever."

"Your wet clothes cannot remain against your skin. If you are unable to remove them, I will need to do it for you."

"I can't take them off...I don't have the strength." I closed my eyes.

He set his hand on my forehead. "I promise I will not look as I exchange your clothes with mine," he said.

Brell pulled my sweatshirt and thermal from my head and arms. The soaked fabric was heavy against my body and cold, and as the neckband stretched over my chin, seawater squeezed from the fabric and dripped down my neck.

He slipped his bare hand under me, and I opened my eyes and arched my back. His fingers, like sticks of ice, unclasped my bra, and when he gently tugged my bra away, he lifted his head and stared at the rocks above us.

Beside him, his ski jacket and sweatshirt laid on a slab of stone. Keeping his head raised, he yanked off his thermal and flipped one of the sleeves right-side-out. He breathed hard, and as his body trembled, I wished I could have reached out my hand to run my fingertips across his warm skin.

Keeping his eyes from my body, he pulled his thermal over my head and gently threaded my arms through the sleeves. Any warmth his chest left in the fabric was gone, and though his shirt was dry, my body didn't stop trembling.

He layered his sweatshirt over the thermal, and got behind me, lifting me onto his lap as he wrapped me in his ski jacket and zipped it to my chin.

Brell's chest against my back was as cold and hard as the stone I'd been laying on. I shuddered, and he drew his arms around me and kissed my cheek. The only sensation I felt was a whisper of pressure.

He lowered me to the ground. Grasping the elastic waist of my thermals and ski pants at the same time, he worked them over my hips and down my legs without looking at me and making sure my underwear stayed where they were. He took off his ski pants, and with his head raised, drew his pants up my legs and sat me up against a large rock.

"How are you feeling?" Brell asked. Wearing only a pair of thermal pants, his knit cap, and boots without socks, Brell stood over me, hugging himself and shivering.

"Better...I think," I said, though besides not being wet, I didn't feel any better. My throat hurt and my words sounded mispronounced and raspy.

"Your words are still slurred. You are not yet free from cold sickness. I must get you to a place where it is warm."

He tied my wet clothes and boots to one of the handles of our weapon bag and slung the backpack across his chest.

"What are you doing?" I asked. My stomach jerked. I turned my head and puked up granola bar, coffee, and sea water.

A gust of wind blew into the shallow cave, and my body stiffened. My hood and its tightly pulled drawstring kept my head from dropping.

"I am going to carry you," Brell said. He put his arm around my back and got me to my feet while holding me against his side.

Bending at the waist, he drew me onto his back, positioned my weak arms around his neck, and with the crooks of his arms under my knees, held me in place.

He took a deep breath, leaned down, and picked up our weapons bag. My body shifted, and he raised his shoulder to work me back into place.

"Are you...sure...you can...do this?" I asked, my voice breathless and weak.

"Yes, Laura. I will not let you down."

My chin slipped from his shoulder, and my eyes closed.

CHAPTER 11

I turned my head. The side of my face sunk into a soft pillow, and the hem of a warm blanket rubbed my neck. My face and head throbbed, the tip of my nose burned, and my ears tingled.

When I yawned, the skin on my cheeks felt tight and raw. A sharp pain pulsed against the side of my head, and a bandage above my right eye and ear stretched, pulling my skin.

Pushing up from the bed, I scooted backward, bringing my lower back against the pillow, and banging the headboard with my elbows when I sat upright. The room was dark except for a small nightlight plugged into the wall next to the bed. In its warm glow, I looked at my aching hands. The tips of my fingers were red, and as I tapped the tip of each one against the pad of my thumb, the skin burned and stung.

I touched my forehead and hit a cushion of gauze, and the pain in my head amplified. With a lighter touch, I followed the wrap of gauze to the back of my head and around the other side where the end of it tucked into place. Running my fingers over my face, I found damp patches of skin on the end of my nose and tips of my ears that painfully tingled.

Thick brown curtains draped the room's only window, and

although the curtains were closed, through the gap where the two panels met, I saw it was dark outside and the sky was free from clouds or falling snow. The taxidermized head of a moose stared at me from the wall across the room.

Someone knocked on the half-open door, and a long shadow grew on the floor where a band of light from the hall entered the room.

"Hello," I said. My throat was dry, but my voice was steady and strong.

"I thought I heard you moving in here," Stan said as he walked into the bedroom. "Mind if I turn on the light?"

"No, go ahead."

He flipped the light switch, and I blinked and squinted. He crossed the room and sat down in the chair next to my bed.

"Where's Brell? Is he okay?" I shifted to look past him and out the door.

"He's fine. He fell asleep in this chair, and it took a lot of convincing from me to get him to leave this room and sleep in a proper bed."

"What time is it?"

He glanced at his watch. "4:22 a.m."

"What time did we get here?" I pushed up on my pillow and winced.

"Yesterday morning at around eleven. Brell told me about the ship and filled me in on everything that happened."

"Oh, my gosh." I took a breath, enjoying the warm air filling my lungs. "I've been asleep that whole time? We've lost two days," I groaned.

"Not asleep—unconscious for most of it. Brell said your speech was slurred, and at times, you seemed confused, meaning you were in the second stage of hypothermia." He rubbed his hands together. "We put your hands and feet in warm water and laid a warm washcloth on your face. Then we wrapped you in an electric blanket, raising your body temperature slowly, so you wouldn't go into shock."

"Thank you for taking care of me," I said, smiling even though it made my face hurt. "I don't remember any of that."

"You were in and out of consciousness. But it wasn't just the hypothermia that did it." His eyes flashed to my head. "Brell said you threw up, the telltale sign of a concussion from that paddle hitting you. It left a nasty slice on your head along with a big lump and bruise. A combination of that and not having slept for over twenty-four hours..." His eyes widened. "And you were out," he said, emphasizing the word "out."

"What about Autka and Prince Pakak?"

"They left here about a half hour after you and Brell did."

"And Ontah? Daveen's horse?"

"They took him with them. Autka said they have stores of dried grasses for the mammoths that Ontah could also eat." Stan gave another assessing glance at me then said, "Brell's also been using my phone to call Todd. Todd told him your mother is doing well and will make a full recovery."

"That's a relief." I touched the gauze, ignoring the pain and pressing the bandage hard enough to feel the bump.

"We probably should have loaded you up on the snowmobile and taken you to the emergency room. Or even called for you to be airlifted to one..." Stan sighed. "But your pupils responded normally to light, and since you didn't have a seizure or any bleeding from your nose or ears, we decided to let you recover here."

"You made the right choice. I would have had to answer a bunch of questions about why I was in the water and where, and it wouldn't have been easy to come up with a believable lie."

"Brell wasn't in any condition to travel either, and he would have wanted to go with you. But he needed to stay here and be treated as well."

"He got hypothermia, too?" My voice rasped in panic.

"He sure did. Brell did the right thing getting you outta those wet clothes and giving you most of his. He showed up here bare-chested and wearing only a pair of thermal pants and boots without socks. He carried you on his back while carrying the backpack and ski bag. With all those weapons, that bag must have weighed at least fifteen pounds. I don't know how he did it." He shook his head. "But then again, he is a Landaffer. That, and his love for you, and I guess that boy can do anything." He smiled and winked.

"So, he's okay now?"

"Yep, a long, warm bath was all he needed."

I touched my cheeks and felt a film of something thick and tacky.

"Aloe vera," Stan said. He gestured to a tube of it sitting on the nightstand next to a lamp that was tiny replica of the Venus de Milo with a lampshade. "The best cure for windburn."

"Thanks, Stan. Thank you so much for everything."

"Anything for Clark's daughter," he said and winked again. "And her fiancé."

I heard footsteps in the hall. Brell walked into the room, beaming, his cheeks and nose as red and shiny as I'm sure mine were. His movements were fluid, relaxed, and light compared to when we were dead tired and dragging our legs through the snow. He combed his hand through his hair at the top of his head, and its longest strands fell into place and exposed his ears. The lobe and delicate conch-like curve of his ear were light peach, but the points were deep red and blistered.

The jeans Stan loaned Brell were too big at Brell's waist and hit above his ankles, but Brell still looked great. Thick grey socks and a white T-shirt layered with a plaid, red button-up shirt completed his look. I smiled, and my chest fluttered.

"I'll let you two talk," Stan said. "And I'll make breakfast."

I pushed up on the mattress to sit a little higher. "You don't have to go through all that trouble, Stan. We still have those granola bars you gave us. Don't you want to go back to bed?"

"Nope. I'm wide awake, and it's no trouble at all. And both of you need a good, hot meal, especially you, Laura. To heal, along with mental and physical rest, your brain needs food."

He got up from the chair. As Brell thanked him again for helping us, they hugged. When Stan left, Brell leaned over the bed and kissed me gently on my jaw line. His warm breath ignited the skin on my neck and sent chills up my arms.

"You saved my life, Brell. I would have died if you hadn't found me and carried me here. And now you're hurt, too. Your poor ears."

"My ears will heal. The important thing is that you are safe and will recover from hypo..."

"Hypothermia." I laughed.

"Hypothermia," he repeated and smiled. "And your head wound." He pulled the chair closer to the bed and sat down. "How are you feeling?" Brell asked.

"Like crap." I sighed. "I have a headache." From under the blanket, I bent my knees and lifted one hand to my lap. "Every muscle in my body aches, and my lips and the skin on my cheeks hurts."

"Stan said that with a concussion, a headache is to be expected. You could have died, Laura." He squeezed his lips together, clasped his hands together, and looked at the floor.

"I know. I'm sorry. I said I wouldn't go on the ship. I didn't plan to, but Daveen and Caylent were talking about where they were going, and I couldn't get close enough to hear them without getting on board."

I slipped my hands out from under the blanket and looked at my fingers. The ends of my fingers were bright red. I inspected a small blister on the end of one index finger.

"And the next thing I knew, the ship was leaving the bay."

"It was very dangerous to go on that ship, especially since I did not know you were going to be on it," Brell said. "When the ship started to leave, and you did not return, I looked for you on the shore. I did not think to search the water."

"I know. I'm sorry. When I jumped overboard, I didn't want to make myself seen and get noticed." I licked my blistered lips. "And then when I was at a safe enough distance to become seen,

I was so focused on keeping my head above water and getting to the beach that I didn't even think about doing it so you could find me." I dropped my hand onto the mattress. "I was just so confused. And I couldn't think straight."

"Hypothermia is the reason for this."

I slumped my shoulders. "I should have been watching the ramp. Then I could have left before they pulled it from the beach."

"You should not have abandoned the shore without telling me. If you hadn't been able to get to the land on your own, you would have become one with the sea."

I lowered my head. "I know," I whispered.

Brell held out his hand for mine. He took it gently, slipping his palm against my mine without touching my fingers. His fingertips were also red, but they weren't as red as mine and didn't have any blisters.

"I love you, Laura." He kissed the top of my hand. "You are The One. You cannot take chances with your life." He blinked his watery eyes and looked down.

I inched closer to the edge of the bed. "I did get some good information for us though," I said in a playful tone.

He lifted his head.

"It's going to take about seven days for them to reach their destination, which means they are only five days away from getting there." I gently shook my head. "And the climate is the opposite of here. Caylent said it had wet heat and rain."

"Wet heat. That is humidity," Brell said. He sniffed the air and smiled.

"Bacon and eggs," I said. "She also referred to the land as being girdled."

Stan popped his head in the room. "Breakfast is about ready. The bacon just needs a few more minutes. I can bring it on a tray if you want to eat in there."

"No, that's okay," I said. "I should get up and try walking around anyway."

My limbs were stiff, and I was slower than usual when I walked to the kitchen table and sat down with Brell and Stan. Each time my frost-bitten toes hit the carpet, they stung, but Stan assured me that, like with my fingers, the skin damage to my feet was mild and would heal on its own in a week or so.

"When I was coming down the hall to tell you about breakfast," Stan said, "I thought I heard you say something about land being girdled." He took a bite of scrambled eggs. "I've never heard anyone use that expression before."

"Yeah," I explained. "When Caylent was talking about where the ship was headed, she said the land was girdled. Why? Do you know what it means?"

"I'm not sure. Maybe." Stan picked up a piece of toast and buttered it while he spoke. "Not a lot of people know this about me." Stan lifted his eyebrows and smiled. "Except for your dad. But I'm a bit of a Greek mythology buff and in one of the English translations of *The Odyssey*— great epic poem. Did you ever read it?" He looked at me as Brell shook his head.

"Yeah, my freshman year," I answered. "It's about Odysseus, the hero of the Trojan War, on his way home to Ithaca."

"Yep," Stan said with a smile. "Well, in this particular translation I read, Poseidon, the God of the Sea, is referred to as 'the blue girdler of islands,' so maybe the place they're going to is an island."

"That makes total sense," I said. "A girdle surrounds a person's torso, so when Caylent said it's a 'girdled land' she meant it's a body of land completely surrounded by something. In this case—water. That's why she'd also feel like she'll be trapped in a cage."

"A grove on an island," Brell said. "It is not in our histories, and it is not in mentioned in any Legend in which I am aware, but that does not mean one does not exist."

"That explains the ship," Stan said. "Seafaring Landaffers." He chuckled. "To travel to a gridled land, Odysseus filled his sails with wind given to him by Aeolus, the king of the wind. And now those Landaffers are doing the same thing but with their own magic."

I took a sip of orange juice and winced as it burned my lips. "That's what Daveen does." I set down my glass a little too hard, and a few drops of juice splashed to the table. "He finds lost groves that are unknown to the collective. He did it with the Tulix. He did it with the Aludene. And then he found another vulnerable, isolated colony that doesn't have access to the truth."

"I agree," Brell said. "It is the only way he is able to get them to join his cause. They believe his lies because they simply do not know any better."

"I also heard them say something else." I folded my arms on the table. "Daveen said he'd have heat magic soon, so this grove must somehow be the source of this magic or else the Landaffens who live there know where to find it."

"I agree that is also true," Brell said. "How many islands are there on earth?"

"Oh, boy," Stan said. "A lot. I'd say at least six or seven hundred thousand."

Brell's jaw dropped. My jaw did the same, but I stopped it mid-drop when a pain shot up the side of my head.

"But not all of them are inhabited," Stan quickly added. "Inhabited brings the number down to about fifteen or sixteen thousand."

"That's still a lot, and we have no idea if the grove is on an island that's inhabited or uninhabited," I said. A headache grew on the side of my head.

"But we do know it is an island with humidity, sweet fruit, and fragrant flowers," Brell said.

"A tropical island. Sounds like Hawaii," Stan said. He rubbed his chin. "But it also sounds like the Bahamas, or Bora Bora, or the Dominican Republic." He looked up and squinted. "Hmm, or even Bali, The Galapagos, or the French Polynesia." He shook his head. "And most of these islands are made up of strings of islands."

"Daveen is always one step ahead of us," I huffed. "How the heck does he do it?"

"I suspect he has been studying our ancient texts for some time, finding clues that lead him to others." Brell sniffed a piece of bacon but didn't eat it.

"The chip of stone!" I blurted, ignoring the pain in my head. "It was in the pocket of the ski jacket I was wearing! Brell, you didn't leave it at the glacier, did you?"

"No, it is here."

"Hanging near the fire to dry," Stan added. "I'll check the pockets."

"When I jumped in the ocean, I wasn't thinking about the stone. I hope it's still there," I said while hugging my knees. "I don't want to go back and get another and possibly jeopardize the magic of the cup."

"Got it!" Stan announced as he came back into the room and opened his hand. The chip laid in his palm like a flake of dull, black rubber.

I picked it up and held it to the light. "The piece of stone Daveen took from the Cup of Queens must be a clue that's leading him to wherever that ship is going. And I bet it's a clue he needs for heat magic."

"Then we also have that clue," Brell said.

"True, but we still have to figure out what island they're going to, beat them there, and find out about heat magic before Daveen does." I slouched in my chair. "If he's there now, I could try to see him with all of my senses and figure out exactly where he is." The thought of concentrating that hard made my head hurt more than it already did. I pressed my palm against the side of my head. "But we have to get there before he does, and we only have five days." I pressed the pad of my thumb against the pressure point between my eyebrows, but it only made my headache worse. "We need to figure this out right now, but I honestly don't know where to start."

"We will start in Wventorin," Brell said. "Using the

information we have, we will study the old text and find the most logical place they are heading, a tropical island that is about seven days from here." He tilted his head. "And do not forget about the Mentsune that rode the wind with us. My father may have been able to get information from him that will help us locate his grove."

"If he's like Koaen, even if your dad threatens to have it beaten it out of him, he might not say much," I groaned. "What if we can't find the right island in time?"

Pressure built behind my eyes, and tears pushed to the corners. I looked up, unblinking, but a big, warm tear rolled down my cheek, followed by another and another. My cheeks stung, and I sniffled hard.

"Laura," Brell said. "We will find the right island. You said Daveen is always a step ahead of us, but now I believe we are a step ahead of him. What will take Daveen seven suns will only take you the working of the wind." He smiled.

"Brell's right, Laura," Stan said.

"But what if we get there, and I can't find another clue that will help me learn heat magic before he does?" My pulse pounded in my temple, and my head hurt even more. "What if we find the island but can't find the grove?"

I took a deep breath and, releasing it slowly, calmed my quickly beating heart.

Brell scooted his chair closer to me. "Laura, Queen Tena's clues are meant for you. She concealed them in places in which only The One could find." He squeezed my knee. "Daveen knew the stone was trapped in ice, but he did not know where or that he'd need merpeople to assist him in the stone's recovery." He wiped a tear from my cheek. "Only *you* were able to accomplish that feat."

"But he found the cup before I did, so he was able to perform quick magic. If what you said is true, he shouldn't have been able to do that." I caught my trembling bottom lip with my teeth and put my head down, staring at the smear of egg yolk left on my plate.

"The Aludene were the keepers of the cup," Brell said. "Yes, he discovered the grove before you, and the cup responded to him, but now it only responds to you. And there is something else you need to remember."

I raised my head.

"Queen Tena did not anticipate any opposition, a faction led by and consisting of Landaffens who believed in a set of new texts; texts written long after she joined the earth." Brell set his hand on my calf. "You are the only one who will be able to find and use the last piece of evidence needed to perform heat magic. It cannot be done without you."

"Brell's right again," Stan said. "Didn't you once say that Daveen wanted you alive?"

"Yeah, he told the Hanllants to capture me. Not kill me," I said.

"Then if what Brell's saying is true, I'm guessing that Daveen is hoping and expecting you to show up to that island." Stan pulled his napkin from his lap and set it next to his plate. "And then once you're there, he's going to try to force you to do whatever magical thing you need to do in order to make heat magic work for *him*, just like he tried to do with light magic and the Cup of Queens."

"If that's the case," I said. "Then Daveen won't hesitate to do whatever it takes to make me comply." I put my hand to my aching head and sighed. "I really don't know if I can go through this again."

"You can," Brell said. "Because you will not be doing this alone. The first queen who gave birth to a half-race has used her cunning and magic to make sure The One will maintain the balance." Brell's eyes grew misty. "Daveen is trying to negate the Legend of Tena, so he can become a legend of his own, but we will not let that happen!" Brell hit his fist against the table.

"Oorah!" Stan shouted.

CHAPTER 12

"I sure wish you could stay a few days to rest and heal," Stan told me when I bent down to zip up my backpack.

My arms hurt. My shoulders hurt. And when I walked, the muscles in my thighs tightened to the point of seizing up and not wanting to move. When I flexed my fingers, they tingled and throbbed like they had hearts of their own. Their tips were still red and tender, and the middle finger of my left hand was white from the dead skin of a popped water blister.

But my head was the worst. It ached, and its pain intensified when I moved. Beginning at my right temple, the pain shot upward and radiated across the crown of my head.

"Me, too." I closed and opened my eyes instead of shaking my head. "But Brell and I can't afford to lose another day."

Brell came down the hall with the rest of our supplies. "Are you sure you have the energy to perform quick magic?"

"Yeah, I'm pretty sure."

We went outside to the porch to say our good-byes, and after a string of repeated thank you and hugs, Brell and I stepped down onto the snow, distancing ourselves just enough from Stan's cabin, so my working of the wind wouldn't sling snow in Stan's direction.

Brell stood behind me, carrying the backpack and our bag of weapons. He wrapped one arm around my waist, and I plucked the air as my hands shook and head pounded. I stopped and took a deep breath, my hands trembling.

"You need more time. Let us wait until the next rise of the sun," Brell said above the whispering wisp of wind surrounding our bodies.

"No, I can do this." I exhaled and closed my eyes.

I pictured the courtyard of the Wventorin grove. The fountain at its center bubbled water through its partially frozen spout. The early-morning sun peaked through the trees, projecting its golden beams while everything in its path produced long, black shadows. Playful shouts and spontaneous giggles cut through the courtyard, bouncing from the trees and cobblestone paths, as Landaffen children headed toward the school. Ignoring the pain in my head, I smiled, inhaling the sweet scent of winter-berry blossoms.

The wind swirled, reaching a speed that encompassed our bodies. In my mind's eye, I saw Brell, his face as fresh and true as the day Daveen chased me, until I found refuge in the Grove during their winter celebration.

Our bodies thinned, and we joined the wind. Brell's grip on my waist lightened, and we settled softly next to the bench where we'd kissed, and I'd first told him about being chased by Daveen.

"You did it, Laura!" Brell set the ski bag on the bench, and with the shrug of his shoulder, slipped the backpack down his arm to the ground. "How do you feel?"

"I'm fine. Just weak and my head won't stop hurting."

"Prince Brell!" shouted a Landaffen child. "He has returned, and The One is with him."

The girl rushed to Brell, her little feet lightly padding across the frost-covered stone. She reached out her hand and stopped short of touching him. "I have not seen human clothes such as these."

Gressim and Farnaway were stationed on the ridge next to the grove's entrance. When they saw us, Gressim jogged down the ridge in our direction, and Farnaway headed toward the palace.

"These clothes are warm," Brell told the child. "But not as warm as a gorthen pelt." He laughed, and the child giggled.

"The One has been hurt," another child said as he pointed to my head.

I readjusted my knit cap, bringing its thick band below the bandage wrapped around my forehead. Smiling, I hid my cringe.

"A bump on the head," I said as the children gathered around Brell and me. "But I'm fine."

A bell rang, its tone bright and magical as its ding lingered and grew stronger before it died.

"And I believe that is the final bell," Brell said. "Off to school," His eyebrows lifted. "For learning brings the darkness to light."

The children lingered, their faces beaming as they stared up at us, but immediately said goodbye and ran toward the school when Gressim appeared.

"Prince Brell! Laura!" Gressim said. "You have returned."

"It is good to see you again, Gressim," Brell smiled. "And it is good to be home. I did not expect to find you and Farnaway in the Grove."

"We traveled day and night to be here." Gressim took both of my hands. "The grove has missed its Prince and The One."

"Thank you," I said. "Is my mother still here?"

"Yes, she is well. Our healer said there is no need for her to be moved to a human healing center. She is in your tree home recovering."

Relief flooded me as I asked, "Is my father here, too?"

"Yes, he is with her. He is aiding in her care."

"And my uncle and Phyllis?"

"They have left the grove. Protectors escorted them to their human dwellings. Dean and Phyllis expressed a desire to stay longer but given the circumstances regarding their abrupt and unexplained disappearance, they felt they needed to leave the grove as soon as possible."

"And Todd?"

"He is here. He has been staying at the palace."

"He needs to go back home," I said, shaking my head, "before he flunks out of school and blows his scholarship. He and I need to have another long talk about that."

Brell looked past Gressim. "My mother and father are here. And so is Bay!"

Bay ran to us, and as Brell crouched on one knee, his faithful wolf companion jumped into his arms. Brell scratched behind Bay's ears. I patted Bay's head, and he licked the underside of my hand. Brell stood, and Bay danced in circles, his eyes full of fire and his thick winter coat shining.

"Go ahead and go to the palace with them, Brell. I'm going to see my parents first, and then I'll join you."

With Bay at his heels, Brell picked up the ski bag and left with Gressim to meet the king and queen where they stood outside the palace. I left for my tree home, acknowledging Brell's parents with a quick smile and wave as I headed toward that section of the village.

As I walked, the ting of metal sounded from the smithy, the working of wood clanged from the carpentry shop, and the eclectic mix of moos, neighs, and clucks from the livery rode the crisp, morning air.

There was hardly any snow left in the grove. Much of it had melted, leaving ice-cold puddles and thick, squishy mud. As the afternoon sun beat against the trees and cobblestones, water dripped from the roofs and naked tree limbs, creating a drip, drip tune of its own.

The Landaffens who saw me stopped to welcome me back to the grove and thank me for all I had already done and was fated to do. Tears balanced on my lower lashes, and I kept my chin raised to keep them from slipping.

Smoke rose from the chimney of my tree home, twisting as it thinned to join the sky. A row of half-melted icicles on the gable caught the sunlight and glimmered. I closed my eyes and smiled, remembering the first time I'd seen my grove home.

A temporary wooden ramp had been erected next to the hanging slabs of stone steps leading to my tree home. I eyed the stone steps as they imperceptibly swung in the light breeze, their dull surfaces absorbing the sun. The thought of climbing them made my head hurt more than it already did, but I needed to hone my Landaffen skills rather than neglect them.

Banging the soles of my boots against the trunk of the nearest tree, I dislodged the snow and ice from the treads and put my right foot on the lowest step. Adding more of my weight kept the stone steady, but when I lifted my other foot from the ground, the step jerked backward, and I almost fell.

I grabbed the ropes, and when the step stopped swinging, I leaped to the next one and then the next. It took three times longer than it normally did, but I finally made it to the landing with only a few bobbles.

I felt faint, and my front door with its beautiful stained-glass window spun and came back to itself when I blinked several times in a row. The door opened just as I reached for the knob.

"Laura," Keena whispered. "It is very good to see you. Your mother is here. She is resting."

I glanced at my couch. A pillow and neatly folded blanket sat at one end. The wood in the fireplace crackled.

"Is my father here?" I leaned to look into the kitchen but didn't see him.

"No, he is at the palace. I have been tending to your mother when he is not here."

"Thank you, Keena," I gushed. "It is so good to see you, too."

I would have hugged Keena, but a lontee sat on her shoulder. We clasped hands instead. I recognized the lontee as the one that belonged to Thriss. I stroked its lizard-like head. It stretched its wings, and its long, vermillion tail curled as it tucked its head under my palm.

"Is this Mheek?" I asked her.

"Yes, Thriss asked me to care for Mheek when she left the grove. She has since given him to me because she said she would be traveling again and would not be able to care for a pet."

"Traveling again? When did she say this?"

"At yesterday's rise of the sun. The half-race, Todd, was with her."

"Did she say where she was going?"

"No, but since their return, Thriss and Todd have spent many hours at the palace with King Vaylen and Gressim." She dropped her voice and wrinkled her nose. "The strange Landaffen they brought back with them is being held there. I think it has something to do with him." She lowered her voice even more, and her eyes widened as she spoke. "His name is Mauka. He is from a place very far from here."

My pulse spiked, and I sucked in a quick breath. "Did he tell them where his grove is? Were they able to get a lot of information from him?"

"I am not sure, but I do not believe so." She pressed her lips together in an apologetic smile. "I only know what Gressim has told others and what those others have told me."

"Has Todd been here the whole time, or has he gone home or to school?"

"I have not spoken to him, but I have seen him come and go from Wventorin."

"That's good to know. Thank you."

Putting most of my weight on my toes, I quietly walked into the bedroom. Mom was asleep. Neatly tucked under a plush blanket, her head lay upon a plump pillow. The top of her right shoulder was covered with a large bandage. Her cheeks were pink, and the corners of her mouth were lifted into a soft smile.

I moved to the ornately carved table that sat under the stained-glass window. The morning light shot through the intricate pattern of colored glass, and I watched the top of my hand light up in red, blue, and green as I ran my fingers across the cover of the book on the table and traced the "L".

E Sheesh eu Landaffia, The Book of Landaffia," I whispered.

A red ribbon marked the page where the Legend of Tena began. I flipped to that page, and the amber glow of the sun spread across the yellowed paper. "I don't want to let you down, Queen Tena. I promise I'll do everything I can to uphold your legend and maintain the balance between both worlds." I turned the page. "I wish I could have met you, my queen."

"Did you say something?" Keena asked at a whisper as she stood in the doorway.

"I was just talking to myself," I whispered back. "Do you mind if I go to the palace?"

"No, please go where you are needed. I will stay here with your mother, and when she awakes, I will tell her you are here."

"Thank you so much, Keena," I said.

When I went outside, Dad was just starting up the ramp.

"Laura! Thank God you're safe." He stopped and let go of the railing. "I was just coming up to see you. Is your mom still asleep?"

"Yeah, I'm going to go to the palace. I'll come back when she's awake."

Walking down the stairs was easier than going up, but with my lack of grace, I wobbled, making the pain in my head throb even more.

Dad came down the ramp. "Your mother and I have been so worried about you." As he wrapped his arms around my shoulders, his hug hurt my aching body, and my knit cap shifted.

"Brell told us about your head. Concussions are serious. You probably should have gone to the hospital," he said as he pulled away from me but kept his hands on my shoulders.

I looked at my feet. "I know...but you know..."

"Yeah, I get it," he said. "How are you feeling?"

"Headache and dizzy off and on." I looked toward the palace, the most beautiful tree home in the grove with its three stories, arched windows, and sharp-peaked roof. "But I'm fine, really." I stumbled on my next step, and Dad took me by the arm.

We walked to the palace together. At the bottom of the stairs, we greeted the protector on watch. Dad sighed and shook his head as he stared at the gently curved, narrow staircase leading upward from the forest floor. When we reached the top, he was out of breath, and I was feeling a little nauseated.

The protector on the landing opened one of the filigreed double doors, and Dad and I stepped inside. "They're in the operational room," Dad said.

As he led me toward the hall, his boots rang against the marble floor. His eyes followed the ivy-bearded walls, his lips parted, and corners of his smile curved upward in awe as we passed the pool of clear water covered with lily pads.

"No matter how many times I enter this room," Dad said. "I'm still wonderstruck by its beauty."

The operational room was the same room I was taken to when I'd returned to the grove with Todd after escaping Daveen when the Hanllants chased us at school. It was also the room where I'd first met Tosh and Caylent, and they'd explained their lack of involvement in Brell's capture and told us about the Hanllants. If I only knew then what I knew now, I would have never believed or trusted Daveen's sister.

We entered the wood-paneled room. King Vaylen sat at the head of the long, rectangular table where a fire burned in a small pit at its center. Rays of sunlight from the room's only window spread across the tabletop illuminating Mauka's leaf necklace and his weapon as they lay near the king. The tips of the long, green leaves making up Mauka's necklace were yellow and began to curl. Several of the teeth embedded into the clubbed end of Mauka's weapon had been removed and now lay scattered on the table.

Queen Sennille, Thriss, her father Blaukk, and Brell were seated at the table. Todd stood next to several large maps that were affixed to the wall with torn strips of masking tape. Bay lay sleeping in the corner closest to Brell.

Everyone stood when I entered, and after a round of welcoming hugs and answering questions about my injury and how I was feeling, Dad took his seat, and I took off my jacket and sat down next to Brell. From a ceramic pitcher, an attendant filled an empty glass full of water and set it on the table in front of me. From under the table, Brell took my hand and we smiled at one another.

Printed on eight and a half by eleven pieces of paper, the maps, like pieces of a puzzle, were taped together in rows and columns to make larger maps. Each map depicted a group of islands, along with Australia, Singapore, the Philippines, and some other countries in Southeast Asia. Several maps, including Australia, were crossed out with big Xs in red ink. The map in the very top right corner of the room was of Alaska.

In the bottom right corner hung a computer-printed picture of a plump, ceramic figure sitting with crossed arms and legs. The figure's closed-lip ear-to-ear smile was so big, its chubby cheeks rose to its eyes, squeezing them shut.

King Vaylan stood, and the gold buttons on his blue, velvet tunic flashed. "Brell told us about the fragment of stone you collected from the Cup of Queens. He also told us about the conversation you heard between Daveen and Caylent when you were on the Hanllant ship," he said in English, since my father and Todd were there.

I pulled the chip of stone from my pocket and set it on the table.

Todd picked it up and held it in the light. "I'll figure out what kind of rock this is and where it came from. Thriss and I will take it to a rock shop in Boston and see if there's a geologist there who can identify it for us. I should have an answer for you later today." He handed the rock to Thriss, and she put it in her bag.

The king sat down and set his hands on the table. "At this

very moment, Daveen is in pursuit of heat magic. We do not know if he has knowledge of its source or knows how to attain it, but we do know this." He inhaled deeply through his nose and turned to me. "As The One, it is your duty and your destiny to find heat magic and learn to use it before he does."

He interlocked his fingers. "While you were in Aludene, Glacion formed a special council, and Wventorin hosted its first meeting. A representative from each grove within a two-week travel radius was in attendance, including Tosh." He lifted his chin and smiled. "And it is understood that The One will continue as she has done without the need for approval or interference and with any level of assistance, protection, and support needed."

King Vaylan looked at me and the apples of his cheeks rose. "Laura, your accomplishments and our promise to your cause have already spread to groves beyond those of the special council and will continue to do so." He tilted his head and smiled. "You are trusted. You are respected. You are the mediator. You are the peacemaker. And we will do everything we can to help you accomplish this feat." He motioned to Todd.

"As you can see, Laura, we've been busy." Todd smiled, and using the red marker in his hand, he pointed to the maps. "Thriss and I have spent a lot of time researching in the library with Phyllis." He swallowed and nodded. "I've suspected all along that they'd traveled by ship. It would be the only way they could have reached the mainland."

"Mauka is the name of the Landaffen you brought back with you," King Vaylan said. "I wish we had more information to help in your pursuit, but he has not been very cooperative. From Brell, we have just learned the name of his grove. Despite giving us his name, Mauka will not speak other than repeating his allegiance to 'Mana' Daveen."

"Do you know what 'mana' means?" I asked.

The king shook his head. "We do not. We have asked, and he will not tell."

"But we have been able to figure out a few things even if he won't speak," Todd said. "The necklace he's wearing is made from Ti plant leaves, and these plants are only native to Australia, Southeast Asia, and the Pacific Islands. And so are these." Todd motioned to a bracelet made from tiny, white disks. "Puka shells. And then there's this." He picked up one of the pointed teeth. "From a tiger shark." He tossed it onto the table. "Based on that information alone, we've been able to narrow down the possible countries where Mauka's grove is located."

"And now with the additional information *you* have given us," Thriss added, "we are closer to determining the precise location."

"Brell described the Mentsune ship to us," Dad said. "It sounds like an ancient Polynesian canoe with a double-haul; a traditional Hawaiian boat."

A pair of numbers connected with a hyphen were written on each map. Todd turned to the wall of maps and put his hands on his hips. He yanked the cap from his pen and drew a big X over each map except for one. "Eight days," he said, reading the numbers next to Oahu.

"We calculated the number of days it would take a ship to sail from Alaska to the Polynesian Islands using the number of miles it would take and a cruising speed of 10 knots," Dad added. "We also factored in, that by working the wind, they could travel day and night without stopping."

"This is the only place that makes sense." Todd drew a star in the corner of the map of the Hawaiian Islands. "Wet heat. Sweet fruit. Fragrant flowers. Girdled by the ocean and about twenty days to get there by ship under normal circumstances."

"So, do you think that's it—Hawaii?" I asked.

"I do," Todd said. He spun back to the table.

I'd never been to Hawaii, but I'd seen it in photos and videos. I pictured a blue, cloudless sky, a turquoise ocean, and palm trees. My skin prickled with the damp warmth of humidity and with my next breath, the fruity smell of mangos, and the soft, creamy floral scent of plumeria blossoms entered my nose.

Perspiration dotted my forehead, and the image shifted to a lush rainforest with gigantic ferns and waterfalls. My nostrils flared with the sweet smell of warm, decaying vegetation, and the acidic smell of damp, swampy soil.

"Laura, are you okay?" Dad asked.

"Yeah, I'm fine." With the back of my hand, I patted the moisture from my head. "I knew I'd seen a necklace like that before. A few years ago, one of my friends brought one back from Hawaii."

"I also believe the ship is headed to the Hawaiian Islands," Dad said. "In addition to the number of off-limit areas in the Hawaiian waters, there are plenty of uninhabited and unused coves and bays, giving them plenty of places to moor their boats. Using their magic to keep their ship unseen when they're not alone on the open water would prevent them from being stopped and questioned by the coast guard for having an unregistered water vessel."

Todd nodded in agreement and added, "Hawaii is made up of over one-hundred and thirty islands, but if we eliminate the atolls and islands without rainforests large enough to hide a grove, that brings the number down to the eight main islands of Hawaii."

"What's that picture?" I asked, pointing to the photo of the jolly figure.

Todd smiled, lifting his eyebrows. "I thought you'd never ask. That's a statue of a mythical race of dwarf people called the Menehune. According to Hawaiian tradition, they live in deep forests and valleys and lived in Hawaii long before the settlers from Polynesia arrived."

"Menehune," I said. "Mentsune."

"Exactly," Todd said. "Like the Alux, mythological Maya creatures living in the Yucatan, hundreds of years ago, when careless, unseen Tulix Landaffens were spotted by humans, the legend of magical, elf-like creatures was born."

"And this has happened world-wide," Todd added. "As human cultures were accidentally exposed to Landaffens living in hidden lands or those of half-race returned to human life, human legends about faeries, sprites, and elves were the result. In the Inuit legend there is a race of people called the Adlet. I believe the Alaskan Landaffens, the Aludene, are the source of that myth."

"That's enough proof for me. We'll start in Hawaii, going from island to island, until we find the Mentsune Grove. We'll leave tomorrow morning," I announced.

"Honey, you have a concussion," Dad said. "You need to take it easy and heal before you do anything."

"I told you, Dad, I'm fine."

"You are not fine. It's affecting your coordination and balance, and, I suspect, your ability to do magic, as well."

"I can handle it."

Dad sighed and set his forearms on the table. "It's not just the concussion, Laura." He didn't start talking until I made eye contact with him. "You don't have enough information to just island hop willy nilly. You need a better plan than that," he said.

"But until we find out more information, that's all we *can* do," I said.

"Do you realize how big those islands are?" Dad huffed, folding his arms on the table.

"Yeah, I do. But the Yucatan region in Mexico is big, too, and we found that grove. I know it sounds like finding a needle in a haystack, but I can do it. I've done it before. Once I'm there I'll be able to—"

"Okay, so let's say you do find it," he said, raising his voice, "then what are you going to do?"

"I don't know—at least not yet. But I will. It's something I'll have to figure out as we go."

"Laura, think about what you're saying," Dad urged. "Flying

by the seat of your pants might have worked once, but there's no telling if it will work again. Don't leave tomorrow, Laura. Wait until you're healed and know exactly where you need to go and what you need to do."

"I can't wait, Dad," I said with growing impatience. "It doesn't work that way. This is the first time we've been one step ahead of Daveen, and I'm going to take advantage of it. As of tomorrow, I have approximately four days to beat the Hanllants to Hawaii and make the Legend of Tena a reality. I can't take the chance of letting that not happen."

Dad stared at the table, breathing heavily from his nose.

"The one called Clark," King Vaylen said gently. "We understand your concern for your daughter, but she is correct. Laura must find and learn heat magic before Daveen is able to do so." He opened his hands against the table and lightly pressed his palms against it. "When Daveen found the Cup of Queens before your daughter, he was able to temporarily harness a power meant only for The One. We fear he will be able to do the same with heat magic."

"He's right, Dad," I said, this time matching the king's calm tone. "I can do this. Yes, I'll be flying by the seat of my pants, but that's the only way. I know it will work again."

Dad's nostrils flared.

"I also believe it will work again," King Vaylan said. "But I understand your reluctance to have faith in your daughter's abilities. You are a smildt, but you are a human at heart. Therefore, you think like a human and will never truly embrace what we know. You are limited when it comes to understanding Landaffen instincts, intuition, and seeing with all of your senses. As a half-race and as The One, Laura is able to—"

"Limited!" Dad seethed. "I might be a human, but I am not limited when it comes to knowing what is right and wrong for my daughter." He made a fist and hit the table. "You know what Daveen is capable of. He has no problem killing or taking people hostage. Your people might be sending my daughter to her death!"

Dad put his hands on the table, pushed up hard with his palms, and stood.

"Dad! Stop! Please!" I shouted, raising my voice to match his. "I'm so sorry you, Mom, Phyllis, and Uncle Dean were taken by Daveen, and you had to go through what you did. You have no idea how awful I feel about that. But King Vaylan is right."

"He's right, and your father's wrong? Laura, you're being reckless and irresponsible!" He gritted his teeth, and his eyes grew misty. "If you don't properly think this thing through, you'll get yourself killed!"

The pressure in my head intensified. My throat tightened, and I blinked watery eyes.

"I'm being reckless and irresponsible?" A tear dropped to the table. "What about you, Dad, the adrenaline junkie? Leaving Mom and me practically every weekend to scale a mountain or hang glide or trek through the wilderness with some bimbo." Heat filled my chest and cheeks. "Bills didn't get paid because *you* spent the money galivanting with other women." I roughly wiped the tears from my face with my shaking hands.

Dad lowered to his seat.

I quickly stood, knocking over my chair. Brell caught it before the chairback hit the floor. "You left me," I snapped. "You moved to Alaska. Never called. Never came back for a visit or sent me a plane ticket so I could visit you. And now you suddenly care about me?" My tone was snarky, and my teary eyes glazed with anger.

"Angel, it wasn't like that. I know it seems like it, but it wasn't. Of course, I care about you. I love you, Laura. I just want what's best for you. I don't want to lose you!" His eyebrows and the corners of his mouth drooped. "We've talked about this before. I thought you'd forgiven me about the past."

"I know what's best for me. This is what I've been fated to do. Queen Tena bestowed this duty to me, and I'm going to see it through. Tomorrow, I'm leaving for Hawaii," I shouted. "And Brell and Thriss are coming with me."

The wall stretched and expanded on all sides as if they were closing in on me. I took a step backward toward the door.

"What about me?" Todd said. "I'm going, too. You can't leave me out of this!"

"Tomorrow is too soon, Angel. Please think this through," Dad begged.

I brought my hand against my forehead and shifted the weight of my upper body to my other hand. "Shut up! Both of you! I can't think!"

The pain in my head spiked. I moaned, closing my eyes and saw Daveen. Around his neck draped a necklace of Ti leaves. He slashed the air with a wooden club embedded with shark teeth. Drum beats thumped in my ears. Smoke burned the insides of my nostrils, and I saw a large block of black rock. I flinched, and when I opened my eyes, the room was spinning.

Brell put his arm around my shoulder, and I fell against him. Taking me by my waist, he lowered me back into my chair. "Laura, what is wrong?"

Dad rushed from his side of the table and took my hand. "Angel, what's happening?"

My head rolled to one side, and I closed my eyes.

CHAPTER 13

I stretched out my hand and tried to touch the rock, to trace its triangular symbol with my finger. But the closer I moved toward it, the farther away the block appeared.

"Hapeye," Daveen growled.

I turned toward the sound of his voice. Daveen walked forward, using his sword like a scythe to cut away tree branches in his way. His eyebrows lowered, and his lips curled. I ran from him, cranking my arms and high stepping to pull my heavy boots from the sticky ground.

I looked down, expecting to see snow, but the ground was wet, brown, and mushy. Water droplets hit my face, and a thick mist formed, impairing my vision. The rock moved farther away, growing smaller and smaller. Daveen was nowhere to be seen. The wet heat made it difficult to breathe, and I stopped to catch my breath.

A bright-red bird landed on the thin trunk of a fallen tree. Its tail feathers and the tips of its wings were black, save for small, white patches under its wings. Its long beak and the skin on its legs and feet was orange. Its curved, needle-like beak unhinged, and it squawked with a high-pitched zeet, zeet, raising goosebumps on my arms and making me take a labored step away from it.

The bird hopped twice and flew away. I looked up. In the distance, the stone was no bigger than my pinky.

"Hapeye! Hapeye!" screamed Daveen, the guttural tone of his voice bringing another set of goosebumps to my arms. My heartbeat quickened, and I spun, searching for Daveen, and saw nothing but mist and trees.

Curtains rustled, and I opened my eyes as sunlight flooded the room. Keena tied back the curtains and bustled past my bed.

"Wake up, Laura," she said sweetly with an ear-to-ear smile.

"How long have I been asleep?" I asked, trying to gauge the time of day by the angle of the sunlight entering the room. "Is it morning or the afternoon?" I'd been changed into a pink sleeping gown.

"It is morning," she said.

"Damn! Then I lost another day." I sighed.

"I think you were having a bad dream. Your breathying is heavy."

I continued to catch my breath and didn't bother to correct her. "Yeah, I was. It wasn't horrible. Just bad. One of those dreams where you're trying to do something or get somewhere, and whatever it is just keeps getting harder and harder to reach." I felt wet under my arms.

"Yes, I have also had those types of dreams. They are very frustrating. But I never remember my dreams, so the emotions do not last long."

"I typically don't remember my dreams either." I shook my head, trying to recall what had happened. "I remember being in the operational room. I was arguing with my dad and then..."

"You fainted and did not respond when Brell tried to wake you. Our healers said your head injury is to blame. How are you feeling now?"

"I'm okay."

As I sat up, Keena helped me readjust my pillow. She wore a plum-colored tunic and gray leggings. Instead of the ballerina-type slippers she usually wore, she had on a pair of boots that hit just above her ankle.

"I like your outfit. I don't think I've ever seen you in leggings and boots before."

She giggled, and her cheeks turned pink. "At the end of this season, I am to be a scout." She clasped her hands together at chest level and bounced on her toes. "The king has approved my change of duties."

"Congratulations. I didn't know you wanted to be a scout."

"I didn't either until I met you and your family. I am now eager to explore the world of humans, and when the time comes for our worlds to meet, it is my hope that I will be able to help."

"That's very sweet, Keena. I will need all the help I can get." I stretched, arching my back, and as my head pressed against the pillow, a dull ache returned to my forehead and then went away.

"Your clothes have been laundered." She pointed to the stack of folded clothes on the dresser. My ski jacket hung on a peg next to the door, and my backpack was on the floor next to one of the chairs. The sword of Tena was sheathed and tilted on its point against the wall.

"Thanks. How's my mom?" I asked. I touched my forehead. My bandage had been replaced with a new one. "Thank you so much for caring for her and staying with her yesterday."

"You are very welcome, Laura. Your mother is doing well. She has much improved. Your father is with her. Your father is very anxious to see you. He has been very worried, and I have also sensed in him feelings of regret and guilt."

"Yeah, I have those feelings, too."

"You will see him soon. King Vaylan has invited your parents to the palace for the morning meal. Your uncle and Phyllis have also returned for a visit."

"Really? My mom, too?"

Keena nodded. "Yes, she is well enough to attend."

"That's great! Wow, she's improved a lot since yesterday."

"Laura." Keena handed me a cup of water that had been sitting on the small table next to the bed. "You did not see her yesterday." Her smiled faded.

"What do you mean?"

"While you have been unconsciousness—"

"Unconscious," I corrected.

"The sun has crossed the sky two times."

"I've been out for two days?" I cried, dropping my arms onto the bed.

Keena lowered her chin.

"I need my backpack." I motioned toward the wall. "Can you bring me my backpack?"

Keena handed me my backpack, and I immediately dug into the side pocket for my phone, pulled it out, and looked at the date on the screen.

"Crap! I should already be in Hawaii by now." I kicked off my blanket, and accidentally spilled my water. "Oh, geez, I'm sorry."

Keena rushed to mop up the water with the cuff of her sleeve, but I beat her to it and smeared the drops with my hand, letting them absorb into my blanket.

"I need to talk to Brell and Todd right away." I handed Keena the glass. "Do you know where they are?"

"I do not, but they will also be in attendance at the morning meal."

A ball of pain and pressure thumped in the center of my forehead, and I grabbed the sides of my head with both hands.

"Please, Laura. There is no rush to enter this day. Prince Brell, Thriss, and the one called Todd have not been idle. They have been preparing for your departure."

Someone knocked on the door, and as Keena went to answer it, I straightened my blanket.

"Laura," Brell said as he and Todd entered.

Keena acknowledged Brell and Todd, gave me a wave, and left the room.

"Brell! I can't believe two more days have passed. We need to leave right now!" I started to get out of bed, but he leaned over me and kissed my forehead.

"Laura, do not be mad at the passage of time. Your body needed this time to heal. Your health is more important than anything else right now." He leaned over me and looked at me with concern. "How are you feeling?"

"I'm fine. I'm ready to go."

"And we are ready, too." On the opposite side of my wound, Brell smoothed my hair with his fingers. "But first there is much we need to tell you."

I lowered back onto my pillow, trying to ignore the pain in my head. Brell gave me a long hug, and he and Todd took seats next to my bed. Brell and Todd were both dressed in traditional Landaffen leisure wear: button-up tunics, thick leggings, and boots. A leather band wrapped around Todd's head, covering the tops of his ears.

"You smell like horse," I told Brell. Closing and opening my eyes, I smiled as the earthy scent of ammonia-laced hay and woodchips filled my space.

"I visited Adiness before I came here."

"I miss Molly."

"I look forward to the day we will once again ride side-by side through the woods." He picked up my hand and kissed it. "And I believe that day will come soon."

"So, what do ya think?" Todd asked. He brushed the front of tunic and tugged at the hem.

"You look great, Todd."

"Thanks," he beamed. "And with the top of my ears hidden, I look like a full-race." He tightened the knot of his headband. "Thriss loves it."

"I'm sure she does. I like it, too," I said.

"Don't worry about us losing two days," Todd said. "It took me two days to figure out the mystery of the stone, so *we* couldn't have left before now anyway."

Todd pulled the chip of stone from his pocket, and with his thumb, flipped it like a coin. To prove I was physically ready to leave, I sprang forward at the waist, and with the swipe of my hand, caught it mid-air. We all laughed, and the pain in my head thumped in time with the bouncing of my shoulders.

"Okay, so tell me, what did you find out?"

"It's lava rock."

"What?" I opened my hand and, using my palm like the pan on a scale, raised and lowered my hand up and down to gauge the stone's weight. "Lava rock is light and rough and has a lot of tiny holes in it." I ran my finger over the surface. "This feels heavier than that, and it's solid and smooth. And the stone in the Cup of Queens is heavy and perfectly smooth too."

"I know, that had me fooled at first, but Thriss and I took it to a geologist, and she looked at it under a microscope, and you won't believe what she found."

"What?"

"I thought it was a metamorphic rock, but it's actually an igneous rock; a rock

that's formed when magma cools and solidifies."

"It's really lava rock? One of my friends in New Mexico had a firepit in her backyard full of lava rock, and it didn't look like this."

"That's because this is a lava rock in disguise. The holes have been filled in with powdered lava rock," Todd explained.

"What? No wonder it's so heavy."

"Yup, someone took the time to grind lava rock into a fine powder. I'm guessing the Landaffen used a mortar and pestle." He demonstrated by pretending his palm was the mortar and his fist, the pestle. "Then fish glue was added."

"Glue made from fish?"

"Yep, fish bones, fish skin, and water are heated together to make a gelatin that can be used as glue. Ancient Egyptians used this type of glue. The glue was added to the lava powder, making a paste, and the paste was used to fill in all the holes—and I mean all of the holes."

I brought the stone closer to my eyes and squinted. It was hard to see, but in a few places, I could see the outline of tiny holes.

"I had the geologist X-ray it. That's why it took two days. I had to schedule an appointment with the geology department at Boston College. The X-ray showed that not only were the tops of each hole filled, like what spackle does to a nail hole, but the paste plugged the entire length of each hole, meaning a thin paste was probably made and dripped into the holes before the thicker paste capped them off. Then the stone was sanded, buffed smoothly, and sealed with a matte lacquer. Without taking it in for a proper analysis, the geologist didn't know what type of lacquer it was, but I told her it was very old, so she guessed it was made from tree sap."

"The lacquer is the reason why one side of the stone is darker than the other," Brell added.

"I had no idea. To look at it you'd never know it was lava rock." I turned the rock over in my hand, amazed. "Were you able to figure out where this particular piece of lava rock came from?"

"No, this type of lava rock is called basalt. Ninety percent of all the lava rock in the world is basalt." Todd's lips turned down in a frown as if determining the rock's origin was troubling him. "I'm sure there's probably some way to determine the exact mineral composition of this chip and match it to others found, but I think it would take a long time to schedule this type of analysis and get the results. Plus, I don't think that it's all that necessary."

"This type of rock *is* found on the Hawaiian Islands," Brell said. "The islands of Hawaii are shield volcanoes. The islands were formed when lava on the ocean floor flowed layer upon layer, building up and out from the ocean to make a land mass." He placed one slightly cupped hand on top of the other when he said "layers."

"Wow, Brell, I'm impressed."

"Do not be impressed." He smiled. "The geologist explained it to Thriss, and she explained it to me. Until that time, I did not know of volcanoes, lava, and of the power, force, and heat contained deep inside the earth."

"Queen Tena sure went through a lot of trouble to hide what it truly is," Todd said, "adding one more layer to a legend to be uncovered."

"It was a mystery she knew The One would solve," Brell said.

I crossed my arms. "I guess, but since Daveen is on his way to Hawaii, he solved it first. He was one step ahead of us like he always has been."

"That doesn't necessarily mean he figured out this is a piece of lava rock," Todd said. "There are other clues that lead to Hawaii. Think about it. Do you really think Daveen thought to take a sample to a geologist?"

"Probably not," I said.

"I also do not believe he would have consulted a human expert," Brell said. "And I do not believe the role of this stone ends solely with the revealing of its origin." He leaned forward in his chair, placing the points of his elbows on his knees. "Daveen already knew the stone from the cup came from one of the Hawaiian Islands. That is how he found the Mentsune grove and recruited its colonists. But he has not harnessed the use of heat magic." He put his hand to his chin. "Since he took a piece of stone from the Cup of Queens, it is only logical to assume he thinks he needs the stone to do heat magic."

"Then we have everything we need, too," I said. "We'll get there before Daveen, and then we have two days to find heat magic and get out of there before his ship docks."

"I've already packed my Hawaiian shirt," Todd snickered. "I bought that thing for the 'Jamaica Me Crazy Day' at school, and thought I'd never have another chance to wear it. Boy, was I wrong."

"Todd." I exhaled, closing and opening my eyes. "There's something else we need to talk about."

His shoulders sunk, and he rolled his eyes to the ceiling. "Laura, I know what you're going to say. You're going to tell me that I need to stay here and finish school."

"Yeah, of course I am." I leaned forward from my pillow.

Todd stretched out his legs. "We don't need to have that conversation because I've already taken care of things."

"How? What about your mom?"

"Everything is cool with my mom. While I was gone, she didn't get any calls from the school because the switchboard has the hardwired phone number to our house, and I unplugged that phone before I left." He folded his arms. "The only calls we get on that phone are from telemarketers, so she didn't even notice."

"Todd." I sighed. "That means she's been..."

"Yeah, I know, she's been drunk the whole time like she always is, so everything's good with her." He swallowed hard and looked at the ceiling again. "When I went home yesterday, she thought I'd just gotten back from the robotics tournament in Las Vegas."

"Okay, so you fooled your mom. But what about school and your grades? I know you were on a two-week independent study contract, but did you even *do* any of the work the teachers gave you?"

"I did." He shifted in his chair. "I finished all of it yesterday when I went home. I submitted the digital stuff and dropped the paper assignments off at the office when they opened this morning at seven."

"So now you have to go back to school. I doubt they'll give you another independent study contract. And even if they do, what about your mom? You can't keep lying to her and leaving her alone when she obviously needs you."

Todd rose from his chair. "Needs me? What about me needing her?" he asked, raising his voice, and poking his index finger into his chest. "All of these years, I've needed a mom, a sober mom. And what did I get? I got having to carry her to bed! I got having to clean up vomit around the toilet when she missed! I got being embarrassed when we went to barbeques and birthday parties, and she got drunk and started arguing with the people who cut her off and wouldn't give her anymore alcohol!" He wiped his lips with the back of his hand.

"I got people looking at me with pity because I had to live with her, and people telling me how sorry they were about my situation," he continued. A vein in his forehead bulged. "And I got people expecting me to step up and be the man of the house and help her," he scoffed. "But I've tried. Believe me, I've tried." A bit of spit sprayed from his mouth. "She won't listen to me. She won't listen to her friends or anyone else who's tried to help her. And she gets mean—really mean—when I try to reason with her. She gets violent. I can't tell you how many times she's slapped me across the face or pushed me away from her. And I just throw up my hands and walk away. That's all I can do until she sleeps it off, and then the bullshit drinking just starts all over again."

"Todd, I'm so sorry. No one deserves to be treated like that." I reached out for him, but he took a step backward.

"I am sorry, too," Brell said.

"I've hidden her bottles of alcohol or poured them down the sink, but she just buys more. If I had access to her bank accounts, I'd pull all the money out, so she couldn't do it, but I don't. My hands are tied. I've given up. It's not fair that her alcoholism is on me! I didn't do anything to drive her to drink. I've been a good son. A great son! I've done all I can do. It's time I think about myself and not plan my life around her. She sure hasn't planned her life around me!" He turned away from me to face the window. "I need to focus on me," he whispered.

"Todd," I said gently. "I agree. I know you've done all you could, and it is time you think about yourself. That's why I don't want you to give up on school and the opportunity you have in getting a scholarship and a college degree."

He spun from the window. "Let me tell you about that scholarship." He shook his head and tightened his lips. "It's not a guarantee. People just think it is. My mom is the one who started the rumor. When she's drunk, she brags to anyone who'll listen to her about how her son has a full scholarship to Harvard. She's been telling people that story since my junior year even though it wasn't a guarantee. Scholarships aren't even given until March," he said, raising his voice again. "I just went along with her bullshit because it's a hell of a lot easier than trying to correct her, especially when she's with her friends."

"I'm sorry, Todd. I didn't know about that until now."

Todd dropped back into his chair. "I submitted my college applications last November, but I won't know anything until the spring. The same with the scholarships. There's a chance I won't get into Harvard. But you know what, I...don't...care!"

Brell put his hand on Todd's back as Todd leaned forward, holding his head in his palms.

"That's not what I want to do anymore," Todd continued. "I only wanted to go to Harvard because that's what everyone expected 'Odd Ninja Todd' to do. But look at me, Laura!" He lifted his head and pressed his hands against his chest. "I'm a true half-race. I don't need glasses to see anymore. I can shoot an arrow five-hundred feet into the center of a bullseye, and when I visited your mom, I climbed the steps and totally kept my balance." He smiled and a dimple appeared in one cheek. "And you don't know this, but Thriss has been tutoring me in the Landaffen language. That coupled with what already comes to me naturally, and I'm practically fluent now."

"That's great, Todd. I've never doubted your abilities." I drew up my knees and adjusted my tone carefully, then said, "I just don't want you to throw away any amazing opportunities you might have as a human."

"Laura, I know you want me to be a strong force in the human world, so I'll be there for you when the time comes. I still want to do that, but I want to do it *how* and *when* I want to and not the way that's been planned for me by someone else."

I nodded my head. "I understand, Todd. I want you to be yourself and do what you want to do. I'm just afraid you don't understand what it truly means to live as a Landaffen."

Todd stared at the floor, and Brell gave him a pat on the back.

"Think about it," I said. "You've never had a girlfriend until now. You've never had this kind of excitement in your life until now. That's why—"

"I know, but don't you get it, Laura?" Todd blurted, lifting his head. "That's why I've never been important until now."

"That's not true," I insisted. "You've always been important. You've always been at the top of your class." I half-raised both of my hands. "Heck, you're going to be valedictorian."

"That's not important to me anymore, Laura." A pair of wrinkles formed between his eyebrows, and his jaw tightened. "Yeah, I'm really smart. I'm a brain. Yeah, I'm a type-A personality. Yeah, I'm conscientious and always strive to do my best and help others, but that doesn't mean I have to go to Harvard." The muscles in his face softened.

"You're right, it doesn't," I agreed, "but it's also something you've worked really hard for. Going to Harvard on a scholarship would be an amazing payoff for your hard work." I inched forward until I was upright with my legs crossed under me.

"Only it's not the reward I want in the end."

"Then what do you want, Todd?" I straightened my back and smacked the mattress with my hands. The pressure in my head was almost unbearable, but I kept a straight face.

He swallowed and licked his lips. "I want to be there with Thriss when you learn heat magic. I'll do everything in my power to protect you, to protect Thriss, to protect Brell, and to protect the integrity of the Legend of Queen Tena. I believe in you, Laura. But until I learned I was a half race and met Thriss, I didn't believe in myself."

He reached for my hand, and I took it. "I promise that I will play a part in both worlds," he continued. "I know I still have responsibilities to my schooling and my mom, and I won't neglect those. When this is over, I will finish school and go to college. It might not be Harvard, but I will get my degree. With everything I've done to help you, Laura, I think I've proved myself. Please let me be a part of this. Let me continue to believe in me."

As he stared at me, his face crumpled, and I stared back at him, unblinking. "What about your mom?" I asked softly.

Todd let go of my hand. "I called my aunt. I told her I couldn't stand living with my mother anymore, so I moved in with the family of one of my friends to finish out the school year. My aunt's retired, so she's flying out at the end of the week to stay with Mom. She's hoping she can do some kind of intervention." He sighed. "And right now, I can't think about being a part of that."

"Then do not be," Brell cut in. "A least not for now." He put his arm around Todd's shoulders. "There is only so much you can do for your mother when she does comprehend, or *wants* to comprehend, the self-destructive results of her actions. I am hoping your aunt will be able to help her with this." Brell swallowed. "A time will come when your mother understands and admits guilt in her role as a parent, and at that time, there will be unconditional love and forgiveness on both sides."

"You really think so?" Todd asked.

"I do. I feel it in my soul." He lowered his arm and patted Todd's back again. "And do not forget. In Wventorin, you are surrounded by those who love and care for you. The grove is also your home, and we believe in you."

"Thank you," Todd said and softly smiled.

The door slowly opened with a squeak. "The morning meal is ready," Thriss said in Landaffen as she stood in the doorway.

"Thank you. We'll be there shortly," Todd said in Landaffen. He spoke slowly, pausing between words and shifting his eyes to the ceiling, but his pronunciation was close to perfect. "I told Laura what we found out about the stone, so we just need to plan our trip." He shot a glance at me and smiled.

"Is Todd coming with us?" Thriss clasped her hands in front of her as she smiled and blinked.

"Yeah, he's coming. We can't separate the four musketeers," I said. "And we're leaving today. Starting with Hawaii, the biggest island."

"Thank you, Laura." Thriss ran into the room, threw her arms around Todd's neck, and dropped into his lap.

"After breakfast, we'll gather our supplies," Todd said. "Brell and I have already made a list of everything we'll need." He kissed Thriss on the cheek.

"I love you, Silly," Thriss said.

Todd gave her another kiss. "I love you, too," he said.

"What is a musketeer?" she asked.

CHAPTER 14

The fire pit was lit. Even though I wore summer clothes under my jacket and had switched out my boots for tennis shoes, the pergola and low clouds trapped enough of the fire's heat, making it warm enough to sit on the cold stone bench without getting a chill. I took off my gloves and held out my hands as I leaned closer to the fire.

Dad sat down next to me. "I'm sorry, Angel," he said. "I know you're too old for me to tell you what to do, but I just couldn't help myself."

"I know." I stared at the flames. "I couldn't help myself either. I know I shouldn't have said those things to you. I was just in a bad place, you know, with my concussion, and being on a time crunch to get to Hawaii, and just everything."

"I understand. And I don't blame you for any of the things you said and for not forgiving me." He rocked forward and rested his forearms on the tops of his thighs. "I was a shitty father. I was a shitty husband. The way I treated you and your mother wasn't fair. I only thought of myself, and not about how it affected you. I was a selfish bastard!" He rounded his back and sighed.

"And I forgive you for all of it. I meant it when I said it

before, and I mean it now," I told him. "Like I said, I wasn't myself the other day."

"When we were in Alaska," Dad said softly. "I felt like we finally connected, and not just on a superficial level because we were spending time together, but connected because I was introduced to the new world you've become a part of and connected because I've got a little Landaffen in me, too."

"You mean because you're a smildt," I joked.

He laughed. "I prefer...um...how about a 'quarter-race' Landaffen?"

"I like that." I nodded in agreement. "We'll go with that."

Dad put his arm around my waist and pulled me in for a side hug. "You have a lot of responsibility on your shoulders, Angel. The future livelihood of the Landaffens is all on you."

I slumped onto the bench. "I know."

"One day you were a high-school kid getting ready to graduate, and then suddenly your whole life was turned upside down. I couldn't have handled that at your age. Hell, I'm not sure I could handle that now." He chuckled.

He gripped his knees with his hands. "And there are Landaffens out there who want you dead. That's a lot for anyone to take in." He dropped his elbows back to his knees and put his head in his hands.

"I can do this, Dad. For a long time, I didn't believe in myself. I didn't think I could live up to my calling. But now I do. Time and time again, I've proved myself worthy of this quest. The Landaffens believe in me. And now I need you to believe in me, too."

He lifted his head, and as our eyes met, I realized I'd given him the same speech Todd had just given to me.

"I believe in you, Angel. I do. I just worry about you. And I'm scared for you."

"I'll be okay, Dad." We embraced, my dad squeezing me long and hard. From over his shoulder, I saw Todd and Thriss walking toward the courtyard with Brell, Mom, Phyllis, and Uncle Dean.

Todd and Thriss held hands while carrying duffle bags. After breakfast, they had gone into town, stopping at my house and Todd's to get some last-minutes things we needed. When they returned, we finalized our plans, checked supplies off our lists, and packed.

My mom and Brell broke off from the group and headed toward my dad and me.

"Remember, I won't be doing this alone, and I also have the support of every colony who knows about me, except, of course, the Mentsune," I said as Dad and I let go of one another. "And I'll text you and Mom whenever I can."

Dad wiped the inner corner of his eyes and flicked away a tear. "I know, Angel, but it's still hard." We rose from the bench. "Oh, there's your mother and Brell."

"Breakfast was wonderful," Mom said as she and Brell came next to us. "Quail egg quiche, fish cakes with a warm, tangy white sauce, buttered wheat biscuits, and fresh-squeezed winterberry juice. I could have that every morning, and not get sick of it." She pressed her lips together. "Um-um."

"I'm so glad you were able to have breakfast with us this morning, Mom. You look great. If it weren't for the sling, no one would even know you were injured." We hugged. "Pink cheeks." I smiled and my face warmed.

"Pink cheeks?" Mom asked. She wore a leather Wventorin coat with matching gloves. She held one hand against her face and laughed.

"Yeah, don't you remember? When I was little and had a cold, you used to tell me you knew I was feeling better because 'my color was good.' You used to say, 'pink cheeks', and talk about how relieved you were because you'd been so worried about me."

"Yes, I do remember that." Her bottom lip trembled, and tears rimmed her lower lashes.

"Mom," I said gently as my own tears threatened.

"You're not that little girl anymore," she sobbed.

Dad put his arm over her shoulder. "No, she isn't, Marg, and we're just going to have to get used to it. She's half Landaffen with a huge role to fulfill, and it's not our job to be sad, but to be grateful that she's got what it takes to get it done." He took a deep breath. "No, she's not our little girl anymore. She is an amazing young woman with extra-special skills and the most incredible life ahead of her." He winked at me.

A group of Wventorins started to gather outside the courtyard. "I guess I'm going to have an audience here, too," I said.

"Yes, and just like the Aludene, you cannot blame them. This is our history in the making," Brell said.

The baseball cap Todd loaned Brell was a snug fit, making Brell's hair pinch against the back of his head and form a C curl, but it concealed his ears, and the bill had already been bent into a fashionable curve. He tugged at the bill, bringing the front of the cap a little higher on his forehead. The T-shirt Todd gave him had a team logo on the chest that matched the logo on his cap.

We'd already said our good-byes at the palace and welcomed hugs, tears, and well wishes, but as more emotions continued to rise now, I knew there'd be another round. It was something we needed, and a part of me didn't want it to end.

A pair of attendants delivered the supplies we were taking with us and set them down in the center of the courtyard. Large, glass bowls filled with flower petals steeped in water and sweet-smelling oils formed a large circle around the place where I was to work the wind and conjure quick magic.

"My neighbor took great care of Molly. You don't need to worry about her," Phyllis said. "I've already moved her back to my barn, and she's happy and healthy."

With his elbow, Uncle Dean gave her ribs a gentle tap. "And..." he said, lowering the tone of his voice.

"And King Vaylan asked me to be Wventorin's official liaison while you are gone," she said. She rolled back her shoulders and smiled. "And I agreed."

"That's awesome! Congratulations! Thank you, Phyllis!" I gushed.

"So anytime you or Todd send a text to your mom, dad, or Dean, they'll tell me, and I'll relay all updates and messages to the king. The same with any calls or texts that come directly to me."

"Are you sure you're okay with this, Phyllis?" I asked. "You know, after all you've gone through, playing a part in this world again?"

"I am. I can't say I'm over what happened to me when I was a teenager, but I can say this ..." She exhaled with a long blow through her lips. "I've been denying and running away from who I am for a long time. I tried to forget it." She smiled sweetly, the corners of her mouth lifting in a soft smile. "But then you came along and made me remember it all over again as if it just happened yesterday."

"I'm sorry," I said, my chest deflating. "I didn't mean for that to happen."

"I know you didn't, honey, and there's no reason to be sorry. It was wrong for me to turn my back on my ancestry. I am a half-race," she said as she adjusted her posture. "And it's time I do my part. Now I know that despite the evil ones, the world of Landaffia is a beautiful place." A set of tears spilled to her cheeks. "And I want to be a part of it now and forever." She grabbed Uncle Dean's hand. "And your uncle is going to join me as we spend time in both worlds."

"Thank you," I said. "Thank you, Uncle Dean."

"It's what I want. It's what *we* want." Uncle Dean rocked back and forth on his feet. His coat opened, and he hooked his thumb around the strap of his overalls.

Dad scanned the crowd, settling his gaze on the king, queen, and Thriss's parents who stood between the fountain and the area reserved for me to work my magic. With his head lowered, Bay sat next to the king.

"Deja vu," Dad said. "But this time, your mother and I aren't going with you," he said softly and hung his head.

"We'll be back, hopefully sooner than later, Mr. Brooks," Todd said.

Brell, Todd, Thriss, and I walked into the circle and stood next to our belongings. The average temperature in Hawaii this time of year was eighty degrees with a low of sixty-five, so our back packs were stuffed with the clothing we'd worn when we were in Mexico. On the way to town, Thriss had also raided my closet. Todd ran home to grab his laptop and some additional clothing for himself and Brell, and when he returned, bragged about how smart he was because he'd also brought several bottles of sunscreen.

The ski bag we'd used to conceal and carry our weapons had been exchanged for a rolling body-board bag with a white wave printed on it. Our swords, daggers, and bows and arrows barely fit, but the Sword of Tena's length and the bag's stiff padding gave the illusion of it containing a body board, a wet suit, and fins.

The four of us took off our coats and gloves and handed them to the attendants who'd brought our bags to us. Thriss put on the baseball cap she'd been holding and looked down at her T-shirt. Like me, she wore a graphic tee with the name of a popular band, which of course she'd never heard of, on the front of it. Todd chose to wear athletic shorts with a plain white T-shirt, but Brell, Thriss, and I were in jeans.

"Damn, I don't know about you guys, but I'm sick of the snow," Todd remarked, and we all agreed. He rubbed his hands together.

"Okay." I sighed. "Let's do this."

We pulled on our backpacks. Todd picked up the duffle bag, and Brell grabbed the handle of the body-board bag. They moved closer to me and put their hands on my shoulders.

I stretched my hands in front of me, trying not to focus on the section of the crowd where Keena stood with her mother and sister. They smiled with eyes full of excitement. Keena clutched the front of her coat closed and smiled at me. I smiled back and shifted my eyes away from her.

"How's your head feeling?" Todd whispered. "You can get us there safely, right?"

"Yeah, I can. I'm fine. I've had plenty of time to rest, and my head doesn't hurt right now," I said, though the dull ache returned as my heart rate increased.

Just in case I messed up, Todd and I had our drivers' licenses and passports with us, so we could travel by plane if we had to. Brell and Thriss still had James and Rececca Walters' passports, so they could do the same if we ended up in the wrong places and separated from one another. We could only hope that the Walters hadn't noticed their passports missing and reported them stolen or applied for replacements.

"Do you need to see the photos again?" Todd shoved his hand in his front pocket and pulled out a piece of folded paper. When he was home and booked our hotel rooms, he'd printed out pictures of the hotel grounds, so I could use the images to help me visualize our destination while I worked the wind.

Todd unfolded a photo of a large, thatched-roof gazebo located on the hotel grounds. A newly married couple walked down the gazebo's steps while the bride held her bridal bouquet in the air.

"No, I don't need them," I said. "I remember."

Opening and closing my fingers, I strummed the air.

Being five hours behind eastern standard time, it was just before six in the morning in Hawaii, so no one should be around to see the four of us miraculously arrive. It was the perfect time to get there.

The gazebo entered my mind's eye, its painted white wood in sharp contrast to the green grass and row of palm trees behind it. The rising sun cut its soft, yellow beams across the wooden floor, through the structure's frame, and against its waist-high walls and railing.

In my line of vision, the colonists became unfocused and blurred, blending in with their surroundings as I worked the wind and kept my eyes on the pocket of air in front of me. Leaf debris and flecks of snow joined the swirl of air I created, and the whirling wind engulfed the four of us.

My head hurt and the muscles in my arms ached, but the whirlwind increased, and the funnel tightened around us. The colonists cheered and gasped in awe. Others shouted our names, wishing us well.

I imagined the dried grass of the thatched gazebo roof rustling in the breeze. Palm fronds tussled, and the giant leaves of monstera plants swayed as the sharp blooms of a bird of paradise remained rigid.

My body tingled and thinned into a whisp of wind, joining the funnel with Brell and my friends. The gazebo appeared, dotted with morning dew, and smelling of sea salt and fresh-cut grass. A blue sky. The crash of waves upon a sandy shore.

As my body separated from the wind and solidified, I landed on both feet but teetered and caught one of the gazebo's beams to stay upright. With their hands out to their sides, Brell and Thriss floated to the gazebo's floor feet first, and Todd hit the railing with his hip on the way down and fell to his rear. The duffle bag and body-board case came last, dropping with a hollow thud.

"You did it," Todd said, as he popped up from the floor and slipped his hand around Thriss's waist. "We are at the Grand Hawaiian Hotel in the exact same spot of the pictures I showed you."

"Yeah, I guess I did!" Inhaling deeply, I put my hands on my hips, and Brell pulled me in for a hug and a quick kiss on the lips. I pressed the medical tape on my head, making sure it was still secure.

In the distance, a team of gardeners tended to a flower bed

and trimmed a hedge wall, but they didn't seem to notice us or look in our direction. Other than the peaceful rumble of waves and the *snap*, *snap* of the gardener's clippers, there was no one else about or any other sounds than the ones we made as we whispered among ourselves and gathered our supplies.

The lobby was in the central building of the resort. From there, it branched into two connecting towers, one to the right of the lobby and the other to the left with the west side of each building facing the ocean. Enveloped by a morning mist hovering at our feet, we headed in the direction of the main building.

"This resort is beautiful," I announced as I took in the massive, glass double doors to the lobby.

"What made you decide to pick the main island of Hawaii as our first destination?" Todd asked. "I think it makes the perfect home base. It's not as touristy as Oahu and Maui."

My mind went blank, and I stopped just short of the entrance. Brell stopped with me, and when Todd and Thriss noticed, they also stopped and turned to face me.

"I have no idea," I said. "Honestly, I just said it without thinking. We probably should have looked at detailed maps and tried to speculate where the best place for a grove would be, but..."

"No, your answer was instinctive," Brell explained. He cupped his palm against my cheek, and the eye contact we made was intense and rang deep into my being as a shiver ran up my arms. "A spontaneous answer without explanation means you were guided by your intuition," he reiterated. "And this is what you must do while we are here."

"I'll text home." In a group text that included my mom, dad, Uncle Dean, and Phyllis, I sent a message letting them know we'd made it.

The morning humidity quickly ripened, and the skin on my arms glistened with sweat. With his slicked-back hair and crisp T-shirt, Brell looked like he'd just stepped from the shower. Thriss appeared cool and collected in her tank top and loose-fitting jeans, but poor Todd was a mess. He wiped a band of sweat from his forehead and with two fingers, grabbed the collar of his shirt, and pulling it in and out, pumped air against his chest.

Brell and Thriss adjusted the baseball hats on their heads, and I helped Brell tuck in the hair that had fallen across his eyes.

"Check-in isn't until three," Todd said. "I can ask for an early check-in, but I'm guessing that will only cut a couple of hours."

The back wall of the lobby was made from glass with two sets of doors leading to the beach. As Todd went to the front desk, we left our bags with Thriss, and I led Brell to the far end of the lobby.

"I promised I'd show you the beach. Seeing it from a plane doesn't really count. Come on," I said.

At the patio, we took off our shoes, stuffed our socks inside them, and with hooked fingers, held our shoes by the inside heels as we made our way to the shore.

The sun hung just above the ocean, a fiery orange ball setting the watery horizon aglow in sparkling shades of orange and red.

"It is soft," Brell said as his feet sunk into the fine-grained sand. "And at the same time, it is sticky." He lifted his foot and looked at the film of sand covering his sole. Like his hands, Brell's feet were smooth and groomed yet masculine and strong, and his toenails were neatly trimmed and buffed. Warm and damp like mine, his skin attracted the tiny grains of sand like a magnet.

"Yeah, but sand gets everywhere and in places you don't want it to be." I laughed. "That's the downside of its beauty."

A series of waves crashed and leveled out, sending a shallow current of water and foam to the shore. In a natural rhythm of its own, the water sucked back into the sea as it rose and fell again and again.

We rolled up our pant legs and waded into the water, jumping and skipping backward when the waves were high enough to wet our jeans.

Brell stood in front of the deflated body of a jellyfish that had succumbed to the lack of water and the morning sun. Its thin, fleshy hood was flattened like a deflated basketball, and its tentacles had withered and dried into stiff, wiry strings.

"The sea is strong yet yielding. Relentless yet forgiving. I sense its power," Brell said. He stared at an incoming wave and lifted his chin. "It can hold the weight of an iron ship yet support and sustain the delicate forms of creatures without bones." He pointed to the jellyfish with his toe. "I respect it but am fearful of the ocean's capabilities."

"Don't touch it," I warned. "It can still sting."

"Yes, something inert and unexpected can still cause pain and misery."

We played in the waves, wading mid-shin when the ocean receded and shuffling backward when the next set rolled in to soak our jeans. We stopped to shield our eyes and watch the sun rise. Misjudging the size of the next swell, we stayed put, and it hit our knees. We laughed and moved into shallower water.

Soft shades of pink and purple spread across the sky, and as the sun rose higher, the colors shifted into yellows, oranges, and reds. Facing one another, Brell took both of my hands. My chest fluttered, and his smile melted my soul like it did so many other times when our eyes locked.

"I love you," Brell said.

As the changing sky cast a warm, yellow glow upon his skin, I cupped his face with my hand and kissed him.

"I love you, too, Brell."

Holding hands, we walked back to the hotel, stopping at a bench on the patio to put on our tennis shoes. People were seated for breakfast, and as the outdoor tables filled up with young couples, older couples, and families, my eyes grew teary.

A small child crawled into his mom's lap as she read the menu. An old man with a cane pulled out a chair for his wife to sit down. A young woman playfully smacked the guy she was with as they looked at his phone screen and laughed.

"I did not get off all of the sand," Brell said as he tied his shoe. "I can feel it between my toes."

"Yeah, me too." I inhaled deeply through my nose.

Brell put his hand on my knee, and I stopped looking at the people and looked at him. He smiled, and I smiled back weakly.

"I know what you are thinking," he said as he gripped my knee a little harder.

"You do?" A tear balanced on my lower lash.

"You are eager to be like them." He lifted his chin in the direction of the dining patio. "Living without the worries and responsibilities that you and I have. You are wondering when we will be able to live as freely as they do."

"Yeah, that's exactly what I'm thinking. From the time we met until now, I can't remember when we weren't worried for the lives of our friends and family and dealing with Daveen and the Hanllants."

"There was a time," Brell said. He put his arm around my waist, and I leaned against him with my head on his shoulder. "When we first met in the woods. And when I gave you the necklace you are wearing today."

"I never take it off. I'll wear it forever."

I pulled the necklace from my T-shirt and held the charm, studying the leaf pattern at its center. Like metallic fluid flowing within a translucent casing, the charm changed hues, sparkling from copper to gold and then silver.

"That day seems like it was so long ago." I laid the pendent in my palm and watched it glisten as it caught the sunshine. "So much has happened since then. I'm not that same person."

"And neither am I. Everyone involved and those whose lives were affected by the Hanllants are not the same as they once were."

I thought of my parents, Uncle Dean and Phyllis, Thriss and Todd, and how just like me, Todd was now a part of both worlds.

"Days like those will come again," Brell said. "Peace will prevail, and we will marry."

"The calm before the storm," I said as I sat up and shifted my gaze to the concrete. I'd tied one of my sneakers tighter than the other. I pulled out the loose bow, yanked the laces, and retied it.

"I do not understand. Is there a storm coming?" Brell asked.

"No. It's a human expression. It means there'll be a quiet period of time when we can relax without big worries. Everything will seem wonderful and serene." I crossed my legs at my ankles. "And then the next thing we'll know, it'll be time for the Landaffens to enter the world of humans, and the chaos and fear and hate and misery will begin all over again."

"Not all storms are destructive and dangerous," Brell said as he wrapped his arm around my back and kissed the top of my head. "If one is prepared, and if the proper precautions are taken, one can 'ride out a storm' with little damage or harm being the result." He smiled, and I knew it was because he'd remembered and used a human expression like I'd done with the 'lull before the storm.'

Brell grabbed my hand and held it between both of his. "We will be ready for the storm. There will be resistance. There will be those who refuse to accept my people. But there will also be tolerance and those willing to make us feel welcomed. And in the end when the storm is over, the lull will come again and this time it will remain."

All I could do was hope he was right. I kissed his cheek, popped up from the bench, and wiped my eyes.

We found Thriss and Todd in the lobby standing in one of the seating areas. On the wall hung a map of the Hawaiian Islands, and Todd and Thriss were in front of Molokai. With each island being a separate metal plaque affixed to the wood-paneled wall, the design was more of a decoration than a detailed map, but the name of each island was labelled in gold script along with some of their major cities and beaches.

"People were forced to live on Molokai because of a disease?" Thriss asked Todd.

"Yeah, they were contagious, so they were quarantined," Todd said. "There's a cure for it now, so people with leprosy aren't sent away from the general public anymore."

"There is only one time a colony of Landaffens experienced an illness so severe that it forced those infected into a state of isolation," Thriss said. "The tale is written in the Legend of Seclusion."

"Brell, maybe that's why there are colonies that the collective doesn't know about. They quarantined themselves and were forgotten," I said.

"That is a possibility," he said.

Brell plopped onto the couch, and I joined Thriss and Todd at the map. On The Big Island, the location of our hotel was marked with a red star. The neighboring islands in the archipelago were Maui, Kahoolawe, Lanai, Moloki, Oahu, Kauai, and Niihau.

I walked to the plaque in the shape of The Big Island, placed my palm against it, and spread my fingers. "The island of inspiration," I mumbled. "From its snow-capped mountains of Maunakea to the lush valley of Hilo and the jet-black sands of Punalu'u Beach, the island of Hawaii will leave you in awe."

Todd laughed. "What did you do? Get a job for the Hawaii department of tourism?" Todd joked.

"I have no idea what made me say that." A pain developed in the center of my forehead. "I must have heard it somewhere."

"What did they say about giving us an earlier time to enter our room?" Brell asked.

"They're going to give us an extra-early check-in. Our room will be ready at noon. They said they'd hold our bags at the bell desk for us, but I figured we shouldn't let anyone else handle them, especially this one." He gave the body-board bag a soft kick with his toe.

"Did you say one room?" I asked.

"Do not worry," Thriss said.

"Yep," Todd said. "I thought it would be safer if we stayed in the same room instead of just being next door." He lifted his eyebrows. "I got us the presidential suite."

"A room meant for the American president?" Brell asked.

Todd laughed, and I joined him in laughing, though it made my head feel worse.

"No," Todd said. "That's just what they call a really big hotel room with more than one bedroom. Our suite has two separate bedrooms, so Brell, you and I will share a room, and Laura and Thriss will share the other."

"Sounds good," I said and lowered onto the couch next to Brell.

"How are you feeling?" Brell asked. "Your lips have lost their smile."

"I'm fine. Quick magic just sucked a lot of my energy. At least there were only four of us this time."

"Thriss and I are going to go down to the beach," Todd announced. "And then we'll find a convenience store and get some bottled water and snacks."

I leaned back and put my feet on the ottoman. "Okay, we'll stay here with our bags."

A uniformed bell attendant pushing an empty luggage cart stopped when he reached the area where we were sitting. He wore a straw hat, and like the employees at the front desk, he was dressed in a short-sleeved Hawaiian-print shirt. The hotel logo was embroidered on the shirt's left chest, and a plastic name tag was pinned beneath it. His name was Koa, and with his dark hair and the shade of his skin, I assumed he was a Hawaiian native. He had to be at least sixteen, but with his round face, smooth skin, and small stature, he looked more like twelve or thirteen to me.

"Excuse me," Koa said, looking straight at me. "Would you like me to hold your bags at the bell station? Once your room is ready, I will send them up."

"No, thank you," I said.

CHAPTER 15

Todd opened the double doors to our suite, and we stepped inside.

I ran to the floor-to-ceiling windows, drew the sheer, white curtains, and opened the sliding glass door. The smell of sea salt billowed into the room, and the curtains did the same as each panel caught the soft breeze and fluttered. "This room is amazing. Check out the view!"

The turquoise waves rolled and crashed, lapping the sand with a roar and crackle. The sun was high in the sky, igniting the flickering ocean waves with a twinkle.

"Only the best for my favorite peeps," Todd said as he slowly turned, giving the room a scan.

"Thank you so much, Todd." I drew him against me in a side hug. "I feel bad that you keep paying for everything. The X-ray of the stone fragment, the additional supplies, and now this. If there was some way I could—"

"Laura, you don't need to keep apologizing every time I spend money. I want to play a role in helping you in any way I can. And if doling out a little cash is part of it, then so be it." He gave my shoulder a squeeze and drew me in for a second hug.

The suite consisted of a living room, dining area, wet bar, and

196

two bedrooms with their own bathrooms. One bedroom had a king-sized bed. The other had two queens. Thriss and I took the room with two queens. We put our bags in our rooms and laid the body-board bag across the dining room table. Brell passed around bottles of water and stowed the rest in the mini fridge.

Todd sat on the couch, grabbed the remote, and turned on the TV. Thriss sunk into the cushion next to him, and I sat in one of the two armchairs.

"I do not understand how humans can enjoy watching pictures that move," she said as she took off her baseball cap and tossed it onto the coffee table. "The emotions are an act and the stories depicted are not real."

"Some of them are." Todd scrolled through the channels.

"It's an escape from reality." I couldn't remember the last time I'd watched television.

"Maybe I can find—"

"Todd, please don't introduce her to reality TV," I groaned.

"I won't." He laughed. "There's nothing good on anyway." He offered me the remote.

"Nah, just go ahead and turn it off," I said. "Let's relax for a bit, and then I want to pull out the maps you brought and start coming up with a game plan."

He flipped off the TV and picked up one of the hotel's touristy magazines that was on the coffee table.

I checked my phone. Mom and Dad were at my mom's house. They said to be careful, text often, and that they loved me. Smiling, I held my phone against my chest.

Brell returned from the bathroom with a wet washcloth. He pulled a first-aid kit from one of our duffle bags. "I want to clean and rebandage your wound," he said.

I moved to one of the dining room chairs. Brell stood over me, peeled the tape from the pad of gauze on my forehead, and lifted it away. Sticking to the dried blood, the gauze pulled my skin, and I winced.

"Sorry." Brell dabbed my wound with the washcloth.

"Hey, what a trip. Listen to this advertisement," Todd said. "The Big Island of Hawaii, the island of inspiration. From its snow-capped mountains of Maunakea to the lush valley of Hilo and the jet-black sands of Punalu'u Beach, the island of Hawaii will leave you in awe," he read and lowered the magazine. "Laura, that's exactly what you said when we were in the lobby!"

"Yeah, it is." I perked up. "You said it's an ad?"

"Yep, for this island."

"Read the rest of it to me."

With a cotton pad, Brell applied an ill-smelling salve to my wound.

"Ouch, that stings," I said, trying to stay still and not wrinkle my forehead.

"It just lists a bunch of attractions," Todd said. "Kayaking on the west coast of the island, hiking the trails in the P valley, whale watching and snorkeling on the Kona coast, ziplining through lush canopies, and visiting the sacred Naha Stone to learn about its legend."

"Naha Stone," I repeated. "I just remembered something," I added as the strange dream I'd had about a large, black rock came back to me. "Does it say anything more about it?" I shot up from the chair and went to the couch.

"Nope."

"Is there a picture of the stone?" My heart raced, and I was a little dizzy.

"Yeah. Why?"

"Last night, I had a weird dream about a big, black rock. A dream that at the time, seemed very real. But I forgot all about it until now."

"What about the dream made it weird?" Thriss asked. She took the magazine from Todd.

Scenes from the dream flashed through my head. I saw the rock. I saw Daveen. My hands shook, and my face grew hot.

"Because Daveen was in it," I said. "He was in a forest. He was mad and yelling...I don't remember what he was upset about though." My wound stopped burning, but the warmed salve melted, and a drop of it slid to my eyebrow. I scraped it off with the knuckle of my index finger.

"But it was just a dream, right?" Todd asked. "Or were you awake, and it was a vision like what happens when you do that thing where you see with all of your senses?"

"I was asleep, so I wasn't seeing with all of my senses. But..." I shook my head. "I just have a feeling that this dream is supposed to mean something." I looked at Brell. "Is it possible to see with all of your senses when you're asleep?"

"I do not believe so. I have not heard of this happening," Brell said.

Todd tapped his chin. "You said Daveen was in a forest, and you had the dream last night, right?"

"Yeah." I nodded.

"Then you couldn't have been seeing with all your senses, or you would have seen Daveen on a ship, not in a forest."

"True, but I know this rock is somehow important! I want to compare it to the rock from the Cup of Queens. Let me see that picture."

Thriss handed the magazine to me. In the ad, there was a collage of photos, a couple kayaking, a group of people hiking, someone on a zipline, two kids snorkeling, and then the Naha Stone. The dark gray rock sat on a concrete slab with smaller rocks wedged underneath it to keep its flat top level. The sides and bottom were also flat, giving it a rectangular shape, and based on the size of the street and building behind it, I'd guess that the stone was the size of a small car.

I closed my eyes, trying to remember more details about the rock from my dream. The image appeared, and I took deep breaths to calm my nerves.

The rock in my dream was shorter and more rounded, its shape organic, unlike the Naha Stone with its flat sides and corners, indicating it had been cut from a larger stone. The rock in my mind was also a darker shade of gray, but the surface of both were rough.

I opened my eyes. "It's not the same rock from my dream, but I still need to see that stone. I need to see it now!" I passed the magazine to Brell.

"Then we will go there," he said. "You might not have been seeing with all of your senses, but your intuition is something that needs to be followed."

"But how did I know the exact wording for that ad?" I sighed. To slow my heart rate, I slowly let out a breath.

"I do not know." Brell put his hand under my chin and lifted my head until we were eye to eye. "But I do know, that in the past, following your instincts was the right thing to do."

Todd got up and dug through one of his bags. "I'll find out where it's at."

"Do you think Daveen knows about the Naha Stone?" Thriss asked.

"I don't think so." I ran my finger across the photo of the stone. "He needed a sample of the stone from the Cup of Queens, so he could find the stone that matched it."

"And if he does not know the stone has been altered, he will not be able to find the stone's source," Brell said.

While Todd got out his laptop and did a search, I looked at my gash in the mirror. The slice ran diagonally from my forehead to my ear. Mid-cut there was a bruised lump, and the skin around the wound was red and puffy. As I stared at myself, I imagined the slice healed, the lump gone, and in its place, a white, raised scar.

"Here," Brell said as he came into the bathroom with medical tape and gauze.

I sat down on the toilet seat, and Brell finished attending to my wound.

"Hey," Todd shouted from the living room. "Guess what?"

Brell and I immediately reentered the living.

Todd beamed then told us, "The Naha Stone is a symbol of

the Naha rank of Hawaiian royalty, and it's a huge volcanic rock, a lava rock, just like the stone from the Cup of Queens!"

"Maybe they came from the same volcano," I wondered.

"That's possible. It was found on the banks of the Wailua River in Kauai, but it originated from Mount Waialeale, also in Kauai. And then in the twelfth century, using a double canoe, Chief Makali'inuikuakawaiea moved it to Hilo."

"Where exactly is it?"

"In front of the Hilo Public Library. It was relocated there in 1952." Todd tapped his phone as he spoke.

"The Legend of the Naha Stone," Todd said as he looked at the computer screen. "This is so cool." His eyes brightened as he smiled. "The Naha Stone was used to tell whether a baby boy was from the royal bloodline of the Naha Clan. Newborn boys were placed on the top of the rock. If the baby was quiet," Todd continued, "he was a member of the Naha. But if he cried, he had to live among the commoners."

Thriss leaned against Todd and looked over his shoulder as he tapped the keyboard. "In the legend of the Naha Stone," he said, "in addition to using it to test boy babies, it was also used as a test of leadership. It is said that whoever could turn over the stone possessed true Naha- leader blood, and that person would be granted the power to unite all of the Hawaiian Islands."

I sat on the chair across from Todd. "Kind of like King Arthur's sword in the stone, but instead of pulling out a sword, it's lifting the stone."

"Exactly."

"How much does the stone weigh?"

"About five-thousand pounds, so it would be like lifting a car."

"Was anyone able to perform such a feat?" Brell asked.

"According to the legend, in the eighteenth century, a fourteen-year-old boy named Kamehameha flipped it over, and later, he became a conqueror and the first ruler of the Hawaiian Island."

"So, he united the islands?" I asked.

"Yep." Todd leaned back with his elbows pointed outward and fingers interlocked behind his head. "Are you all thinking what I'm thinking?"

I rubbed my chin. "Yeah, but I don't want to jump to conclusions."

"But it makes sense, Laura," Todd said.

I glanced at Brell. "You have lifted a stone before, Laura." Brell said. "In Mexico, there were two statues with missing heads. One in the human Maya temple in Yaxchilan and its twin in the Tulix Grove. Using move magic, you restored the balance between our worlds by resetting the heads."

"So, you're thinking that just like the statues, there might be two Naha Stones. One in Hilo and the other in the Mentsune grove?" I asked.

"Yes, I believe that it is possible," Brell said.

"I do, too," Thriss said.

"Yep, totally," Todd said. "To get heat magic, you need to turn over both stones—the one in Hilo and the one in Mentsune."

I rubbed my chin again. "I don't know. That seems way too easy. And why would Queen Tena set up the same kind of task for me to perform? And if the Mentsune have a sacred stone in their grove, Daveen would know about it."

"That is true," Brell said. "And since the Hilo Naha Stone is an attraction for visitors, I believe Daveen would also know about it."

Todd shrugged his shoulders. "Yeah, I guess you're right."

"I do not think the stone needs to be lifted," Thriss said. "Daveen would need to force Laura to perform move magic, and he did not try to bring her with him."

"Unless he figures you're going to follow him here," Todd said.

"But Daveen can't count on capturing me once I'm here because he doesn't know that I know where he's going," I said.

"That is also true," Brell said. "But we cannot take the chance that the Hanllants do not know you are here or *will* be here. We must not let our guards down or take unnecessary risks."

I opened the magazine to the ad. "I agree, but I still want to see that stone."

"It's only a one-and-a-half to two-hour drive from here. We can rideshare to the library. I'll download the app and request a ride."

I filled a tote bag with bottled water and sunscreen. We changed into shorts, took the elevator to the lobby, and stood outside the hotel waiting for a black SUV to pick us up.

"I do not like how these flippies fall from my heels with each step," Thriss said. "And I am not used to my feet being exposed when I am around people I do not know."

"They're called flip-flops." Todd laughed. "I warned you about them."

"I know," she whined and wiggled her toes. "I think I would like to paint my toenails like humans do."

Our ride pulled up, and we got inside. After our experience with Juan in Mexico, we'd learned not to discuss anything related to the Landaffen world in front of people who weren't privy to us and our plans. Other than small talk and commenting on how beautiful the island was, we didn't say much.

We passed flowering trees and bushes, ferns, lush grasses, and, of course, palm trees. With my window down, I smelled a mix of dewy sweetness, fresh fruit, and earthy floral notes. The sea's aqua waters shimmered beneath a bright-blue sky and wispy clouds streaked the horizon. When the SUV cut inland and onto a two-lane road, I marveled at a green mountain range looming in the afternoon sun, its patchwork of colors in shades from emerald to lime.

From half a mile away, Brell spotted the stone. He pointed, and I leaned across his lap to look at the window. The stone sat on a grassy traffic island between the main road and an asphalt turn in front of the library. The driver turned off the road and pulled into the turnout.

Since we were just there for the stone and wouldn't be there very long, the driver said he'd wait for us in the parking lot. We slipped from the vehicle, and he pulled away as we walked to the traffic island.

A small group of people were at the stone. A couple read a plaque mounted on an adjacent rock. A family of four took pictures as they took turns trying to lift the stone, and a little boy climbed on top of it and laid on his back.

"Look at me. I'm not crying, so I'm royalty," the boy said.

A tween girl tapped the rock with the toe of her sandal. "You're too old. It only works on babies," she sneered.

"Hey, get down from there!" his dad snapped.

The boy rolled from the rock, and the family headed to the library, freeing up a spot for us.

I ran my hand along the top of the Naha Stone. Though it was rough, porous, and patchy in color, the stone held its own beauty as its legend, travels, and tonnage gave it a magnificence all its own.

The chip of stone from the Cup of Queens was in my pocket, but I waited until the couple left before I pulled it out for a comparison. The last thing I needed was for someone to think I'd chiseled off a chunk of the Naha Stone for a souvenir.

I held the chip against the Naha Stone, and Brell, Todd, and Thriss gathered around me.

"One side of the chip is a lot darker than the Naha stone," Thriss said. She tilted the bill of her ball cap higher on her forehead and leaned closer.

"That's because the lacquer on that side makes it the same color as if it was wet," Todd explained. "If it was raining, the Naha stone would look black, too."

"Well, they're both lava rocks, but there is no way to tell if this chip came from the same flow of lava that the Naha stone came from."

Todd read from his phone: "It is believed that the person who could overturn or move the rock, possessed mana, or spiritual power to rule the land."

I took a sharp breath. "What did you say?" I put the chip of stone in my pocket.

"It is believed that the..."

"No, what was that word you said for spiritual power?"

"Mana." Todd tapped his phone. "In native Hawaiian culture, it means spiritual energy in strength and power."

"That's it, Brell! Remember? The Mentsune called Daveen, Mana Daveen. We didn't know what they meant because 'mana's' not a Landaffen word. It's Hawaiian. Now we know for sure that the Mentsune Grove is on one of the Hawaiian Islands."

"It also tells us the Mentsune believe Daveen possesses magical strength and power. It is the reason why they follow him," Brell said.

"Place your hand upon the Naha Stone, Laura," Brell suggested. "See it with all of your senses. You will sense more than us, but Thriss and I will also try."

The three of us placed our right hands atop the stone and closed our eyes. I spread my fingers and concentrated, focusing on what I heard, felt, and smelled.

On the road behind us, vehicles buzzed past the library in varying ranges of motor roars, from the higher-pitched drone of motorized bicycles to the deep growl of semi-trucks. Car exhaust drowned the sweet native odors of flowers and fresh fruit, and under my hand, the coarse Naha Stone was warm from the beating sun.

As if a switch was flipped, the smell of exhaust was exchanged with the smell of something acrid and bitter like the scent of rotten eggs. My eyes burned. I held in a cough, and in my mind's eye, I saw a rock. Gray smoke clouded my vision, making its edges undefined.

Orange to yellow to white—a series of bright colors illuminated the rock in a heated glow like a horseshoe over a farrier's forge fire. White hot and slick, melting and pouring, a river of deadly liquid heat, a stream of lava crept into the ocean, its fingers sizzling. The outer layer hardened, turning it into ash and rock, as the molten layer beneath it cooled, turning from yellow to orange to gray. Crackling and cracking, lava solidified and steamed as the ground popped and bubbled.

My heart beat hard in my throat. I tried to scream, but the words clogged, and I held in another cough. Sweat dripped from my chest to my cleavage, pooling between my breasts and on the band of my bra.

"Ouch, it got hot," I heard Todd say.

"Yes, it did," Thriss said.

"The heat came to me, too," Brell said.

I shook my head and refocused, taking deep breaths and shifting my senses away from their voices.

Palm fronds, the elephant-ear sized leaves of ferns, the slick wet heat of a rainy, sunny day. Mangos ripe and sweet. A red bird with a needle-like hooked beak, its squawk ringing in my ears. Rain and more rain. Another stone, dark as the night and smooth. Etched upon it were three deep-cut lines, a triangle.

I'd seen that triangle before, but where? My headache returned, beating like a miniature drum in my temple, but I ignored the pain and concentrated. The triangle reappeared, but from a different angle than the one I'd just seen. It was the same triangle from my dream!

The hard pounding of my heart pulsed up my neck, and I yanked my hand from the stone and opened my eyes. "I saw—"

Todd poured water over Brell and Thriss's hands as the three of them stood behind me.

"Are you okay?" Brell asked, his eyes hard and searching for answers. "Let me see your hand. Is it burned like ours?"

"Oh, my gosh! You got burned?"

"I saved some for you," Todd said. He held one of the bottles of water I'd brought with us. Three-quarters of its contents were gone.

"I'm fine. I don't need it."

My palm was redder than it usually was, but the skin was soft and unblemished. When I pressed the pads, it didn't hurt or feel any differently than it usually did.

As Todd poured the remaining water over their burns, their jaws tightened, and Todd sucked in air through his teeth. Their palms were bright red, and the skin across their palms' heels and the pads of skin stretching across the base of their fingers were white and swollen.

A water-filled blister had formed below Brell's index and middle fingers, and Thriss had a raised blister on the last pad of her pinky. Her hand shook. She winced, taking deep breaths, and I sensed she was about to cry. Todd's hand wasn't as red as Brell's or Thriss's. His palm was void of blisters, but the skin was obviously tender and probably stung.

"Second degree burns," Todd said.

"This is terrible! I'm so sorry!" Tears pushed to the inner corners of my eyes, and my voice cracked.

"Do not be sorry." Brell said. "It is not a fault of yours. We did not know our senses would take us to the time when the stone was newly created."

"I'll get you some ice," I said as I noticed a convenience store on the other side of the street.

"Tell our driver to keep waiting for us," Todd said.

I told the driver. I sprinted to the streetlight, ran across the road when it was clear instead of waiting for the "walk" signal, and slowed to a jog when I entered the store. At the self-serve soda fountain, I ripped a bunch of napkins from the dispenser and filled three jumbo paper cups full of ice. With noticeable tears in my eyes, I convinced the clerk to give me the cups of ice for free.

I dashed back to the library where I found Brell, Thriss, and Todd sitting in the shade on a bench near the front of the library. With his uninjured hand, Todd cupped the back of Thriss's, cradling it tenderly.

Wrapping several cubes of ice in a double layer of napkins, I made three ice packs, and Brell, Todd, and Thriss used them to soothe their burns.

"I do not like these flippies," Thriss said. She slipped them off and set her feet on top of them. "The skin between my toes hurts."

"They're giving you blisters," Todd said.

"Todd, I still don't understand how *you* were burned." I joined them on the bench.

"He put his hand on the stone after we did. I have been teaching him to see with all of his senses," Thriss said and kissed Todd's cheek. He turned his head for a kiss on the lips, and she gave it to him.

"Touch was the only sense the three of us experienced," Brell said. "But I am sure, Laura, that you experienced much more."

"Yeah, unfortunately *we* got 'touch,'" Todd whined. He started to stretch the fingers of his burned hand and stopped when they were half uncurled. He clenched his teeth. "Damn, that hurts."

"I did," I said as I rounded my back and rested my forearms on my knees.

I told them what I'd heard, smelled, and seen, explaining how the scenery changed from one of fire and lava, cooling and hardening into rock, into a vision of the green vegetation of a rainforest, the red bird, lots of rain, and the triangle on a stone.

"I panicked when I saw the triangle," I said.

"Why is that?" Todd asked.

"Because I'd seen it before."

"Yes, there was a triangle on the sail of the Mentsune ship," Brell said.

"Yeah, but that's not what I'm talking about. It was in one of those dreams about Daveen that I've been having!"

"You did not tell me about the triangle carved in stone," Brell said. He scooped ice from the paper cup and added the cubes to his soaked napkins.

"I would have, but I didn't remember that part until now."

"Okay, wait," Todd said. He stood up, and with one hand on his chin and the other thrust inside the cup of ice, paced the sidewalk in front of the bench and stopped. "Dreams are not real, but seeing with all of your senses is real, right?"

"Yes," Brell and Thriss said at the same time.

"But Laura saw the same symbol in both. That means either both *aren't* real, or both *are* real. It can't be one or the other."

"Following your logic," Brell said, "Laura's dreams are real."

Thriss and I looked at one another but didn't say anything. My headache was gone, and I didn't want it to come back.

Todd poured some water from the cup onto his palm. "In one of the dreams with the stone, are you one-hundred percent sure Daveen was in a forest?"

"Yes," I said.

"And we know he's not in a forest...so the only thing that could mean is that your dreams are a glimpse into the future."

"Do you think that's possible?" I gasped.

"You are The One, Laura. Anything is possible." Brell set his hand on my thigh. "Now we know that seeing the stone in your dream was more than intuition. It also explains how you were already familiar with that advertisement. You saw it in your future. I believe you have the ability to see the past, present, and future."

"Well, if that's true, I know where we need to go next—Mount Waialeale, the origin of the Naha Stone." My body trembled with the thought.

"Todd, is Mount Waialeale a volcano?" Brell asked.

"Yeah, it's not currently active, but it's a volcano." He chucked a piece of ice into his mouth.

"The triangle on the sail was divided into three colors: red, brown, and green." Brell set his ankle on top of his other knee. "The Tulix had a symbol—three circles in a row, one smaller than the next."

"The perilune," I said.

"And the symbol of Aludene—"

"A half circle, flat side up with a smaller circle inside, representing the Cup of Queens!" I exclaimed.

"And the Mentsune. A triangle," Todd said.

"Red, brown, and green—lava, mountain, and the rainforest below," I said. "The triangle is a volcano."

"Elementary, my dear Watson," Todd said in a British accent.

CHAPTER 16

"What symbolizes Wventorin?" Todd asked Brell. He held his hand over the concrete and poured more water onto it.

"Our grove is not recognized by a symbol. Other than Tulix, Aludene, and Mentsune, I know of no other grove that uses a figure or shape to represent their grove."

"Why only those three groves?" I asked.

"To make it easier for The One to find. That is what I believe."

My cheeks warmed, and with my next breath, I shivered. "Queen Tena—she did it. I can feel it."

"Okay, guys. Prepare to get wet," Todd said as he read from his phone screen. "Mount Waialeale is under a trade wind inversion layer, so the winds can't rise and escape before the rain falls. Due to this, it's considered the wettest place on earth."

"How many inches of rain does it get a year?" I asked, remembering the warm rain from my vision.

"Four-hundred-and-fifty inches!"

"Is that a lot?" Thriss asked.

"Yeah. Back home we only get around forty."

"That's crazy. What else does it say?" I made new ice packs

with the napkins that were left, squeezed the water from their old napkins, and dropped the squeezed-out balls into Brell's cup.

"Well, um, it says there are flash floods, difficult terrain, and narrow paths with a sheer drop off one side. It's muddy and slippery. Temperatures can go from one extreme to another. Hikers need to be in optimal physical condition, and the inexperienced hiker should hire a guide." Todd bent his arm and made a muscle. "We don't need to worry about being in excellent physical condition."

Thriss gave him a teasing slap on the shoulder.

"We're going to need hiking gear," I said.

Todd swiped the phone screen. "People have also disappeared while hiking this trail. It's assumed that they slipped and fell into an abyss of vegetation and their bodies were never recovered. People also get lost."

"If someone was hiking close to the grove, the grove's magic would cause humans to lose their sense of direction," Brell said.

"It also says these are sacred grounds and hikers must be respectful of the environment. In ancient times, the Hawaiian chiefs and priests used to climb the mountain and leave offerings of wreaths and flowers to their god."

"How long does it take to get to the top?" I asked.

"It seems to vary. Some people can make it to the top in one day, but most people take two."

I thought quietly for a moment, then said, "I'll use quick magic to take us to the base of the mountain in Kauai. We'll start climbing and search for the grove, and if we don't find it by night fall, I'll get us back to the hotel, and we'll try again the next day. Hopefully we'll get there before Daveen."

"How is your head feeling?" Brell asked. "Will you able to perform quick magic again so soon?"

"Yeah, it won't be a problem. What about your hands?"

The three assured me that the cold water and ice had extinguished the sharp stinging in their hands and only a dull burning sensation remained.

Todd looked up the nearest sporting goods store. We went to the parking lot and asked our driver to take us there and wait for us until we were done. He stared at Brell, Todd's, and Thriss's hands but didn't ask any questions.

The driver parked, and we headed to the store.

"We will make ourselves unseen," Brell said. "Todd, you need to hold one of our hands at all times, especially when we are leaving."

"Laura, I know it bothers you to steal. It bothers me, too, even if we take money from a bank. Let's actually buy it this time," Todd said.

"But you've been spending so much of your own money," I said. "I know it's wrong, but sometimes Landaffens don't have a choice."

Thriss looped her arm around Todd's. "Landaffens only take from humans what is needed for us to spend time in the human world. It is something we must do in preparation for joining them in the future. It is not done in meanness or spite. We do not take items meant for our pleasure, leisure, decoration, or entertainment." She patted his upper arm. "But when humans steal, it is often done for many of those reasons."

"I get that," Todd countered, "but whether it's humans or Landaffens, it's still stealing. What would you think if humans secretly walked into your groves and took things?"

"Every time a human does something to upset the balance of nature such as deforestation and emitting pollution, it is as if they are stealing from the groves." Thriss pulled him against her. "Since the beginning of humankind, groups of humans have also stolen land from other groups of humans, using force and taking lives. Landaffens have never taken land from one another. You cannot argue with that, now can you, silly?"

"No, but I'm still paying."

Following a list of recommended supplies and equipment Todd found online, we grabbed hiking pants, shirts, and jackets made from quick-drying fabrics, rain jackets, wide-brimmed sun hats, sunglasses, hiking shoes, flashlight, a rechargeable electric lantern, reusable water bottles, a trail map of the mountain, and mosquito repellent.

We also bought a tent, so we could use the storage bag for our weapons. We already had the backpacks we'd used in Alaska along with my dad's compass. With the sunscreen and first-aid kit we'd brought from home, we were pretty much set.

When the clerk gave Todd the total, I gave him a nudge and whispered, "Now you're probably wishing we'd done it the Landaffen way." I laughed, and he over exaggerated bugging out his eyes when he looked at the receipt.

On the way back to the hotel, we made a pit stop at the grocery store for nutrition bars, beef jerky, dried fish, and fingernail polish for Thriss. In our room, Thriss applied a bitter-smelling salve to their burns, and she painted her toenails pink.

🙚🙙

A ray of sunlight poked its way between the curtain panels and lit up the living room. I pulled the drapes open, and a wash of light illuminated our pile of supplies next to the door. The swelling on Brell, Todd, and Thriss's palms had subsided, and other than being tender, all three said the pain was minimal, and they were ready for anything.

Todd took Thriss's hand and led her to the window where they stood arm in arm admiring the view. Brell reached for my hand, and we joined them.

"Do you ever wonder what your life would be like if you'd never met me?" I asked as I cuddled against him. Bands of coral and pink light ran the length of the horizon. Feathery clouds tickled the sky, and below, the purple sea waltzed with the rise and fall of each swell.

"I do not. There is no reason to question a past that has given rise to a future of ultimate happiness and fulfillment."

My chest warmed, and I snuggled closer. "When it is time to unite with humans, there will be death on both sides."

"I know." He held me tighter. "But we will be together."

There was a soft knock at the door. Todd looked out the peep hole.

"Who is there?" Brell asked.

"I don't see anyone." Todd opened the door and stuck his head in the hall.

I came behind him and did the same. Except for the bell attendant named Koa from yesterday, no one was there. Koa pushed a luggage rack with two suitcases on it. He turned his head and smiled at us.

"Did you knock on our door?" Todd asked.

"Yes, I am sorry. I had the wrong room. I transposed the last two numbers."

"No problem," Todd said and closed the door.

"I think we should go," I said.

"Wait, wait, wait," Todd said as he jogged to the coffee table and picked up his laptop. "Take one more look at the place you're taking us to."

"Todd, I looked at it for half an hour last night. We're just hopping from one island to another. Nothing is going to happen."

"I know, but...how's your head feeling?" Todd fumbled with his laptop and shoved it in my face.

"My head's fine," I said, "but if you keep bugging me, you'll give me a headache."

Last night after hours of toiling with the map of Mount Waialeale, Brell and Thiss determined that there were three areas on the mountain with the ideal terrain and level of isolation that could most likely harbor a grove. Todd figured out which trails would take us through each. From his laptop, he pulled up photos of the trailhead, and I memorized the landscape and the worn wood sign with an arrow that marked the trail. Behind the sign, between a cluster of trees and a jagged row of bushes, was the perfect place for us to arrive.

Referencing a website dedicated to listing the fauna and flora of Kauai, Thriss and I identified many of the trees we'd see there and learned their names.

"I definitely don't want to give you a headache." Todd closed his laptop, set it on the table, and sent a text message to Phyllis, telling her that we were still safe and well and asked her to relay the message to my parents.

Using one of Todd's belts, Brell fashioned an additional strap to the tent bag, so he could carry it across his back. I stuffed the chip of stone from the Cup of Queens into my front pocket. We put on our raincoats and backpacks and headed to the gazebo where I'd have three-hundred-and-sixty-degree access to the wind, and where no one would see us mysteriously disappear.

The level of humidity, temperature of the air, and sounds of the ground crew's clippers echoed the morning from the day before. Thriss, Todd, and Brell held onto me as I closed my eyes and worked the wind, weaving a cone of warm air around us. My sun hat blew sideways and with one hand, I straightened it and tightened the string under my chin.

"Hold onto your hats," I said and envisioned an area between shrubs and groups of trees.

A rainbow eucalyptus, its exposed bulk of roots covered with moss. Hibiscus flowers, a peppering of bright-red blooms upon a woodsy shrub. The limbs of a strawberry guava exploding with waxy, green leaves and red balls of fruit.

Raindrops pelted my body, and with my face to the sky, I opened my eyes.

"You did it," Todd said and pointed. "There's the sign."

"Of course she did it," Thriss said. "You need to stop doubting her."

Brell hooked his finger under the tent-bag strap. "It is very beautiful here."

A jeep was parked at the trailhead in a bare patch of mucky

soil overrun with the tread of many vehicles. As the rainfall increased, puddles formed in the deepest grooves.

"I guess we aren't the only ones who decided to climb the mountain today," Todd said.

A thin, muddy trail started up a slope, disappearing behind a group of giant ferns as it twisted to the right. Shrouded in clouds, the top of the mountain wasn't visible.

"Okay, let's go," I said and zipped my raincoat to my chin.

With Brell in the lead and Todd at the rear, we started up the path. Exposed from erosion and rain, large round stones poked up from the slop of mud blanketing the trail, and without any plants to slow it down, water rushed down the path like a waterfall.

Brell bobbled, and his foot hit the ground with a splash.

"The stones are slippery," Todd said. "I almost fell when I was walking from one to another."

"Maybe we should switch places, and I can catch you if you fall," Thriss said in a flirty tone.

"We are not used to this kind of terrain," Brell said. "I, too, almost fell when I set my foot upon a stone."

The rain stopped, and as the water soaked into the already-saturated ground, the mud thickened into a thick, slippery clay. Ferns and ohia lehua trees lined our path, and at one point I wobbled to the side and grabbed a branch to keep myself upright.

"What exactly are we looking for?" Todd asked.

I put my hands on my hips and stared at the ridge of lush jungle in the distance. "I'm not sure. I'm hoping I will know it when I see it."

"We can sense when a grove is close," Thriss said. "But the Mentsune colony does not know about the Velletsemn, meaning it has not been in communication with the collective for the turn of an unfathomable number of seasons. Because of this, I fear we will not see the grove with our senses when it is near."

"Crap," Todd said. "Then this is worse than looking for a

needle in a haystack, or should I say a toothpick in a jungle. We've got almost two-thousand acres to search through."

"I fear I also might not sense it," Brell said, drawing my hip against his, "but I do not fear that The One will."

The trail veered left and descended to a waist-deep stream that cut across the trail we were taking. Brell stopped at the river's edge.

"I read about this," Todd said. "This is where we boulder jump."

Boulders of various sizes zigzagged across the stream. The suffocating heat had dried the tops of the largest rocks, but the smaller ones glistened with the splash of rushing water.

"I have never seen brown water," Thriss said. "It looks like the tea that humans drink."

"It's from the tannins, compounds in wood and leaves. As they decay in the water, their tannins are released and turn the water this color."

Brell pulled one strap of the tent bag over his shoulder and went first, stepping onto a boulder, and leaping to the next two. On impact, he bent his knees and straightened his legs as he stuck both landings. He turned to wait for me, and when I'd made it to the second rock, he leapt to the next, repeating the process. When Brell reached the last boulder, he stretched out his hand and pulled me onto it with him. We kissed and jumped to the ground together, making deep prints in the mud but not slipping.

Todd and Thriss followed, Todd imitating what Brell had done for me, including giving Thriss a kiss when they reached the final boulder.

The trail stopped where a fallen tree and an uprooted bush lay in our path. We stepped over them, holding back the foliage that was destined to scrape our arms and legs.

"Ouch," Thriss said.

Thriss pushed up her sleeve, and Todd inspected her arm where a needle-thin scratch drew blood. "Well, no wonder,"

Todd said. He tugged something from a bush and popped it into his mouth. "Wild blackberries. Their vines have thorns."

The trail beyond us had been washed out or overgrown and wasn't visible. But just as Todd was going to consult the map, Brell found a log with an arrow cut into it, and Todd explained that he'd read hikers often helped each other out by marking the trail themselves.

"I see something," Brell said. He picked up his pace, the tent bag banging against his back. Breaking into a controlled sprint, he avoided mud holes, batted back the low-hanging foliage, and stopped at a Mokihana berry tree.

When we caught up with Brell, he was holding a frayed, faded ribbon tied to a tree limb. "And there are more." He let go of the ribbon and pointed ahead. "The trail begins over there."

"Markers left by hikers," Todd said. "If I'm remembering correctly, at one point we'll eventually come across a fence about so high." Todd held his open hand horizontally across his chest. "Meant to keep the feral pigs from entering this part of the rainforest."

"I can totally imagine how destructive pigs would be," I said.

From a pocket on his backpack, Todd pulled out the trail map and unfolded it. "But before we reach the fence, we need to go through a swamp," Todd said. "And then we'll do some more rock hopping up the river to a crater wall with a bunch of water falls that is supposed to be the most beautiful place on earth."

The jungle thickened, and we entered a forest of shoulder-high ferns. Mist curled at our legs, creeping into my raincoat and sending a chill across my back. The longer we walked, the muckier the soil became, turning from a thick, frosting-like mud into a spongy, waterlogged path of peat moss and long, shallow puddles.

A torrent of water cut across the trail. Brell jumped the deluge and turned with an outstretched hand to watch me. I made the leap, landing short, and Brell pulled me next to him as stream of water rushed against the back of my right heel. Mid-sprint, Thriss sprang from one foot, clearing the stream, and Todd's running start and leap was almost as graceful as hers.

Hours passed, and the terrain grew steeper, more rugged, and wet. Todd consulted the map off and on, nodding from the rear and giving a thumbs up each time he folded up the map. As the rain started and stopped, we zipped up our rain jackets and threw them open again when the rain turned to a mist we couldn't escape.

The muscles in my thighs burned and water soaked through my hiking shoes to my socks. A palm frond that I'd pushed aside snapped back and one of its leaves made a paper-thin cut across my palm that burned but was too shallow to bleed.

Brell stopped and wiped his forehead with the back of his hand. He was atop a large rock with a semi-flat top, and I stepped onto it and stood next to him. He put his arm around my waist and kissed my damp cheek.

"How are you doing?" he asked.

"I'm fine."

"We can stop and rest."

"No, we should keep going."

To our right, running along the ridge with a steep cliff, the trail narrowed. A thick forest of lush jungle was to our left. Studded with moss-covered rocks and marinated by gushing water, this path of slop and runaway leaf litter was the most challenging we'd met so far.

"It is extremely slippery," Brell warned as he shifted the tent bag's strap onto his shoulder, so it hung vertically.

I watched him lift one foot from the muck, lower it slowly, and twist his toe like he was putting out a cigarette before dropping his heel and shifting his weight to his newly planted foot. His next step was just as smooth. But when he lowered his heel on the following step, it slipped from under him, and he had to shift his weight to the other foot. He shot his hands out to his sides to balance himself.

I copied Brell but moved much slower and kept my hands

raised. Teetering when my toe hit a rock, I shot a glance down the cliff as the rock skated to the edge of the path and dropped. Grabbing a branch above my head, I caught my balance.

An undulating sea of green one-hundred feet below, the jungle canopy quaked with the wind and rain. The stone I'd hit punched through the foliage without making a sound and disappeared. At the cliff's edge, a finger of water sprung from the failed integrity of sediment, sending a trickle of water to the trees below. The tree branch gave, and I let go before it broke in my hands.

The rainfall increased, and a mist rose from the canopy, swirling in a witches' brew of treetops and the acrid smell of rotting wood. I pulled the hood of my raincoat over my sunhat, but it did little to help me see beyond the drops of rain.

Water rose, drowning my feet, and I held onto another overhanging branch to secure my footing.

"Flash Flood!" Brell shouted from over his shoulder.

"Aaaaaah!" Thriss screamed.

Twigs snapped and water rumbled.

"I got ya!" Todd shouted. "Whatever you do, don't let go of me!"

I twisted my upper body, replanting one foot, so I stood sideways on the trail. Brell did the same and sidestepped closer to me.

Thriss dangled over the cliff, digging the toes of her boots into the eroded cliff face, and using her free hand to grasp the cliff's edge. Holding a tree limb with one hand and Thriss's wrist with the other, Todd was the only thing preventing Thriss from tumbling to the jungle floor.

A stream of water rushed over the edge, hitting Thriss's face and spilling over her backpack. She shrieked and spit, opening and closing her eyes. As the soil gave in her hand, clumps of mud broke from the earth and fell. The rain slowed and stopped, but the water continued to run.

Todd braced his feet against a tree trunk, fighting the pull of her weight. Rain pelted his face, but he didn't flinch or blink. Grinding his teeth, he grunted as he heaved, squeezing her wrist, and telling her to take his.

"You're slipping!" Todd screamed. "Grab my wrist!"

"I am trying!" she cried. "My hand hurts!"

Her fingers dug into his skin, but Todd's hold upon her wrist included the base of her thumb, making it difficult for her to move her fingers.

Brell dropped the tent bag onto the trail. "I am coming," he said.

I backed into the trees, taking a thin trunk in each hand as I tightened the muscles in my legs, resisting the force of the flood against my lower legs.

"Brell, be careful," I cried. "Thriss, hold on! Brell's coming to help!"

As Brell waded past me, his left foot flew forward with the current, and he fell backward. I reached for him, but he caught a tree branch and pulled himself up before he needed my help.

"I cannot hold on any longer," Thriss cried.

Todd lowered to one knee and then the other. As waves of water crashed against his chest, he drew his legs behind him and dropped to his elbows.

"Todd, what are you doing?" I yelled.

Hooking his feet behind a tree trunk, he inched backward and crossed his ankles, locking the trunk against the insides of his lower legs.

"Grab my hand!" Todd shouted.

He lowered his head and stretched his other arm below the edge of the cliff. Mud plopped, rocks dropped, and water rippled over Todd's head, spilling onto Thriss. Thriss swung her other arm upward and caught Todd's hand, so he had both of her hands in his.

"I am here." Brell crouched next to Todd.

Todd lifted his head from the water, and in a single movement, pulled while bending his elbows and rising onto his knees. Thriss rose up the cliff face and flopped onto the trail as Todd backed into a row of ferns and dropped to his rear.

Brell helped Thriss to her feet, and Todd pushed up from the mud. Thriss had lost her hat, and her raincoat and head were caked with mud and decaying leaves. Between tangled strands of mud-clad hair, the points of her ears were visible.

"Todd, you saved me!" she screamed, throwing herself against him. They hugged for a long time, and Brell and I did the same.

"Are you okay?" Todd asked Thriss.

"Yes, my knee hurts where I hit the ground when I fell, and my wrist is sore, but I am fine."

Brell kissed my lips, and as he rewrapped his arms around me, I forgot my shoes and pants were soaked.

"I love you," Brell said.

"I love you, too."

When the water stopped flowing and our nerves settled, we continued our hike. The trail widened, veering from the cliff, and dropping into a ravine. As we walked, Thriss and Todd pulled clumps of mud and twig bits from their hair. A few worn-out ribbons continued to mark the trail, but in places where the trail had previously washed out, Todd consulted the map.

"Oh, you're gonna love what's up ahead," Todd announced and smiled. Thriss picked a tiny twig from his hair.

"What is it?" I asked.

"I can hear it," Brell said. "There are waterfalls. Many of them."

"It's called the Blue Hole. It's supposed to be the most beautiful place in the world," Todd said.

We found a small stream and did our best to clean our hands and faces.

"Cool! We're the only ones here." Todd put his hands on his hips and stood wide legged and in awe.

Water dropped from a three-thousand-foot-high cliff, beginning as several, wide waterfalls and splitting into a collection of twenty or more. As the water flowed against a curved stretch of a craggy, moss and plant-covered wall of rock, at the wall's base, clouds of mist rose from a clear pool of water.

"It's called the weeping wall," Todd explained, "because it looks like it's crying."

"Absolutely breathtaking," I said above the roar of water. I lifted my head and saw the blue sky through a round hole made from the curved cliff face. "And this is the Blue Hole." I closed my eyes and took a deep breath, filling my chest with the fresh scent of moist plants and cool water. "I think they're right. This is the most beautiful place on earth." As I opened my eyes, my head spun, and I took a baby step backward.

"How are you feeling?" Brell asked. He set his hand against my lower back.

"I'm fine. I think I'm just dehydrated."

Among the myriad of moss-covered boulders, we found a pair of flat rocks, took off our backpacks, and sat down. The blister on Thriss's hand had peeled open when Todd pulled her up from the cliff, and the two sat facing each other while Todd applied a bandage to her palm.

Brell replaced the soggy gauze pad and loose medical tape on the side of my forehead, and I guzzled water while staring at what I thought should be recognized as the eighth wonder of the world.

Todd stood and pulled Thriss up with him. "We're going to get closer to the falls," he announced.

Holding hands, the couple made their way toward the soft mist blooming from the bottom of the cliff. Keeping their steps firm and steady, they planted their feet against the clusters of greenery growing between the field of rocks and boulders.

I covered my mouth and yawned. "After all that hiking, I need a nap," I joked.

"Here, lay against me," Brell said.

I rotated, bringing my back against Brell's chest, and he held me.

Thriss and Todd moved from rock to rock, Todd stepping carefully as Thriss sprinted on her toes. I closed my eyes, and taking long, deep breaths, enjoyed the sun on my face, the cool mist from the waterfalls, and Brell's warm chest and slow heartbeat against my back.

Zeet, zeet.

I heard the gentle beating of wings and opened my eyes. Across from the falls, a red bird was perched in a tree. It opened its curved beak and chirped again.

Goosebumps rode up my arms. I popped up from Brell's chest and stood.

Zeet, zeet.

Keeping my eyes on the bird, I walked toward the tree, gently placing my feet as I moved across a rocky bed of moss and small plants.

"Laura, where are you going?" Brell asked.

I heard him stand and sling on his backpack.

The bird chirped, and its head turned in my direction.

Quickening my pace, I jumped over rocks and fallen tree limbs. As I grew closer to the cluster of trees, the earthy smell of wet wood grew stronger. The bird ruffled its feathers and came still, sitting on a limb like a ripe, red fruit.

"Where's Laura going?" Todd shouted.

"I do not know," Brell shouted back. "But we need to follow her. Take your things."

Slowing to a walk, I crept forward with an outstretched hand. The bird's beady eyes were on me. Its beak unhinged.

Zeet, zeet.

The bird's wings flapped, and with a hop, the bird took to the air, flying through the lush jungle, weaving in and out of tree limbs.

I ran after it, cranking my arms, ignoring the mud, ignoring the rocks, and ignoring Brell calling my name. The thick vegetation brushed against my legs. Low-hanging branches hit my head. Twigs poked my arms, but I remained steadfast, running without a slip or bobble, my stride mechanical but smooth.

The bird slowed, beating its wings in place as it brought its feet forward and landed on the limb of a giant banyan tree. I stood, catching my breath, staring at the magnificent tree and taking in its inimitable beauty.

Creeping aerial roots descended from its limbs, coiling and twisting to the ground, adding girth to its multiple trunks and spreading across the jungle floor in a tapestry of thick tendrils. A series of tall, thin surface roots at the tree's base curved like satin ribbons from the trunk to the ground, creating deep, tall nooks between them.

"Laura, are you okay?" Brell asked.

Staring at the bird, I took deep breaths through my nose.

Brell set his hand on my shoulder and set the tent bag at his feet.

"Don't scare it," I whispered.

"Scare what?" he whispered back.

"The bird. I've seen this bird before. It was in one of my dreams."

The squish and clomp of footsteps came up behind us, and Brell held his hand up behind him. "Shhh—"

"What's going on?" Todd asked.

The bird extended its wings, and with a series of short flaps, it lifted from the branch. I dashed toward it, but it took flight, disappearing behind the banyan tree and into a dense web of heavy foliage before I could follow it.

"Damn it!" I spun, dropping my shoulders. "Todd, what the hell! You scared it away."

"What? That red bird?"

"Yeah, that red bird," I snapped.

"It was in one of her dreams," Brell explained, "So she believes its presence was significant in some way." He set down our bag of weapons.

Todd slipped his backpack from one shoulder and my backpack from the other. "I'm sorry. I didn't hear Brell in time before I opened my big mouth." He lowered his head. "Maybe it will come back. We'll help you find it again."

"No, I'm sorry. Thanks for getting my backpack for me." I lowered my head. "I shouldn't have run off like that without saying anything. I don't know what came over me."

"I know what it was," Brell said. "You need to see this."

Brell stood against the Banyan tree in a nook between two thick aerial roots. Fused to the tree, the roots overlapped in an arch at the top of the trunk where they parted and ran the length of the trunk to the ground.

I walked forward. Brell moved aside and pointed. Deep within the nook, a triangle was carved below the arch of roots. Standing on my toes, I ran my finger over the symbol. The names Brad and Maria with a heart between them were also cut into the trunk. Below were the names "Margo," "Kimo," and "Jasmine," but unlike the crudely etched names and heart, the triangle was perfectly symmetrical, and its edges were black and smooth like they'd been carefully seared into the wood.

"The grove is close," I said. "It's past this tree and straight ahead."

"What do we do now?" Todd asked.

"Brell and I are going in, unseen by all, and you and Thriss will wait for us."

I ran to the tent bag, unzipped it, and dug inside.

"Thriss and I should go, too," Todd said, folding his arms.

"I would love that, but I don't have the energy to keep all four of us unseen by all for very long, and it would be too hard to explore with the four of us holding onto each other," I said as I pulled the sheathed sword of Tena from the bag and tied its belt around my waist. "I also need to save my strength to get us back to the hotel."

"She is right," Brell agreed. "And if we do not return, we will need you to come to our aid." He strapped his sword to his waist and slung his quiver and bow over his shoulder.

I rolled up my pant leg and tied a dagger to the outside of my calf, and Brell did the same.

Pushing tree branches aside, we walked behind the mammoth banyan tree. As the sun burned through the lush canopy of trees, the thick, dew-dropped vegetation glistened, and the vibrant colors of fresh bark on the rainbow eucalyptus trees appeared to glow.

"We're getting close. I can feel it," I said as I walked through a row of tightly packed trees and ferns.

"I feel it, too." Brell said. He took a deep breath while opening and closing his eyes. "It is old magic."

"Very old magic," Thriss added.

As if my body was a tuning fork that had been tapped, my nerves vibrated, and my ears rang with a deep hum.

"I found it." I stopped and faced a wall of trees.

"Where?" Todd asked, coming next to me.

Thriss slipped in front of him, tucking the top of her head

under his chin. She took his wrist and lifted his hand, so his palm faced the trees. "Do you feel it now?"

"Yeah, I think I do," he beamed. "It's like I can feel the air." He patted the space in front of him. "It's soft and pillowy, and it's kinda pulsating, too."

"It is the magic you are feeling," Thriss explained.

"And humans can't feel this?"

"No, and they would not have been able to get as close as we are. The grove's magic would have redirected them."

"Brell and I are just going to go in, get a look around, and see if we can find out anything about heat magic and what they plan to do when Daveen gets here," I said. "We shouldn't be any longer than an hour or two."

It started to rain again, a spattering of warm drops. Thriss pulled on her hood. "We will wait for you here. What should we do if you do not return? We cannot enter the grove. We will be seen."

"We can enter," Todd said. "We just have to wait until it's dark."

"Be careful," Thriss said, and we exchanged hugs.

Brell took my hand, and I made us unseen by all.

"That's so cool," Todd said as Brell and I became invisible.

Walking toward the thickest part of the jungle, our feet met a patch of bright-green moss. We closed our eyes, and the air swirled around our bodies, sucking us into the Mentsune Grove.

Brell squeezed my hand. I opened my eyes and gasped. There was no rain. We stood on a ridge below a banyan tree many times larger than the banyan tree on the other side. With thousands of fused trunks and hundreds of aerial roots like smooth, gray fingers digging into the moist soil, the tree had probably been there since the first existence of the Mentsune Grove.

A small range of rolling hills flanked the far side of the grove, and at its center, a row of waterfalls dropped against a silvery rockface, creating a miniature Weeping Wall. Birds chirped, water babbled, and the smell of ripe fruit and flowers rode the wet heat, enveloping us with sweet goodness.

The ground at our feet was spongy. Thick moss ran along a stretch of earth sloping downward and flattening to a community of several hundred homes. The homes were made from wood with thatched roofs of dried palm fronds. Window shades of woven jute hung in their glassless windows; some blinds were pulled, and others were half raised and swinging in the warm, light breeze. Rustic surfboards of various lengths were tilted against homes and lay in wood racks next to the houses.

Built upon stilted wooden platforms, the homes stood proudly above the damp earth by two to three feet. Stone steps led from each door to paths made from horizontal planks, and flowering plants, bushes, and trees sprinkled between buildings and along the wooden sidewalks, made Mentsune the most beautiful grove I'd ever seen.

A Landaffen next to a stack of palm fronds was repairing a roof, two small children were picking papayas from a tree, a young female with a surfboard under her arm jogged down one of the paths, and chickens roamed freely as they pecked the ground.

The Mentsune wore necklaces of Ti leaves or puka shells, and brightly colored cloths wrapped around their bodies made loin coverings, skirts, and dresses. Some Mentsune were barefooted, and others wore jute sandals.

To my surprise, protectors weren't stationed at the grove's entry, but I made our voices unheard by all before I spoke.

"I think I see the palace," I said as I walked to a higher point on the ridge.

Enclosed by a circle of palm trees, one structure was larger than the rest, a grand thatched home three-stories high with double doors and an entryway of arched wood. A field of boulders spread before the palace. With their tops flattened and the cracks between them grouted with smaller stones and moss, the boulders created a large patio that extended from the palace to make a small courtyard. A large firepit filled with lava rock was at the courtyard's center.

"Look," Brell pointed to three rows of long, thatched-roof buildings, and a large vegetable garden. "Areas of trade, a school, and farmland."

"Let's go and see what we can find out," I said.

Heading from the ridge, we took long steps, avoiding the mud and placing our feet on stones, so we wouldn't make footprints. Winding through the grove, a rushing river cut across the bottom of the ridge. We walked to a spot where the river narrowed, tightly locked our hands, and leaped with a running start.

Clearing the river and hitting the earth simultaneously, it was a clean landing, but the ground of moss sagged under our weight like a taunt sheet with nothing beneath it.

"What the hell?" I spoke.

From under our feet, the moss tore. Still holding hands, we dropped. Brell landed feet first, and pulled me up to do the same, so I wouldn't stumble. We stood at least ten feet below the ground in a cave, staring up at the blue sky. A tunnel to our right led into the darkness.

I closed my eyes and held my breath. My body tingled. "We're still unseen and unheard by all," I said. "They set a trap! How did they know we were coming?"

"They might not have known. This trap could be meant for anyone who found a way to enter their grove," Brell said.

The heat was thick. The walls were slick and dripped with ground water, but Brell ran one hand on the cave's surface, hoping to find a rough patch where we could place our feet and climb out.

Brell stopped searching and drew his sword with his left hand. "We cannot climb from here. We can wait here for them and fight or..." He nodded in the direction of the tunnel.

I pulled the Sword of Tena from its sheath. "I don't like

being a sitting duck. I think we should take our chances with the tunnel."

"I hear something," Brell said.

I heard it too, the sound of wood sliding and a repetitive, rhythmic *click click* of heavy gears turning. Above us, a trail of water dripped from the split moss.

"The river is being diverted," Brell shouted. "Run!"

Water gushed into the hole, a violent torrent, knocking us from our feet. Still holding each other's hands and clinging onto our weapons, we tried to stand, but the gushing water was too powerful as it waterfalled into the tunnel.

We lost our footing and dropped into the water. Coughing and spitting, we popped our heads to the surface but were dunked again and again as the current pulled us with it. Riding the river, we entered the tunnel, our bodies banging against the tunnel's walls as we yanked each other with each twist and turn.

"Brell!" I shouted when my head came to the surface. I squeezed his hand. Even with Landaffen eyes, it was too dark to see anything.

The current jerked me down again. As my wrist rotated, the Sword of Tena scraped the wall, and I almost dropped it. I rolled, turning sideways, and bashed into the wall, my wet clothes and raincoat making my movements sloppy and awkward.

Brell banged against me. I hit the wall, and when I was able to come up for a breath, I realized he and I were no longer holding hands.

"Laura!" Brell shouted.

"I'm here!" I yelled.

Another surge of water drew me under, and I crashed against the cave wall. As I tried to get upright, the side of my head smacked the rock in the same place where I'd been hit with the paddle. I sunk while riding the current.

Behind my eyes, my head hurt, and the pressure in my lungs from holding my breath was unbearable. My feet hit the cave floor. I bent my knees and sprung upward, gasping as my head shot from the water.

"Laura! Do not fight it! Swim with it!" Brell's voice pinched off with a gurgle.

"Brell?"

Bringing the handle of my sword under my chin, I pinned the blade against my body and with my other hand, I scooped the water. Kicking my legs with the current, I fought to keep my head above the surface as its strong current threatened to drown me.

The tunnel curved right. Continuing to kick and paddle with one hand, I managed to push from the wall before I slammed into it again. Sunlight shot into the tunnel. Squinting against the light, I dropped from the tunnel and into a pool of clear water.

The pool overflowed, bottlenecking into a larger expanse of water. Mist rose from the surface of the second pool, and a stream ran from it, winding into the jungle.

My muscles were tight, trembling from overexertion, but the pleasant tingle I'd hoped to feel from being unseen and unheard was gone. I staggered to my feet.

Facing me, a row of twenty Mentsune stood along the edge of the pool. Brell was between two of them. They held his upper arms while another tied Brell's hands together with a rope. A third held Brell's sword and dagger, and through the waist-high water, another pair walked toward me. Like the Mentsunes in Aludene, they wore woven helmets with a mohawk of tightly packed red feathers.

"Laura, are you okay?" Brell asked.

"Yeah, I'm—"

A Mentsune slapped Brell's face, and Brell licked his bloody lips.

Brell and I had lost our sun hats, and as the water guzzling from the tunnel slowed to a drizzle, a small wave drove our hats to the pebbled shore. As the pool drained, its water joining the stream, I saw Brell's bow and arrows floating at the pool's edge.

I raised the Sword of Tena, and one of the Mentsune holding Brell set a dagger against Brell's throat. As I lowered my sword, a Mentsune yanked it from my hand, and the pair grabbed my arms. Like Brell, I didn't fight their hold. They patted me down, found my dagger, and took it away.

Blood dripped to my lips. My bandage was gone, and my wound had reopened. My legs wobbled, and I was dizzy, but the Mentsune holding me kept me upright.

A Mentsune moved aside, and another Landaffen stepped to the pool's edge.

I gasped, and my knees buckled. He was tall with broad shoulders and blond hair. A necklace of Ti leaves hung around his neck, and a red cloth wrapped his waist, hitting above his knees. He was barefoot and bare-chested with a lean, muscular build and rippling abs. A helmet with a mohawk of feathers sat atop his head, but instead of red, gold feathers filled the crest. With his square jaw, high cheek bones, and full lips, admittedly, he was handsome.

The arch of one of his eyebrows lifted, and I grew sick.

"The One called Laura." He nodded and half bowed. "And Prince Brell of Wventorin." He turned to Brell, nodded, and half folded at the waist. "Welcome to Mentsune. I am Mana Finnlen," he said slowly. "You know my older brother, Mana Daveen."

A face flashed through my mind, an angry face shouting the word "hapeye." The more I looked at him, the more I realized he and Daveen could practically be twins.

It wasn't Daveen I'd been seeing in my dreams. It was Daveen's brother!

CHAPTER 18

"They are dripping on the palace floor. Do something about it!" Finnlen ordered.

He sat down on a wooden chair with images of palm fronds and hibiscus flowers carved into the top rail of its tall, arched back. Wearing helmets similar to Finnlen's, a couple, whom I assumed were the king and queen of the grove, sat apart from Finnlen on a bench with the same carvings.

With its open windows and woven shades, the palace was like the other buildings we'd seen, though on a much grander scale. Arched beams along the ceiling gave it a baronial flare, flowering trees in wooden planters perfumed the air, and woven mats painted with sea life covered much of the floor.

A Mentsune hurried from the throne room and returned with two large white cloths. As Brell and I stood side by side with our hands bound behind us and mouths gagged with a twist of rope, the attendant daubed the towel against our pants and mopped up the puddles we'd made on the lacquered wooden floor. Brell and I stood firm and didn't move, making the attendant's job harder.

As anger pulsed through my body, I bit the rope hard and fidgeted with the cloth binding on my hands.

Finnlen motioned with his index finger, and the Mentsune behind me untied my gag.

Finnlen laughed and shot me a snide glare, reminding me of his brother. "The One wants to speak, so speak. I am sure she is overwhelmed by my royal presence and has much to say."

"I didn't know Daveen and Caylent had a brother." As I spoke, the corners of my mouth burned where the rope had rubbed. "Your father never mentioned you." I lifted my chin. "Now I know why. Like your siblings, you are a disappointment. A disgrace to all of Landaffia."

"My father is the one who is a disgrace." One of his eyebrows rose. "Tosh never mentioned me because he has never acknowledged my existence." He drummed his fingers against the arm of his chair. "I am my father's mistake. I am his inbred 'bastard' son."

I sucked in a breath. "Inbred?"

"Yes. My mother was a cousin of the King." He laughed. "What do you think of the Laramiss king now?"

Brell and I looked at each other.

Finnlen rubbed his chin between his thumb and index finger and laughed, throwing back his head. "My father is a liar and a cheat," he snarled.

"And so are you. With your lies and misrepresentation of what is just and true, you have fooled the Mentsune, just like you once fooled the colonists of Tulix and Aludene," I said strongly. "But now the Tulix and Aludene know your evil, and soon the Mentsune will turn from you just like the other colonies did."

My face was hot. I licked my lips and tasted blood as the gash on my head continued to bleed and ooze. The room spun. I closed and opened my eyes.

"They are loyal to me and will remain so." The corner of his mouth lifted as he glanced at the Mentsune king and queen. "My mother's husband, the one I had believed was my father, died at the turn of my seventh year. Then eight seasons ago as my mother lay dying, she told me Tosh was my real father. Following my mother's wishes, I have kept her secret, with the exception of Daveen and Caylent, of course, and did not tell Tosh that I knew the truth. I left Laramiss. My purpose—to acquire the Magic of Tena before The One was able to do so."

I narrowed my eyes.

"Once Heat Magic is mine, at your death, all forms of higher magic will be transferred to me. And King Tosh, who thinks I am living in another grove, will know what his blood-son is capable of doing."

"Heat Magic will never be yours! You'll never use the Magic of Tena to upset the balance between humans and Landaffens." The pulse in my temples pounded. Brell huffed from under his gag.

"That is where you are wrong."

A young boy entered the throne room and stood next to the queen. With a red cloth wrapped around his waist, puka necklace around his neck, and helmet of gold feathers, he was dressed similarly to the other royals. On his shoulder perched a red bird. Its beady eyes met mine, and I knew it was the same bird I'd seen earlier. Strapped to the boy's waist was the Sword of Tena.

The boy pulled seeds from a woven bag at his hip, dropped them into his palm, and offered them to the bird. With its needle-like curved beak, the bird pecked the seeds from the boy's hand.

Smiling, the boy looked at me, and I immediately recognized him as the young bell attendant from our hotel. Brell and I exchanged glances.

"Using a boy prince to do your dirty work," I said. "That's how you knew I was in Hawaii. You must be so proud of him," I sneered.

The queen blinked like she was trying to halt a tear, and she and her husband lowered their heads.

"Our scouts are many. They have infiltrated human spaces throughout the islands, establishing employment and building relationships with our enemy as a means to eventually rule over and destroy all humans." He licked his deep red lips. "From the time you left the land of ice mountains, we have been on high alert, anticipating your arrival." He motioned for Koa to leave his mom's side and stand next to him. Finnlen put his arm over Koa's shoulder. "Young Koa has been more than willing to prove that the Legend of Queen Tena is a lie."

"It is not a lie! You are the one who is full of lies and spreading them!" I screamed, trying to pull my wrists apart. The protector next to me clamped my arm harder. Brell rose on his toes while struggling against his bound hands. Another protector grabbed Brell's shoulders. "Heat Magic will never be yours!" I shouted.

Prince Koa lifted his chin, and Finnlen patted the top of his head. "You are wrong," Koa said. "Yesterday I followed you. You led me to the stone that we must lift and bring to Mentsune where the stone originated. It will be returned to the top of the mountain where fire once flowed like water."

Brell and I looked at each other.

"And with the Magic of Tena, Mana Finnlen will unite the groves and destroy all humans." Koa folded his arms.

The queen put her hand over her mouth and turned her head from her son.

"Don't you see how Finnlen is poisoning your son's mind?" I said to the queen as I thought of little Pakak and how he'd been so full of revenge. "Making him hate and want to kill? That is not the Landaffen way. But this can end now. Take back your colony! Forget about the velletsemn. It is an archaic practice and is no longer used. Nalaan and Caylent aren't married yet! Break the engagement and allow him to marry for love. Break your allegiance to the Hanllants."

The queen lifted her head.

"Queen Tena possessed a deep magic to maintain the balance," I continued. "She knew it wouldn't happen in her lifetime, so set it up for a descendant of both races. We need to work with the humans—not kill them. Landaffens and humans living together peacefully—that was Queen Tena's goal. And now it is mine. I will make sure that happens. This is the only colony that does not believe this, but it's not too late to do what is just and right."

"Claiming to be The One is a disgrace," Finnlen sneered.

"A disgrace and a half race. That is why she talks of peace," Prince Koa said. "Humans will not care about us because they do not care about the earth." He put his nose in the air. "They pollute our oceans with slicks of deadly oil and trash that does not decay and become one with the land. Instead, it is rejected by the earth to trap, injure, suffocate, and poison animals."

"I have seen seals dead on the beach with nets wound tightly around their necks. I have seen sea turtles with human trash caught in their mouths and noses. I have seen sea walls of coral turn white and die from the toxins produced by humans."

"And you talk of balance and peace? Humans have upset the balance of our seas. They do not know what it means to be equal and fair. They deserve to die!"

"No! They do know what is means to be equal and fair. I promise you they do. Humans have made mistakes, but they're trying to change things and fix the damage they've caused. Landaffens can help us do it. We can learn from you. You can teach us—"

"Enough!" Finnlen put up his hand. "Humans are too vain and too self-absorbed to take lessons from anyone but themselves. Heat magic will be mine."

"No, it won't. The stone is too heavy," I urged. "You'll never be able to bring it here from another island and lug it up the mountain. Even with my magic, it wouldn't be possible."

Finnlen shook his head at me. "Magic is not needed to move the stone. The Mentsune engineers have solved that problem. As we speak, the hapeye system they made to move the stone and trailer they designed is on its way to the biggest island in this archipelago. By high moon, the stone will be on my ship, and when it arrives, we will celebrate."

"Hapeye?"

"Yes, it means 'lift.' That is what I will do to the stone, and then heat magic will be mine."

I imagined Finnlen's evil face, his teeth exposed and chest heaving. I remembered him shouting the word "hapeye" in my dream and knew what I'd been seeing was a glimpse into the future.

Finnlen clapped his hands in the air above his head. "Take them away," he ordered. "Enjoy your last hours of life, Laura. Breath remains in your lungs only because I need the power of Heat Magic before you die, and then you and your prince shall become one with the earth."

Brell jerked his shoulder from the protector's grasp and turned to me. His face was red and eyes full of anger. But with the gentle lifting of his eyebrow, his eyes softened, reassuring me that everything would be okay, and we'd find a way to escape.

Two protectors led us to a windowless room with a door made from the rib bones of a large animal, probably a whale. Hanging vertically in a wooden frame, the bones were spaced about three inches apart. Three additional bones ran horizontally, one at the top, another at the middle, and the third at the bottom. Straps of leather wrapped where the bones crossed, holding them together.

A third protector, wearing a necklace with a tusk-like tooth pendent, came down the hall holding a wooden rake and pulling a cart full of sand. He threw open the bone door, entered, and dumped the sand in the center of the room. With the rake, he groomed the sand into a thick, wall-to-wall layer. When he was done, he stood outside the door, and one of the other protectors pushed Brell and me inside.

Sand flew from under our feet as we reluctantly shuffled into the tiny space.

"You cannot trick us with your ability to be unseen by all," the protector with the rake said. He tossed the rake into the cart and picked up a coil of rope. "Footprints cannot hide in this sand. We will know where you are even if we cannot see you." He looked at me. "And you will not be able to work any of your magic."

While two protectors held Brell, the third Mentsune untied my wrists and retied them separately with long lengths of rope. On opposite sides of the room, iron rings hung on the walls. He threaded one rope through one loop and the other rope through the other, forcing my arms up at my sides when he pulled the ropes and tied them in place.

"Ouch," I said when he yanked the rope.

"Appreciate the pain of a tight rope," the protector said. "To prevent your magic, Mana Finnlen wanted to cut off your arms, but Queen Noeli convinced him to use this method instead."

When he was done, he took a bottle from the cart and poured a thick amber liquid onto the knot. The fluid wicked into the rope, quickly absorbing into the fibers. He left enough slack for me to sit down with my hands up and out to my sides, but not enough for me to bring my hands together and work the wind.

"This is unnecessary," I said. "Can't you see that I'm injured? Working magic in this condition is impossible."

"You lie," he grumbled.

But I wasn't lying. Just the thought of trying to concentrate long enough to rouse a whisper of wind made me ill. My head throbbed and my wound was hot and numb.

They slammed the door behind us and fastened it closed with a long strap knotted beyond our reach. Two protectors left with the cart, leaving the protector with the tooth necklace to guard our door. We sat down in the far corner of the room.

"You know how I feel about sand," I said, and half laughed.

It stuck to our moist skin and wet clothes. Brell rolled onto his back and worked his bound hands under his body and into his lap. With his fingers, he pulled down his gag. He twisted his wrists in opposite directions and untied his rope.

"I will untie you," Brell whispered.

Using what little fingernails he had, he tried to scrape away the syrupy liquid that kept the knot in place, but the liquid had hardened and was impossible to chip away.

"I believe it is tree sap," he said. "I am sorry, but the knot will not come loose."

"It's okay. We'll have to find another way."

Brell sat next to me and took me into his arms. I lay my head against his chest, his damp raincoat cold against my cheek. My hands started to tingle from my arms lifting above my shoulders, but I didn't care.

"Now we know why Daveen was always one step ahead of us," I whispered. "His brother is the mastermind. What are we going to do?"

"We cannot assume Thriss and Todd will come to our aid. And we are not going to wait here to die." Brell whispered back. "We will find a way out."

"If Todd and Thriss come after us, they'll fall into the same trap."

"I have the same fear," Brell said.

I leaned closer to Brell's ear. "Do you think they really believe the Naha Stone will give Finnlen heat magic if they bring it here and he turns it over?"

"I do. Since many human myths originated from Landaffen truths, I am certain they believe the story of the Naha stone is based upon an older Landaffen legend."

"The Naha Stone is sacred to the Hawaiian people. It shouldn't be moved."

"I understand," Brell whispered. "But we cannot tell them it is the wrong stone."

"What do you think he'll do to us when the Naha Stone doesn't give him Tena's magic?"

"I do not know, but I am afraid he will assume you have the

answer." He stroked my damp hair, brushing it from my face. "But no matter what happens, you cannot tell him there is another stone. He cannot have the magic that Queen Tena meant for you."

"I won't." I rose higher against Brell's chest, bringing my numb hands a little lower. "Were you watching the king and queen? The queen kept her head down, and I sensed a lack of confidence, like she was conflicted and unsure."

"I felt the same emotion in her." Brell flashed a glance toward the door. "I also noticed something different about the protector guarding our door. Did you?"

"No, not really. Although, I do sense he's feeling...unsettled."

Brell got up, went to the door, and stood, holding the bone bars in his hands.

"You are not from Mentsune," Brell said to the protector. "You wear a piece of walrus tusk around your neck. You are from Aludene."

The protector blinked nervously but didn't say anything.

"Your Mentsune accent is strong. I suspect you have been here for many seasons," Brell continued.

The protector's chest expanded.

"You must long for your family and friends," Brell said softly. "You must miss the reflection of the morning sun upon the carved palace ice, the snow-capped mountains appearing purple under a pale blue sky, and the playful trumpeting of woolly mammoths."

The protector's chest sunk. He turned to face Brell and folded his arms. "You do not know anything about me," he sneered.

"That is not true. I know you were once an Aludene Protector, proudly serving King Mutu and Queen Jussik even on the coldest of nights."

The protector brought his hand to his ear, and I saw the unpleasant result of frostbite and the sign of an Aludene protector, the scarred flap of skin that used to be an earlobe.

"What is your name?" Brell asked.

"Sukan," he grumbled.

"You took a vow to protect your colony, but now you are here, Sukan, an enemy and traitor of the ones who brought you first breath."

The protector looked down the hall before he spoke, his voice low and gruff. "I did not come here by choice. Five winters ago, I was captured at my post outside my grove. I was taken to a Mentsune ship, brought here, and questioned."

"What did they want to know?"

"They asked me about the Cup of Queens. They had hoped my colony had the stone or knew where it was located. But we did not."

"Did you ask them to take you back to Aludene?"

"I did not. There was no reason to return. Aludene vowed their allegiance to the Hanllant's cause. My home grove and this grove are one and the same. When Mana Finnlen returns the rock, he will be granted the magic he needs to unite all groves in a fight against humanity. It is at that time when I will return to Aludene and fight alongside my people."

"You've been lied to," I said, rising onto one knee. "Aludene has not aligned with Finnlen. Neither has Tulix. The only grove being manipulated by Finnlen is this one." I pushed up and stood. "Daveen led the Hanllants in a surprise attack against the Aludene. Many colonists were killed. The queen's walrus, and one of their dolphin companions, were slaughtered." I swallowed and licked my lips. "The Aludene's allegiance is not with the Mentsune. It is with me."

"I do not believe you," Sukan said, raising his voice.

"You need to believe me," I said with a tight jaw. "We're telling you the truth! Aludenes were killed, the palace destroyed, and little Prince Pakak barely escaped with his life."

"It is Laura who saved him," Brell said.

Sukan flicked his eyes from mine. "When did this attack take place?"

"It has been five turns of the sun," Brell said.

Sukan counted on his fingers and shook his head. "Do you know the names of those who met the earth?"

"No, we don't. I wish we could have stayed to pay our respects and mourn with the colony but..."

"I understand." He lowered his head and rounded his shoulders. "Twenty suns ago, I was asked to draw a map of Aludene and I told them how to enter Aludene unseen. At the next sun, our ship left for the land of ice mountains." He shook his head. "I fear the information I provided was used in the planning of this attack."

"It was!" I spoke.

"Then I have failed my colony."

I widened my stance. "If you help us escape, you can make up for what you've done."

He lifted his head, moved closer to the cell door, and whispered. "Then I will help you. A ship carrying the Naha Stone will return to our shores tonight. Twenty protectors are needed to lower the trailer to the beach and pull it to the grove. Mana Finnlen, the king and queen, and most of the colony will be watching." He looked down the hall. "At that time, I will set you free."

Sukan straightened his back and stepped from the door. The sound of footsteps came from the hall, and Finnlen emerged, followed by a protector.

"Queen Noeli is much too soft," Finnlen said. "I would prefer to see you with bloody stumps." He shifted his eyes to my hands. "Perhaps that will still happen."

"What do you want?" Brell asked.

"To gloat and give you my apologies that the two of you are not invited to tonight's feast."

"No apology needed. We wouldn't attend even if we were invited," I said.

"If my brother's ship arrives early, the celebration will double as we acknowledge my sister's engagement to Prince Nalaan."

My knees buckled, and Brell caught me before the ropes stopped me and yanked my arms.

"She is not well," Brell said. "Please, release her arms, so she can lay down and rest."

Finnlen laughed, a cocky laugh that started out strong and faded.

I placed my head on Brell's shoulder and closed my eyes.

⚜

I felt Brell's arms cradling me, one across my back and the other under my bent knees. I opened my eyes. The room was dark. "What's happening?" I gasped. "Where's Finnlen?"

"He is gone," Brell said. "How are you feeling? Do you think you can stand?"

"I'm fine. Yeah, I can stand." A torch in the hall threw an orange flicker of light against the whale bones, and the bones threw long shadows across the sand.

He lowered my feet to the ground. When I was stable, he let go of me and stretched, arching his back, and bringing his hands over his head.

"How long was I out?" I asked. My hands tingled. I tried to bend my fingers, and they barely moved.

"I am not sure. I believe it was for many human hours."

"Were you holding me that whole time?"

He rubbed his lower back.

"Brell," I whined. "You should have set me down."

"Sitting down, your arms would have been above your heart. They needed to be below to help with the flow of blood. Your hands should not be that color."

Even in the dim light, I could see that my hands were several shades darker than my arms. "Where did Sukan go?"

"I am not sure. At sun drop, he lit the torch. Another protector was with him, but Sukan looked at me and nodded, so I believe he still intends to set us free."

"I hope Todd and Thriss are okay."

"If they are in the grove, they have not been discovered and captured, or they would have been brought here. Not only for Finnlen to gloat..." Brell went to the door and looked down the hall, the slight curve of the rib bones allowing him to see slightly beyond the door's frame. "But I believe this is their only containment room. That is why we were not separated."

Drumbeats echoed down the hall, followed by rattles shaking and the strumming and plucking of strings on some type of guitar, in a rhythmic, repetitive beat. A female voice joined the music, but like the other sounds it was too muffled to hear clearly.

"The celebration has begun," Brell said.

"That means the Naha Stone's here."

A bright light filled the hall, and we heard footsteps. Sukan appeared with a torch in one hand and my sheathed sword in the other.

"I dared to take one weapon," he said. "I assumed you would want this one."

"Thank you," I said. "You're doing the right thing, Sukan. The Aludene would be proud."

He set the Sword of Tena against the wall, started to unlatch the gate, and stopped. "Before I release you, I need you to make me a promise."

"If it's a promise I can keep, I'll do it. I swear," I said.

"Then when heat magic is yours and the Hanllants are defeated, please, do not forget about me and what I have done for you. Use quick magic to take me back to Aludene."

"I will. I promise. And I will tell them about how you helped us."

Sukan opened the door, and Brell stood against it, holding it ajar while Sukan cut me free. He used a dagger with a short blade, avoiding the hard, sap-caked knot, and cutting the rope at the top of my wrist. Unable to slide the blade beneath it, he cut the rope from above, slowing down the closer he got to my skin.

I closed my eyes, counting on his Landaffen precision and accuracy.

The last thread of rope snapped, and my right wrist dropped free. Brell took my hand, massaging the muscles in my palm and fingers as Sukan cut the rope from my other hand. My hands burned and tingled, and within minutes of their release, I could move my wrists and hands without any residual pain.

"Thank you," I said, giving Sukan a hug. "I promise I will take you home as soon as I can."

"I believe in you," he said as we let go of each other. "I believe in The One."

The music continued booming down the hall, a celebratory melody of heavy drumbeats, the sporadic, yet intentional pluck on guitar strings, and the chant of many voices.

"I will lead you from the palace to the stream. Following the stream will take you to the shore of Mentsune Cove where you will find unattended canoes and paddle boards. Use one of these to follow the coast up Mentsune Beach and into human territory. It is the only way you can leave."

Brell had pulled the torch from its holder on the wall, and with Sukan in the lead, we sprinted down the hall. To restore my blood-restricted hands, I rotated my wrists as we ran, and though my head hurt and at times my vision blurred and the hall appeared to tilt, I kept going, cranking my arms and springing from my toes with each step.

Sukan slowed to a stop and pointed. "I will leave you here. The stream is just outside that door."

The celebration continued, drums beating, a choir of voices singing, and guitar strings strumming in a soothing and hypnotic melody, conflicting with its insensitive celebration of stripping the Hawaiian people of a sacred monument in the hope of destroying them in the future.

"Thank you, again," I said. "Your allegiance to the Legend of Tena will not go unnoticed or untold."

Slowly, Brell opened the door. Ahead was the pool where

Brell and I had been trapped and detained. The pool was a quarter of the way full. Brell's bow and arrows were gone. Our sunhats were still there but had sunk near the edge of pit and were half-covered with mud.

Riding the wind, rain came down in angled sheets, lightning cracked, and thunder boomed. We pulled on our hoods, ran to the far end of the pool, and followed the stream. Running along its muddy bank, we pushed palm fronds from our path and sprinted over rocks and fallen branches.

We heard waves crashing on the shore and smelled the salt of the sea. The lush forest thinned, the muddy earth turned to sand, and through a gap between the trees, we saw the beach. Slowing to a walk, Brell took my hand. We stopped when we reached the last set of palms.

"I can try to use quick magic and take us back to the weeping wall, but if Todd and Thriss entered the grove, we need to stay here and find them. What do you think we should—"

"I hear something," Brell whispered.

The blade of a sword pushed through the trees and slashed the air in front of us. Brell jumped in front of me, shielding me with his body. I reached for my weapon. The sword made a second swipe, its blade flashing in the moon. Brell sprung backward, taking me with him.

"It is Brell and Laura," Todd said.

I spun to find Thriss behind us. She lowered her sword and threw her arms around my neck. In front of us, Todd stepped from the trees, and he and Brell patted each other on the back.

"Thank goodness you're alive!" Todd said.

"And you, too," I said. "How did you get here?"

"Let's get our things, and we'll tell you," Todd said.

Brell and I followed Todd and Thriss to the bottom of a rocky cliff overlooking the beach. Clouds covered the moon and the weepy rain continued, making it difficult to see, but there was enough light to make out the dark shapes of canoes and paddle boards on the shore. Beyond the breakers sat a small, rocky island, its craggy silhouette ominous and foreboding.

"We found the perfect place to stash our stuff," Todd said, pointing to a narrow gap within the cliff face.

Lightning cracked, filling the sky with a webbing of bright light. Turning sideways, we squeezed through the opening and entered a small, shallow cave. Inside lay our backpacks and tent bag. While Brell and I munched on granola bars and guzzled water, Todd and Thriss explained how they ended up on Mentsune Beach.

Under the cover of night, they'd entered the grove and immediately saw the torn patch of moss leading to a cavern below. Suspecting it was a trap, and that Brell and I had fallen inside, they decided to investigate. The music began, and the Landaffens they could see from the ridge headed to the center of the grove.

With Thriss waiting above, Todd followed the tunnel to the pool and the stream to the beach. He saw our sunhats and knew Brell and I had been there. Todd went back for Thriss, and they decided to wait until the Mentsune were asleep before trying to find us. When they heard footsteps on the trail, they decided to confront and threaten who was there; an attempt to force the Mentsune to tell Todd and Thriss where Brell and I were being held.

"What should we do now?" I asked.

"Get us out of here, Laura. Use your magic," Todd said.

"I'll try. But I hit my head again."

Exhaling, I closed my eyes. Brell, Todd, and Thriss put their hands on my back and shoulders. As I concentrated, my head pounded with pain. A drop of liquid rolled down the side of my forehead, and when it hit the corner of my mouth, I tasted blood and not rain.

I worked the wind. A small funnel of air developed, and the wet sand it picked up pelted against my legs. My hands tingled and burned. The throbbing in my head intensified, building with an unbearable amount of pressure and pain. The swirl of wind puttered and died. I opened my eyes.

"I can't," I cried. "It's not working."

Brell took me in his arms, as I sobbed on his shoulder.

"We must leave by boat," Brell said.

"Thriss and I already explored the beach," Todd said. "You can't see it from here, but that bluff cuts off the shore. There's no way to go around it or climb the rock face. To the south, there's a jetty, so the only way to get out of here is to follow the coastline up the beach."

"Yes, Sukan told us that would be the only way," Brell said.

Todd stuck his head from the cave. "Oh, no!"

Brell took a look and dropped his chin.

"What's wrong?" I grabbed Brell's hand.

"The Hanllant ship," he said. "It has arrived."

CHAPTER 19

Staying in the shadows, we walked to the shore. The wind whipped, stirring the palm fronds, and sending rain against our faces.

"The ship wasn't there ten minutes ago," I said.

Brell pointed. "It must have been sailing behind that island of rocks when we were on the beach."

As the ship, a silhouette against the horizon, slowly turned toward the shore, two of its three billowing sails appeared as one, making it look like a black dragon floating upon the water. Lightning flashed and the dark shape illuminated and flickered. Thunder rolled, sending chills up my arms.

"We need to leave now and before this storm gets worse." Brell set his hand on my shoulder. "Laura, what about making us unseen by all. If it becomes necessary, do you think it is something you can do?"

"It's easier than quick magic. I can always try." I nodded emphatically, cringing at the pain in my skull.

Todd and Brell found a canoe with four seats in a row running down its haul. We put our backpacks inside and laid our weapons along the haul. Thriss and I hopped onto two of the four seats, and Thriss held the oars while Brell and Todd pushed the canoe into the water. With a final running shove, the canoe floated free from the sand. Brell and Todd jumped in, and Todd sat in the center seat and took the oars.

A wave crashed, sending the canoe back toward the shore, and Todd thrust an oar in the water, hitting the sand and driving us back toward the open sea as the water receded.

"Have you ever rowed a boat against the waves?" I asked Todd.

"No, but I know we just need to ride them out and cut through them at a forty-five-degree angle." He fastened the oars in the oarlocks and rowed.

A series of waves hit the canoe. Staying on top of the surf, the canoe tossed and bucked, water splashing into the haul. The next set of waves were bigger, rising above our heads and crumbling over us.

"Hold on," Todd shouted above the rain as another wave tumbled against the canoe.

We grabbed the top edge of the boat and ducked. The boat rocked, rose, and fell, water continuing to spill into the canoe as the rainfall increased, pounding us with water from all directions.

"Are we past the breakers?" I shouted, raising my head. Water hit my face, and I spit the salty water from my mouth.

"Yeah," Todd shouted. "But the water's rough, and the current's driving us toward the jetty." The canoe bucked, spinning on the crest of the wave. "Damn it!" Todd screamed. "I just lost an oar."

"Todd! Take us away from the ship!" Brell shouted.

I drew away my hood and pulled my hair from my eyes. As the waves rose and fell, the Hanllant ship came into view. Lightning cracked, and in the blink of the light, I saw teams of Mentsune behind each bulging sail, working the wind with their fingers, driving air and rain against the fabric. Oars dipped into the sea, stroking the waves in a coordinated rhythm, and at the rear of the ship, a Mentsune beat a drum we couldn't hear.

Thunder rumbled. "I'm trying!" Todd pulled the oar from its lock and plunged it into the ocean on the other side of the canoe. Rowing with both hands on the oar, he switched sides as the current forced the canoe in the wrong direction. "The current's too strong!"

I looked toward the shore. A group of Mentsune stood on the beach, holding torches, and facing the sea.

"The drum! I hear the drum! They're getting closer!" Thriss screamed.

Brell took my upper arm. "Laura, try now before they see us!"

Todd and Thriss clasped their hands on my shoulders, and I closed my eyes and concentrated. My head tingled, the ache in my temple thumping. A wave hit the canoe, carrying us closer to the ship. As the canoe jerked, my body shifted, and I slipped from my seat to the floor of the haul.

Brell pulled me to my seat, and a beam of light hit the water in front of us. With the next roll of the sea, I saw three figures on the bow of the ship. One held up a concave metal plate while another held a lit torch in front of it while using another plate to shield the flame from the rain, creating a spotlight that hit our canoe.

Lightning flashed, and the three figures on the bow became visible. Nenmie held the torch and Daveen the plate. Next to them was Caylent's fiancé, Nalaan. He pointed toward the canoe. Thunder crashed and another streak of lightning cut across the sky.

"They see us!" Thriss screamed above the roaring of waves.

"Todd, get us out of here!" Brell yelled.

Todd struck the angry ocean with the oar, sweeping the sea with hard pulls. The rain was thick and the swells rough and constant.

"I can't!" Todd shouted as the boat rocked, rearing and bucking in place.

"The ship's going to hit us!" I cried.

The beam of light bounced across the waves and

disappeared. From the ship, indistinguishable shouts rode the wind. The drumbeats stopped, and the sails deflated, but the ship kept moving under the power of the sea.

"Take off your shoes and as much of your clothes as you can!" Todd screamed. "The only thing we can do is swim to the shore!"

As we struggled with our shoes and clothes, the canoe rocked, knocking us against each other and against the inside of the canoe. I ripped off my shoes, throwing them overboard, and Brell helped me yank off my raincoat.

"Jump! Now!" Todd hollered.

I reached for the Sword of Tena.

"Leave it!" Brell shouted. "It will make you sink."

The bow of the ship hit the canoe, and I let go of the Sword of Tena. Grabbing my hand, Brell jumped into the ocean, pulling me with him. Holding our breaths, we sunk, and I looked up, watching the ship's triple hauls move over the surface.

Brell let go of me, and I kicked, scooping water with my hands. My head popped to the surface. "Brell!" I screamed. The ocean slapped my face, and a wave forced my head back under water.

I treaded water, kicking and moving my hands back and forth at my chest to keep my head up. My clothes made my limbs heavy and my movements awkward and ineffective.

"Brell!" I shouted before my head sank again.

With a hard kick, I shot to the surface and started to swim. Waves splashed over my head. I swallowed water, my body dipping deeper. My heart beat hard. Between waves, I tried to catch my breath, but each inhalation was a combination of air and water.

I coughed and gagged and could barely move. My kicks were labored and infrequent. My arm strokes didn't pull me forward. Exhausted, I rolled onto my back and tried to float. The moon glowed behind a sheet of clouds, and paddling my hands at my sides, I watched a section of the clouds thin to reveal a patch of stars.

"Brell! Brell—"

A swell broke over my face, and my feet were pulled under, dragging my upper body with them. I held my breath and kicked weakly as my head dropped into the sea. My chest hurt. I blew bubbles from my mouth, scooping the water with my hands, beating my heavy legs, and looking up through the water. I searched for the glowing clouds and couldn't find them.

I closed my eyes and kicked. But my breath was gone. My lungs were tight. I opened my mouth. In my mind's eye, I saw the summit of a mountain. Grass. Small palms. The stone from my dreams. My body went limp.

❧

I gasped and someone rolled me onto my side. Water spilled from my mouth. I coughed and gagged. My nose and throat hurt. A hand on my shoulder rolled me to my back.

My eyes fluttered open. Two women stared down at me, their long, wet hair glistening in the dim moonlight. Reaching out her webbed hand, one woman touched my forehead, and my body tingled. She removed her hand, and the other woman placed something cold and wet against my head wound.

"Please save my friends!" I cried.

"We are here," I heard Brell say.

My heartbeat slowed, and my muscles relaxed against the rock beneath me.

The mermaids' features were delicate—small nose, thin lips, and smooth, sculpted cheekbones. A set of gills ran diagonally across the sides of their long necks, and pointed ears pushed through their dark hair.

A string of puka shells adorned each mermaid's neck, hanging above their small, firm breasts. I pushed up on my palms, rising to my elbows, but one mermaid reached out her hand and stopped me.

We were at the end of the jetty. It was no longer raining, but the wind blew in gusts and the clouds were stormy. Water dripped onto my cheek as another mermaid joined the others. It was a male. He lifted his arm and combed his wet hair back against the top of his head. He was muscular, broad shouldered, and the skin on his upper body was hairless and smooth.

He placed his palms on the rock on either side of me and lowered to kiss my forehead. When his lips hit, I closed my eyes and held my breath. Warmth traveled from his lips, through my head, and down my neck. Lifting away, he set his hand on my chest, and a cool sensation trickled into my abdomen, arms, and legs.

The three merpeople pushed from the rock, diving head-first into the water, barely making a splash as their smooth, gray, dolphin-like tails slipped into the water.

Brell rushed to my side and knelt next to me. "Did the merpeople save you, too?" I asked him.

"Yes, they saved all of us." He glanced over his shoulder at Thriss and Todd.

"When I was in the water, I saw it, Brell. I know where to find heat magic."

"What did you see?" he asked as he picked up my hand and helped me sit upright.

The merpeople poked their heads from the water, a fourth head joining them. It was a female with hair to her shoulders. She lifted the Sword of Tena from the water. Its blade caught the moonlight and flashed. In her other hand, she held the sword's sheath.

"My sword!" I gushed. "Thank you. Thank you for everything!" Brell leaned over the water. She handed him my sword and sheath. Without a splash or ripple, the four sunk below the water and disappeared.

I rose to my feet, and Brell and I hugged.

"Oh, no!" Todd said. "We've got company."

A group of Mentsune with plumed helmets stood on the beach in front of the jetty, blocking our path to the shore. A boat full of Mentsune rowed in our direction. The Mentsune ship had already moored, and the crew were in the process of lowering the ship's small sailboat into the water.

As the rowboat approached, I strapped on my sword, ran to the edge of the jetty, and stepped down its rocky bank until I was inches from the water line. Holding my hands over the water, I worked the wind, creating a small whirlpool in the water. As I raised my hands, the cone of spinning water rose into the air and widened.

The Mentsune stopped rowing and the others braced themselves against the inside of the haul. A flick of my fingers pushed the rotating body of water toward the boat. It engulfed the small vessel, drenching its occupants and sending it into a frenzied spin. The boat capsized, and the Mentsune came to the surface and swam for their overturned boat.

"Where did you learn to do that?" Brell asked.

"It's something I saw Autka do," I explained. "He never taught me. Somehow, I just knew how to do it."

"You'll need to do it again," Todd said. "That sailboat is headed this way and look who's in it!"

Fighting the surf, the boat raced toward the jetty where we stood. Three Mentsune worked the wind, forcing air into their sails as three others rowed and worked the rudder. At the bow sat Daveen. He drew back his lips like a growling dog and stared at me.

He screamed, and though I couldn't hear him through the roaring surf, I read his lips and knew he'd shouted: "You are mine, half race!"

Spreading my fingers over the ocean, I worked the wind into a small funnel and drove it into the water. A tiny hurricane formed, spinning with more force than the last. Daveen's eyes grew wide, and the rowers stopped rowing. Daveen shouted behind him, and the Mentsune picked up their oars and continued rowing toward me.

A swipe of my hand sent the hurricane against their boat.

The boat spun and rocked. Ripped from their hands, the oars flew into the sky. A last violent swirl pulled Daveen and the Mentsune from the boat. Flailing their arms and legs, they soared through the air and dropped in the water, Daveen landing closest to the jetty.

Bringing my hands together, I slowed the funnel and lowered it into the sea. The water twisted and spun in a violent swirl. With short, desperate arm strokes, Daveen swam toward the jetty, cutting right to avoid the whirlpool while the others swam for the boat.

Anger pulsed through my core, and I remembered all he'd done to me and those he and the Hanllants had killed. Pressure built behind my eyes.

Raising my hand, I drove the spinning water toward Daveen. He struck his hands against the water, fighting the current, but the raging sea sucked him into its swirling center. He spun, slowly sinking, desperately scooping the water to keep his head above the surface.

My nostrils flaring, I strummed the wind, tightening the vortex. Gasping for air, Daveen's head dropped below the ocean. He poked one hand from the water, his fingers spread and raking the air.

"No!" I screamed.

With the swing of my hand, I lifted the funnel with Daveen's limp body inside of it. Daveen spun toward the jetty, and as I lowered my hands, he fell to the rocks. The whirlpool collapsed and the water drained back into the sea. Daveen spit and coughed, his body rolling from side to side against the rocky base of the jetty.

The muscles in my face softened and my shoulders relaxed. Brell came up beside me.

"Killing him won't take back all he's done," I said. "Though there is a part of me that wants him dead."

"Doing so would only bring you guilt. Revenge is never the answer," Brell said.

"Laura!" Todd hollered.

A group of protectors ran up the jetty and another boat headed our way.

"Hurry! Get over here. Let's go!" I announced.

"Where are you taking us?" Thriss asked.

"To the top of the Mount Waialeale."

Brell took my hand. "Are you sure you are well enough?"

"Yeah, I'm sure. I don't know how to explain it, but I feel perfectly fine—better than fine."

"It was the kiss," Brell said. "I believe the merpeople must have their own special magic."

"Let's do it!" I shouted.

Brell, Thriss, and Todd put their hands on my shoulders and formed a half circle around me. Using my fingers, I raised my hands and worked the wind. The summit of a mountain. Grass. Ferns. Small palms. The sweet swampy smell of decaying foliage. Warm rain on my face. A cool mist swirling about my legs, and the stone from my dreams, its carved rectangle illuminating like a red flickering flame.

Our bodies stretched and thinned. I closed my eyes, and we joined the wind.

Landing smoothly, my bare feet hit the soft ground, but the other's touchdowns were less than graceful. Brell steadied himself by grabbing hold of a small tree, and Todd and Thriss were on their rears.

"There it is!" I screamed.

A large block of rock lay before me. The surface was rough, but the edges and corners were smooth and rounded.

"Don't you see it?"

No one answered me.

Placing my hand on the rock, I ran my fingers across its top as I walked around it, looking for the carved triangle. The ground shook, a rumbling deep within the mountain, almost knocking me from my feet. Putting out my arms, I widened my stance and tightened the muscles in my legs.

Thick, black smoke snaked around my ankles and rose, obscuring my vision.

"Brell?" I shouted. "Where are you? Thriss! Todd!"

I looked down. The grass was gone. The ferns were gone. The stubby little palms were gone. The ground was hard, black, and craggy. The mountain shook, vibrating under my feet, and the deep rumbling sound continued, followed by a piercing boom and sharp snap.

The stone rocked as the earth next to it cracked and split. Hot, black smoke spewed from the five-foot long crevice. I smelled the putrid scent of sulfur. Stumbling backward, I wiped the sweat from my eyes.

"Brell!" I screamed, but the rumbling and booming of the earth was so loud, I couldn't hear myself speak.

Smoke burned my eyes and throat. I pulled the neckline of my T-shirt over my mouth and nose and coughed.

"Brell! We need to get out of here."

A tall, slender figure rushed through the billowing smoke. I fanned the smoke from my eyes and followed the figure to the block of stone.

It was a woman with long brown hair. She wore a white dress, tied at the waist with a rope and belted with a sheathed sword. On her head, she wore a wreath made from pine needles and Ti leaves.

"Who are you?" I asked.

She placed her palms on the top of the stone, and as she leaned over it, her puka shell necklace swung and her dress ballooned against the smoke.

"Hey!" I screamed and tried to grab her shoulder.

Though her body appeared solid, my hand pushed through her, and I felt nothing as if she was a ghost. Watching her every move, I took a step backward.

Facing the stone, she drew her sword. I gasped. It was the Sword of Tena. I looked down at my waist. The Sword of Tena hung there in its sheath.

"Queen Tena!" I cried and coughed as more smoke entered my lungs. The ground burned my feet.

Using the length of her dress, Queen Tena wrapped the blade of her sword with fabric. She set the handle of the sword against her shoulder. With both hands, she gripped the covered section of the blade and, with its tip, carved into the stone. I moved closer, watching the delicate expression on her face change as she worked.

The muscles in her jaw were tight and her plump, plum-colored lips pulled thin as she maneuvered the heavy blade. As she forced the blade's tip into the chunk of lava stone, her thin, arched eyebrows came together and sweat beaded on her forehead.

The mountain continued to quake, and the crack in the ground behind the stone lengthened and separated. Thick smoke wrapped my body. I gagged and coughed, blinking my stinging eyes, but Queen Tena appeared unaffected.

Lava rose to the top of the crevice, a river of orange, but Tena kept working, carving lines, and going over them again and again to make them deeper.

"A female half-race taking first breath with a crown of laurel on her head," Queen Tena said as she dug the blade across the stone. "She will have full magic, and she will bring what is fated to be—peace."

Lava shot from the crevice. I ducked, covering the back of my head with my hands. Blobs of lava landed near my feet, and another gob landed on the stone. Queen Tena watched as the lava spilled into the carving she'd made, igniting the shape with a tiny, bubbling river of red.

"Queen Tena, we need to get out of here! Now!" I screamed.

Meeting her eyes with mine, the queen turned and lifted her head. Tears pushed to the corner of my eyes, and I saw she, too, was crying. Her essence twisted with mine, combining into one until I knew her desires, her fears, and how to use the magic she'd intended for me.

She shifted her eyes to the triangle she made and then shifted them back to me. My pulse spiked, and I swallowed hard.

"The One," she said. "The true keeper of the cup."

Instinctively, I shoved my hand in my pocket, pulled out the fragment of stone from the Cup of Queen, and set it on the rock.

The ground shook, the crevice grew, and my feet burned. Smoke blackened the sky, blocking the sun. It was hard to breathe, but I stepped forward, and stood next to Queen Tena.

"Your wrist. Press it against the stone," she said, gesturing toward the triangle. Queen Tena's eyes softened, and the corners of her lips gently rose. "Trust me."

I nodded, took a deep breath, and lowered my wrist to the stone, pushing it against the carving.

Drawing back my head, I screamed into the black sky. My head spun and knees buckled. I ripped my arm away and dropped to the ground. The earth shook and the stone vibrated, rocking in place.

Queen Tena put her hands on the stone's edge and pushed, and I stood and joined her, bracing my feet and pushing with all my strength. The stone rolled over once, and we pushed again, turning to our sides to use our shoulders. The stone tumbled, dropping into the crack.

Lava splashed from the fissure, spraying our chests, burning our clothing and skin, but we didn't move. The stone sunk into the lava and disappeared.

"We did it!" I screamed.

But Queen Tena was gone. The sky was clear, palm fronds rustled in the breeze, and the sweet smell of flowers filled my nose. Taking a deep breath, my heart settled. I ran my hand down my chest and didn't see or feel any burns.

Brell ran to me. "Laura! Are you okay?"

"Where were you?" Todd asked. "You just like totally disappeared."

I lifted my chin to the rising sun. Below us, the mountain was covered in mist, but the sun had risen above the horizon, turning the sea as bright as lava. "I was with Queen Tena. She gave me heat magic."

And then I showed them the triangle the lava had burned into my wrist.

ABOUT THE AUTHOR

Karri Thompson, a native of San Diego, attended San Diego
State University where she earned her bachelor's degree in
English and master's degree in education. When she's not
writing novels and teaching high school English, she can be
found nerding out at San Diego Comic-Con and cooking
delicious meals for her family. Karri is the recipient of the San
Diego Book Awards Best Published Young Adult Novel for 2014.

For more information, visit
www.KarriThompson.com